THE INDISCRETIONS OF ISABELLE

'Dry me a little, then powder me please Isabelle,' she asked, quite oblivious to the effect she was having on me. 'I can never get at all the little crevices.'

'Don't you think it's a bit rude showing yourself to me like that?' I said, but I was already climbing onto the bed behind her.

'Don't be silly, I haven't got anything that you haven't got too,' she answered.

THE INDISCRETIONS OF ISABELLE

Penny Birch
writing as Cruella

Nexus

Dedicated to BE, RM, JG
and all other Isabelle enthusiasts

First published in 2004 by
Nexus
Thames Wharf Studios
Rainville Road
London W6 9HA

www.nexus-books.co.uk

Typeset by TW Typesetting, Plymouth, Devon

Printed and bound by
Clays Ltd, St Ives PLC

ISBN 0 352 33882 2

You'll notice that we have introduced a set of symbols onto our book jackets, so that you can tell at a glance what fetishes each of our brand new novels contains. Here's the key – enjoy!

cp (traditional)

cp (modern)

spanking

restraint/bondage

rope bondage/hojojutsu

latex/rubber/leather/enclosure

fem dom

willing captivity

medical

period setting

uniforms

sex rituals

One

Oxford has yet to come to terms with the idea of girls spanking each other for pleasure. Lesbianism is fine: there are societies dedicated to it. Corporal punishment is just about acceptable, at least among the more traditional elements of the university, so long as it is never mentioned. Combining the two is definitely beyond the pale.

However, it is an essential element of who I am, and so long as it remains consensual, I defend my moral right to do it. Besides, girls ought to be spanked. There is something about the shape of the female bottom which simply cries out for chastisement. Sex is sin, especially for women, or so my parents and a string of preachers did their best to instruct me as I grew up. So if sex is sin, what better way to precede it than with a good spanking?

Thus the crime is absolved before it takes place. Not that either my parents or my preachers would see it that way. Then again, if they can twist logic to suit their ends then I can do the same. So, as I sat in my tower room in the beautiful and ancient St George's College at the beginning of the Hilary term with my slave girl, Jasmine, bent bare-bottom across my knee, I was entirely happy with the situation, but also cautious.

1

The question was: how noisy could we afford to be? She takes it well, quite well anyway, not squealing too badly, although she does rather wriggle about. The problem was the spanks, which were going to be noisy even with the window closed, and being square and surrounded by buildings, the quad does tend to echo rather. I could take care of the squealing at least, and with luck nobody would understand that the smacks were the result of a palm being applied to a bottom.

'I think we had better have these right off,' I told her, taking hold of the silky black panties I had already adjusted to the level of her upper thighs, down just far enough to show the little blood-red 'I' tattooed on her bottom to mark her as mine.

Her response was a sigh. She knew full well where her panties were going. In her mouth.

The panties were the reason she needed to be punished. She knew she was supposed to wear full cut, white cotton underwear, which she finds hideously embarrassing. Turning up in a black set with the panties barely more than a thong counted as deliberate provocation. She'd known she would be inspected, and not to have spanked her would have been out of the question.

I'd made her take her bra off too. Not that it made much difference with her elfin figure, but it was cold enough outdoors to make her nipples perky and they showed through her jumper. The jumper was now up, her top too, leaving her little apple shaped breasts dangling forlorn under her chest, a detail I find always adds a certain something to a girl's feelings during a spanking.

'Open wide,' I instructed as I began to strip her lower body.

Boots, tights, panties, it all had to come off. If that left her in just her rucked up skirt and lifted top with not a stitch besides, then that was all the better. Generally I prefer a girl not to be fully nude during punishment, to make her more aware of what is showing. That doesn't mean she should be allowed to hide anything – just the opposite.

Jasmine was hiding nothing. Her natural shape, slim thighs and her bottom, twin eggs of firm, only slightly cheeky girl flesh, means that even when she is just casually bent across my knee her pussy shows from behind. Her bottom hole shows too. She has a very rude bottom hole, pink and slightly everted, like a woman's lips puckered up for a kiss. Making her show it is particularly satisfying, although I could wish she had a little more modesty to break down.

She kept her mouth open, as obedient as ever, while I stripped her lower body. Her panties were sticky, no doubt because she'd been anticipating what she would get for wearing them, but that wasn't going to stop them going in her mouth. Wadding them into a ball, I pushed it in, leaving her gaping, with a little scrap of black material hanging out between her lips.

'There we are,' I told her, laying my hand on one neat little bottom cheek, 'all ready. Stick it up.'

Her bottom lifted immediately, making the display of her anus and pussy more deliciously indecent still. I could smell her excitement, and the flesh between her sex lips was puffy and moist, tempting me to slip a finger in. I resisted. Punishment comes first.

I began to spank, firmly, but using just my fingertips to make it sting as much as possible without being too noisy. She immediately began to make little muffled sounds through her panty gag, and to squirm, wiggling her bottom in a way that put a grin straight on my face. I adore the reaction of a spanked girl, all that chagrin and shame, helpless sexual arousal and yet more shame because of it. She wasn't the only one getting aroused either, and as I laid in harder I was thinking of how I'd make her strip off her last few clothes and go down on her knees to me, licking pussy in the nude at my feet . . .

The knock at the door came as a dreadful shock. I hadn't given her more than fifty or sixty, and she was just starting to colour up nicely, and to kick about properly as well. I stopped, my heart hammering, answering diffidently and wondering who it was. A male voice answered, coarse, local and suggestive.

'Best stop that, Miss Colraine. I can hear you down in the quad.'

It was Stan Tierney, my scout and an unpleasant side effect of my determination to express my sexual dominance. He was a dirty old man, no question, in looks and in behaviour. He stood maybe five foot seven, four inches less than me, and had a dreadful shabby look about him. He was always leering and making suggestive comments, and I was sure that while clearing girls' rooms he took every opportunity to have a good rummage through their underwear drawers. He'd found out about my tastes while I was still trying to find my feet, and had reacted just the way you'd expect a dirty old man to. Just thinking about it made me blush.

Fortunately he now knew I didn't stand any nonsense, and could be relied on to keep quiet so long as I had Jasmine or her friend Caroline help him with his cock occasionally, something they would do just as long as I kept them in role. Inevitably that was what was going on in Jasmine's mind, and she had stiffened over my lap. If she'd kept quiet she would have got away with it. She didn't, immediately spitting out her panty gag to plead with me.

'No, please, Isabelle, not Stan, not again.'

There was a catch in her voice, deep, genuine humiliation. He was still outside my door. I paused,

4

my hand on her warm bottom, feeling the subtle trembling of her body. She would do it, I knew, however much it disgusted her. I had the power, and it was just too tempting to use it.

'Well, if I can't spank you . . .'

'No, please Isabelle . . . Mistress . . . please?'

'How would you suggest you be punished, then?'

'Take me home. You can do as you like!'

'I'm sorry, Jasmine, I'm not sure I heard that correctly. Do you seriously expect me to walk halfway down the Cowley Road for the sake of your modesty?'

'No, but . . . OK, but don't let him do it in my mouth, please?'

I just laughed and stood up, dumping her on the floor. She stayed put, curled on the carpet, looking wide-eyed from the dishevelled bird's nest of her pretty blonde hair. I pulled the door open, revealing a grinning Stan, and quickly shut it behind him, pushing the catch to. He licked his lips at the sight of her, and squeezed his crotch.

'Hello, Jas, been a naughty girl, have you?'

She didn't answer, just biting her lip. Her skirt was still up behind, but she had pulled her top down, and even if being bottomless made her cuter than ever, I wasn't having it.

'Top up,' I ordered.

Her jumper and top came back up, lifted shyly over her little breasts as if she had never shown her chest to a man before. It was an act, at least in part, but her embarrassment was real.

'Sit down, Stan,' I offered, indicating my armchair. 'Could you really hear us from below?'

'Loud enough,' he answered, 'but not that any what didn't know would think you were up to spanking.'

The way he said 'spanking' was so lewd, so dirty, that I felt the blood go my cheeks and had to turn to the mantelpiece to hide my reaction. However much I do it, I can never get used to that word, said aloud, and still less the way he said it.

'Do I get a piece of the action, then?' he demanded, speaking to me but with his eyes on the naked curve of Jasmine's hip where the reddening of her skin showed.

'You're not spanking her, no,' I answered.

'Let me watch, then,' he answered immediately, 'and you can both give us a toss after.'

'No,' I answered firmly. 'You know I don't, Stan, and I'm going to postpone her spanking if it's that noisy.'

Relief and gratitude washed over Jasmine's features. Stan gave a disappointed grunt and was going to say something, probably a veiled threat, but I got in first.

'She can do it on her own. In her mouth. Go to him, Jasmine, on all fours, and get sucking.'

Her face fell, her mouth coming wide in horror at my deliberate crushing of her will. She went, though, throwing me a single resentful look as she began to crawl across the carpet, her red bottom showing behind with the glistening pink flesh of her aroused pussy on plain show between her thighs. I sat down again, cool and poised but trembling inside as she began to undo his fly, her face set in utter disgust.

His cock came out, balls and all, with him helping her ease it through the opening of his fly. She stared for a moment, gave me one last, imploring look, which I ignored, and went down, her cheeks sucking in as she took his cock. Then she was sucking, a truly revolting sight, with her beautiful, delicate face working up and down on his wrinkly old penis. He was actually quite big, fleshy and a good shape, but that only made the sight of her sucking him all the more obscene. So did her nudity, with her showing everything and him with just his cock and balls bare, the minimum amount needed for her to attend to, while she was left without the slightest scrap of modesty. I wanted to come, but I was not going to, not in front of him. That would happen later, once he had finished and I could picture the whole, repulsive spectacle in my mind as she licked me to heaven.

'You're to swallow,' I instructed, 'every drop.'

Her expression of disgust grew just that little bit fuller, but she kept sucking, now bobbing her head up and down on a fat, pink erection. His cock skin was glossy with her saliva, and his balls were moving sluggishly in his scrotum as it grew taut, fat and round within the ugly, hairy, wrinkled sac, something that definitely belonged in Jasmine's mouth.

'Suck his balls,' I ordered.

She gave me one heated, sidelong glance and pulled her head up. His helmet was so swollen it looked fit to burst, with bubbles of pre-come already mixing with her spit at the tip. A few more good sucks and he'd have come in her mouth, but she dutifully went down on his balls, gaping wide to take in the full bulk of his scrotum, her eyes screwing up as she began to work her mouth on it. He wrapped a hand round his cock, nursing it, his face set in a slack leer as he watched her work on him.

The temptation to just pull up my skirt and stick a hand down my tights and panties was almost too much. It took all my will-power to hold back, but I was determined to be aloof, cool and dominant, my body inaccessible to him. I almost broke, but he came, the whole experience suddenly too much for him as he finished himself off with a flurry of quick jerks.

A fountain of thick white come erupted from his cock, all over the top of Jasmine's head. She jerked back with a squeal of revulsion, which was exactly the wrong thing to do. His second spurt caught her full in the face, in one eye, across her nose and into her open mouth. Then he had stuck his erection back in, milking himself down her throat, his hand on the back of her head, smearing sperm into her hair as her face worked in horror at what she was doing.

I was trying not to laugh, because I knew it would break the moment for her, her soiled ecstasy in being made to degrade herself by me. Sure enough, the moment he let go of her head she rocked back on her heels and twisted, spreading her sex to me. Her fingers went to her clitoris and she was masturbating, utterly shameless, rubbing at herself with his come rolling slowly down her face, one eye shut with it, the other wide and moist. It took just moments, and then her pussy and bottom hole were in contraction and she was coming, her mouth wide, showing off the pool of white sperm inside, and at the very peak calling my name.

The instant it was over she was in my arms, cuddled close, sobbing her heart out at the sheer emotional intensity of what I'd put her through. I held on, soothing her by stroking her back and trying not to think about the mess she was making of my top. She was close to tears, and would have let them go if only Stan had left, would have cried freely as she licked my pussy, something I find so loving.

He didn't go, as insensitive as a lump of rock, but simply reached down for her discarded panties, wiped his cock on them and sat back with a satisfied noise halfway between a grunt and burp. Unable to let my feelings show in front of such crass behaviour, I pushed Jasmine gently away. She stood, suddenly embarrassed as she covered her bottom and breasts. He watched, managing to seem intrusive despite having just come with her. Then, as she went for tissues, he turned his gaze to me.

'How about you, Isa? Going to make Jas lick cunt or what?'

'No,' I answered, 'not now. Could you . . .'

He cut me off with a laugh.

'Well up yourself these days, aren't you? You'd of made a good Rattaner, you would.'

'Rattaner?'

'Yeah. Don't tell me you ain't heard of Margaret Coln?'

'No.'

'I'd of thought she'd be right up your street . . . up your passage too, with her fingers, given half a chance, front and back, I reckon. Dirty old bitch.'

'I've never heard of her. She was at Oxford?'

'Sure she was. Lady Maud College she was at, back when it was St George's Hall. I used to be the boots there, I did. Forty years back, that would be, more, when I first started.'

'So who was she? What did she do?'

'What did she do? Same as you, girlie, only worse.'

'She used to spank girls?'

'The least of it. The cane, that was her favourite, her and most of them others. Not them what got it though. Fuck me, how they used to howl!'

'Slow down, Stan. So this was some sort of society, up at Lady Maud College?'

'Yeah. Old Dr Coln, she had the Old Mill, you know, past St Catharine's.'

'I know, yes. It's accommodation now, isn't it?'

'That's right, changed it over in '82, they did. If some of those students knew what used to go on there!'

'What exactly?'

'Whipping and stuff, what you're into.'

'Yes, you said, but how was it organised? How did you find out?'

'You can't keep dirty stuff like that from the college servants, not easy.'

He was right, as I knew only too well.

'I bet you used to peep,' Jasmine put in from where she was trying to get her tights back on without showing off too much to him.

'Yeah,' he answered proudly. 'Took a bit of guts, that did, 'cause they'd have had me if I'd let 'em catch me.'

'What did you see?' I demanded, fascinated by the idea.

'This and that,' he answered. 'Never too much, 'cept for one time. They were dead careful, they were, and used to do it late at night with the curtains shut and that, and you know how the place is. Noise didn't matter so much, 'specially with the singing.'

'So how did you find out?' I asked. 'And what singing?'

'He was probably sneaking around in the hope of a bit of eye candy anyway,' Jasmine suggested.

'No,' Stan answered, 'I figured out something was going on, I did. I had to do the errands for the butler, and on the first Wednesday of every month I used to take a half-dozen of hock and a half-dozen of claret out to the Mill. When I'd done it I'd get shooed away double quick, and never so much as a farthing to thank me. Then these other old birds would turn up, and one or two young ones and all. Oxford Ladies Choral Society it was, which was what all the singing was about, but really it was to drown out the screams.'

He chuckled, his wrinkly old face creased up with mirth at the memory, then went on.

'What a sight, eh? Seven mad old bags pumping out 'Jerusalem' at the top of their voices, one on the piano, while the eighth gives some poor little scrap of a thing what for across her knee!'

'You saw this, close up?'

'Close enough. Like I said, there was just the one night they left a curtain open a crack, but I saw it all. Cunt and arse, every fucking detail. They had her drawers down, they did, and this big dress up over her head so it was like she was in a bag, with her little white arse sticking out and her legs going like fucking crazy! Then they caned her, six each while two others held her down. I forget what they sang to that. That was all I saw, but I've heard plenty, other times.'

He started to sing, badly, and to slap the arm of his chair. Only he wasn't singing a hymn but a slightly smutty American folk-song. It mentioned President Clinton, so it was not from the 50s.

'When was the last time this happened?' I queried. 'It's still going on, isn't it?'

It was a suspicion, but he immediately stopped singing and shook his head, looking shifty.

'Nah, not for years. Not since the 60s.'

'You're a very bad, liar, Stan. Tell me the truth.'

'I am!'

'No. The truth, Stan, or no more Jasmine for you.' He shook his head.

'Can't do, miss. Not any more than I could tell another what you get up to.'

'You know they're still going? For certain?'

He shook his head and smiled.

'You do, don't you. Come on, Stan, it's not as if I'd disapprove, or that they need know you told me anything. I . . . I could pretend to stumble across them by accident. Do you think they'd have me?'

He laughed.

'Oh, they'd have you, all right, Miss high-and-mighty Isabelle Colraine. They'd have you, right over their knees with your pretty panties at half-mast, that's where they'd have you.'

I was blushing immediately.

'What do you mean? If they were a society of dominant women, surely they would recognise me as one of their own?'

'Oh, no, not that lot, they didn't believe in all that bollocks. Young and pretty and over you go, skirt up, drawers down for a smacked arse, that's the Rattaners' way.'

'Yes, but presumably the girls who are punished want it?'

'Don't think so.'

'How would they get away with that? I mean, didn't any of the girls ever complain?'

'Nah. They wouldn't dare, would they? I reckon some of them was tarts from the town, but more than half was students. Little favours, ain't it? You want a good result in your mods, whoops over you go. You want a few shillings extra to see you by, whoops over you go. You don't want Pater and Mater to find out what you've been up to with the boys from town, whoops over you go. Oh, she had plenty, did old Dr Coln. Nowadays . . .'

He stopped again, at the brink of revealing more than he was supposed to.

'Nowadays what?' I demanded. 'Come on, Stan, you've no right to keep this from me! It's me . . . it's who I am! I need to know!'

'Oh no you don't. I've said too much already.'

He got up, now looking more than a little irritable. The moment he'd gone I turned to Jasmine.

'So what do you think?'

'He's full of shit.'

'Why should that be?'

'I'd have heard of them, or Walter would.'

Walter Jessop had introduced us, another dirty old man, but with more refined tastes.

'Just because they're into corporal punishment doesn't mean they're into corsetry, or Victorian underwear,' I answered her.

'How do they get their girls then?' she retorted. 'Caroline would have heard if they were after submissive women in Oxford.'

'From London?' I suggested. 'On the net maybe?'

She shrugged.

'I still say he's full of shit.'

'Maybe,' I admitted, 'but I love the idea. Just think, I could take you, and Caroline too. I'd have you passed around for spanking, or make you serve tea and cakes in just your corsets, stockings, suspenders and gloves maybe, but bare chested, and with your red bottoms showing.'

I chuckled, thinking how wonderful it would be to show the two of them off, and to indulge myself with other submissive girls too. Between Jasmine, Caroline and my cousin Samantha I'd only ever spanked three women, and it wasn't enough. She didn't answer, but she was looking wistful and I could tell that even if she didn't believe Stan Tierney the idea still appealed to her. I turned to check that the door was on the latch, then beckoned to her.

She smiled and once more got down on all fours, not needing to be told what I wanted. I tugged up my thick woollen skirt and pushed my tights and panties down as one, a bit undignified, but I was too aroused to bother about poise. Not that she minded, now kneeling at my feet like a good little puppy, all eagerness as I slid forwards in the chair and let my thighs come apart.

13

'Show yourself,' I ordered.

She quickly pulled her top up, pushed her tights down at the back and lifted her skirt, baring her breasts and bottom.

'That's better,' I sighed as she went down, her face between my legs, to kiss my pussy mound, then my lips. 'Make it slow. I want to think what I could do with you.'

She began her task, teasing me with her lips and tongue, kissing and dabbing at my sex, and lower, on the tuck of my bottom and where my cheeks meet. I knew she would lick my bottom if I told her to, an act that to her was the final, deepest submission, but I wanted her to do it by choice, when she needed to. I closed my eyes and let my thoughts drift, to her spanking, to her sucking on Stan Tierney's cock, to a girl in a full dress, held down, her bottom on show, kicking helplessly under some stern old matron's cane . . .

It was good, very good, an idyll, really, and with clothing almost as appealing as Victorian wear was. I could imagine their victim's shame as her great big panties were peeled down, strong even compared with what Jasmine suffered. Modern girls don't mind showing their bottoms, even if most do mind being spanked. For a girl in the 50s, some proper, well brought up student, highly intelligent, highly sensitive, it would have been agony.

'. . . think of how she would have felt,' I breathed, letting my thoughts become words. 'Even if she had agreed to it she might not have known it was going to be on the bare. They'd have had to hold her down to get her stripped, two big, strong women on her arms. Imagine her feelings as her dress came up, the awful helplessness of not being able to do a thing about it as she was put on show. She'd have had a girdle, I suppose, and stockings held up by suspender straps, and big white panties, thick cotton, with a gusset, ones that hid everything, at least until they were pulled down.'

My pussy tightened as her lips found my clitoris, just briefly, bringing me a hint of the glory of orgasm, no more. Her hands came up under my hips to take hold of my bottom, kneading gently as she once more began to explore my sex with her mouth. I pulled my jumper up, taking my bra with it, to free my breasts into my hands, teasing my stiff nipples just as she was teasing my pussy and bottom.

'Think how she'd feel,' I sighed, 'as those big, big panties were peeled down over her bottom, her cheeks coming bare, her bottom hole, her pussy. Think how she'd fight to stop it, how she'd struggle and beg and whine, but they'd come down all the same, right down, showing every rude, secret detail of her body. She'd know it wasn't just for her own good. She'd know they wanted her, to see her, to relish her body, her exposure, her pain . . .'

I broke off with a gasp. She had pushed her face between my cheeks, to plant a firm, willing kiss on my anus. Now she was licking me, no longer teasing but right on my clitoris, intent on making me come, on giving me the ecstasy I so badly needed. I'd hit a soft spot, I had to have done, to make her kiss my bottom hole, and I knew what it was. She liked to feel helpless, physically subdued, the way she can be with me. It was good for me, too, and as my orgasm began to rise I was babbling.

'I'd love to do that to you, Jasmine, to hold you down while a dozen women you've never met stripped you, spanked you, fingered you . . . Stan said she fingered the girls, didn't he? Up their pussies . . . up their bottom holes too . . . Think of it, Jasmine, held tight in my arms, women you've never met before, maybe whose names you don't even know, stripping off your clothes, pulling off your panties, spanking your bottom, sticking their fingers into your body, and last . . . last . . . holding you down so the biggest, the strongest, could sit on your face and make you kiss her anus . . . her bottom hole, Jasmine . . . her . . .'

I broke off, crying out in ecstasy as I came under her tongue, my fingers flickering over my erect nipples, my back arched tight, my thighs locked hard around her head. Her thumbs found my pussy just as I began to contract, and slipped in, one finger tickling my bottom hole at exactly the right moment. It left me on a long, glorious high, holding her in tight, forcing her to lick me and lick me until at last I was done and could allow myself to go limp.

She came up bright-eyed and smiling, her face wet, with a little white moustache of pussy juice on her upper lip. I had already decided that I was going to find out everything there was to know about the Rattaners.

Two

There had to be the possibility that Tierney was lying, but I didn't think he was. One or two things didn't ring true, but in general the story made sense. After all, people have always been into corporal punishment and, with enough determination, will always find an outlet for their passion. I knew, because I had.

One anomaly was that 'Rattaners' seemed an odd name, old-fashioned, yes, but too obvious for a secret society dedicated to corporal punishment. It sounded more like something from one of the old Victorian underground magazines Walter Jessop collected, but while it was unlikely that somebody with Tierney's education, or lack of it, would have read *The Pearl* and so forth, I could easily imagine Dr Margaret Coln doing so – assuming she had ever existed.

Another question was whether the society still existed. Forty years is a long time for any organisation, especially a secretive one in which new members would have to be very carefully selected. Against that, Oxford boasts dining societies dating back to Regency times and learned ones from earlier still. Also, a don like the supposed Dr Coln, with life tenure, might well be in residence for over thirty years, maybe even forty. Therefore, in order to survive with around eight members they would only have to find a new one every five years or so. That seemed feasible, especially as there were sure to be girls among their victims who would in time want to be members. Indeed, some might even have been willing to endure the suffering in order to dish it out at a later date. Again I knew that was possible because I'd taken the same route. Regardless, if Tierney had been lying, then the stage had lost a fine actor when he decided to become a college servant.

What I had to do was check the facts. Had there ever been a Dr Margaret Coln at St George's Hall? If so, had she lived in the Old Mill? Had she run a choral society? If all the answers were yes, then it pretty well had to be true. Tierney was what the Irish so delightfully call a 'gobshite', but he was no genius. If he'd made it up, then it had to have been on the spur of the moment, and any tale made up by him on the spur of the moment would have more holes in it than a Gruyère cheese.

Reason aside, I wanted it to be true. I also wanted to become a member, very badly indeed. There was so much I wanted to learn, about my sexual feelings, about the way I am, and I really had nobody to talk to. Jasmine and Caroline were more experienced, but not all that much so, and with them as my slave girls I needed to maintain my authority. Stan Tierney was just a dirty old man, Walter Jessop little better. The last member of my little spanking clique, Dr Duncan Appledore, was far more intelligent but little more experienced, and ultimately a man. I needed a woman, older than me yet prepared to accept my equality in terms of dominant sexuality. If the Rattaners did exist, the senior members would not only fill that role for me, but also have the collected wisdom of the society over perhaps as much as half a century.

Then there was the prospect of punishing new girls. Not that I could approve if it wasn't done with the victims' consent, but undoubtedly that would be a thing of the past. Certainly no modern student was going to allow herself to be physically disciplined, not unless she wanted it. Then again, there had to be those who did, and the internet would have increased the scope for finding new girls enormously.

That led to my first avenue of research. From what Tierney had said the Rattaners were discreet in the extreme, but it had to be worth feeding a few key words into a search engine. I drew a blank, but that only left me feeling mildly disappointed. After all, in their position I would never have made it so easy to find out about my activities.

The other person I could ask was Dr Appledore, who had the advantage of being my tutor. He had been around Oxford for a couple of decades and might have picked something up, but it was not very likely. After all, I had manoeuvred him into spanking me in order to escape Tierney's malice when the scout had first discovered my predilections rather than the other way around. He still spanked me, too, something I was very keen to keep from Jasmine but could not easily put an end to.

I had managed to avoid it since the beginning of term, but I could see he wanted to do it. Nor could I very well deny that I enjoyed it, physically if not mentally, but I did feel it was no longer part of who I am, and that therefore it should stop. I had also decided to become fully lesbian, so being spanked by men was out of the question. So I had to tell him, but in such a way that I didn't upset him or lose his trust and friendship.

It was not easy, and I had been putting it off, always finding an excuse for why I couldn't be dealt

with after our tutorials, which had been the traditional time for my panties to come down. Yet if I was
going to present myself as a serious candidate for the
Rattaners, strictly lesbian and strictly dominant, then
I had to do it.

My tutorial was on Thursday afternoon, the last of
the day. Duncan greeted me as ever, with a big smile.
He was like a bear, huge and hairy, only more of a
teddy-bear than the grizzly variety, at least until he
got me over his knee. Then his sheer power came into
play. I'm nearly six foot, strong and fit, but he
handled me physically as easily as I handled Jasmine,
and that was both appealing and disconcerting. It is
also very hard not to feel submissive to a man who
has held you squealing and kicking across his knee,
but I was determined.

The tutorial was the usual, a purely academic
discussion of my latest essay, this time on the
emergence of the Dutch banking system. His detach-
ment was real, but it made no difference to his
underlying feelings, or mine, and as the hour drew to
a close I had one eye on the fine old clock on his
mantelpiece. He didn't, but as it chimed six he sat
back in his chair and offered me a sherry. For the
previous three weeks I had always made an excuse at
that point and the temptation to do so again was
close to overwhelming. I fought it down, telling
myself not to be so cowardly and that it was best to
get the unpleasant moment over.

'Please, yes,' I answered.

'Not in a hurry this evening?' he queried, moving
for his sideboard and the collection of decanters on it.

'No, not at all,' I answered him. 'I was hoping to
talk to you, in fact.'

His sideboard was just a couple of paces from the
door, and he paused to reach out and slip the catch

before taking up the glass. There was no mistaking his intention in locking the door. He wanted to spank me. It was time to speak.

'I . . . I'm really not sure we should . . . should do this,' I said, putting on an embarrassed smile and praying he would take it well.

He simply passed me my sherry and sat down in the middle of his settee, his favourite place for disciplining me. For one awful moment I wondered if he might not be going to just do me anyway and to hell with my prissy objections, but he was smiling and relaxed, taking a leisurely sip before speaking.

'The college does rather a good Amontillado, don't you think?'

'Yes, but about my . . . my spanking. I'm really not at all sure it's appropriate any more.'

'Ah, yes, I had been concerned you might feel that way. It can be hard enough to come to terms with one's sexuality as it is, given the constraints imposed upon us by society, and doubly so in your case.'

'Thank you, Duncan. I'm so glad you understand.'

'Do I understand? Perhaps, at least to an extent. Yet am I not right in saying that you always enjoyed our little sessions?'

'Of course, you know I did.'

'And your reason for calling a halt?'

'I feel I need to express myself solely as a dominant, and as a lesbian as well.'

'I see. That is your choice, naturally, but might I respectfully suggest that rather than exchange one set of conventions for another you should simply go with your feelings?'

'How do you mean, conventions?'

'Well, in accepting your sexuality as sadomasochistic in nature and primarily lesbian, you are flying in the face of modern social convention. Yet it seems to me that in doing so you are replacing the conventional conventions with unconventional conventions . . . if you will forgive the rather clumsy phraseology.'

'I don't see what you mean. It's how I feel I should be.'

'And yet in contradiction to what brings you pleasure? Since our pleasant little encounters last term I have been reading up on this, and it seems to me that there is a considerable degree of peer pressure among sadomasochists, notably in the United States of America. This obliges conformity, and in particular as regards being one thing or the other, dominant or submissive. Hence I ask if you are not simply allowing yourself to be made to conform?'

'No . . . not consciously, anyway. But yes, there is a contradiction between being dominant and allowing myself to be spanked. Sexual dominance is my nature, it is who I am!'

'Oh, without doubt, yet surely if you are to be truly dominant, truly in control, you should do as you please, not do as you are told?'

'Yes, of course.'

'Including having your bottom smacked?'

'No!'

'Yet you enjoy the experience? Does this not imply that you are allowing yourself to be manipulated?'

'You're the one who is manipulating me, Duncan, you just want me over your knee!'

'Naturally, I believe that is also where you would like to be, not as an act of submission, but for the sake of the pleasure it brings.'

'The pleasure is in the submission . . . some of it.'

He paused to take another sip of his sherry, his eyes bright with the light of debate as much as lust, then spoke again.

'It seems to me that the true dominant behaves as she wishes, not as others think she should. So I ask you this. If you truly wish to express your independence and your dominance, is there any reason you should not come over my knee right now?'

He set his sherry glass down and patted his lap. It looked so inviting, his whole body so big, so powerful. Nor could I fault his reasoning. I did like it, and yes, my desire to call a halt to the spankings was not for my own need but to make myself more acceptable to Jasmine, and potentially to the Rattaners.

'Furthermore,' he continued, 'there is no reason our arrangement need go outside these four walls. Jasmine need not know, nor anybody else.'

He was right. I knew I could trust him, and I did want it, maybe even need it. Still I hesitated, my lips pursed in doubt, until I realised I was making silly faces, and that he was waiting. I could walk away. He wasn't going to stop me. I also suspected he would never ask again. He patted his lap one more time. I stood up, shaking, my stomach fluttering, telling myself I was pathetic even as I stepped the short distance to the settee and draped myself across his lap with all the elegance I could muster.

If he'd crowed over his triumph I think I might have backed out, even at that late moment. He didn't, but stayed absolutely silent as he set about preparing me for my spanking. I closed my eyes as it was done, feeling the trembling of my body and wishing that being stripped for punishment wasn't quite so irresistibly arousing. My skirt came high, rolled up my thighs and over my bottom, so that I had to lift my hips to help him get it up. There was no question at all that my panties were coming down, they always do. I kept my bottom lifted as he dealt with my thick winter tights, peeling them down from around my waist, over my hips, over the swell of my bottom, taking my white silk panties with them, and I was showing.

23

He began to stroke me, just caressing my cheeks, as if to calm me down. It worked, breaking down the last of my bad feelings as I settled onto his lap, my naked bottom ready for punishment. He went on stroking, a little more firmly, to make my cheeks part. I let out a sob at the realisation that he could see my bottom hole and the rear of my vulva. It was all too easy to imagine, my sex lips pouting out between my thighs, my vagina showing as a wet patch amid the fleshy pink folds, my anus a wrinkled brown knot, ruder even than Jasmine's, and infinitely more shameful, because it was mine.

I was shaking badly, and trying to get my bottom cheeks together even as I felt silly doing it. He had seen it all before, every detail, but somehow that didn't seem to matter. To be bare in front of him, so intimately bare, was so awful, so inappropriate, yet so exciting that I would simply not have been able to hold still had he not taken me firmly around the waist. Then I was helpless, trapped beneath his massive arm, held tightly down as he continued to explore my bottom, his huge paw squeezing my cheeks, spreading them once more to stretch my anus, and at last starting to spank.

My tears had already been welling in my eyes, and they burst at the first firm swat, running down my face as I dissolved into hysterical sobbing, relief flooding through me as I gave myself up to punishment. He ignored my tears, letting me pour out my emotions into my hands as my bottom bounced to the firm, stinging spanks, each and every one sending a jolt right through me.

It hurt, a lot, but I knew it had to, and I knew where that pain was going to take me. I let myself go, kicking my legs and wriggling my bottom in a lewd, undignified display, no better than any other girl who has needed her bottom spanked down the years. He didn't laugh, even though I must have looked pretty ridiculous, but just kept on spanking me, smack after smack, each catching me full across my cheeks, until at last the pain turned to warmth and I had begun to come on heat.

I stuck my bottom up, as lewd and promiscuous as a she-cat, wanting my tail warmed, my pussy frigged off. He knew, and he obliged, cupping his big arm under my tummy to get at me, burrowing in among my folds and starting to rub, still spanking all the while. I just went wild, squirming in his grip, bucking my naked bottom up and down to flaunt myself for the spanks, rubbing my pussy on his hand, just too out of control to find the focus I needed for orgasm.

He dealt with it, tightening his grip to lock me into place, my bare red bottom thrust up, my pussy spread over his fingers. My thighs slipped wide and I had surrendered, utterly, giving him my body as he dealt with my need, rubbing and spanking, harder and harder, my bottom jiggling wildly, my legs pumping, then tense.

I was coming, brought off under his hand, spanked to orgasm, biting on the cushions of the settee to stop myself screaming as it tore through me, the most wonderful ecstatic climax. It was perfect, true ecstasy, with me surrendered utterly to the man who had had the guts to spank my bottom for me, the man who had taken me through my pain and beyond, who knew so well what needed to be done to me.

He held me tight as I shook in orgasm, still spanking and rubbing until at last my spasms stopped and I went limp in his arms. Only then did he stop and let go, but I made no effort to get up, just lying there across his lap, spanked and masturbated and quite unable to feel anything but gratitude.

It felt so good, to have given in, to have let down my armour and accepted a spanking. He was so, so right. I did need it, regularly, just to allow me to come down to earth now and then. He was definitely the man to do it, every time, big and strong and reliable, an authority figure for me, the ideal spanker.

'Was that not pleasant?' he asked softly as he once more began to stroke my now smarting bottom.

'It was beautiful,' I admitted. 'I did need it. Thank you.'

At last I got up, to stand a little unsteadily as I reached back to take my hot bottom in hand, feeling the heat of my skin and the strange, thick feeling of spanked flesh. It was smarting, a lot, and what I really wanted was to be creamed, but I had my duty to perform. He deserved me, and he could have me, as he pleased, his choice. When he spoke he was as polite as ever.

'I will understand if you no longer wish to perform fellatio, Isabelle, but it would be a great pleasure, and appropriate, I think.'

I nodded. Oral sex is the perfect reward for a spanking, the ideal way for the punished girl to acknowledge her willing submission to what has been done to her, to thank whoever has done it, and to provide the relief for the sexual tension she has caused. He gave me a knowing smile and undid his fly, to pull out his cock, thick and heavy above a pair of large balls. I went straight down, still shaking, into a kneeling position with my red bottom stuck out behind so that he could admire what he had done to me. He took his cock, offering it to me, and I gaped, taking him in.

He was swelling immediately, growing in my mouth as I sucked obligingly on him, doubtless as he thought of how he'd spanked me and how I now looked on his cock. I took his balls in my hands, playing with them to help him on his way, just gently, and began to lick the underside of his erection as he came fully hard. He had fucked me before, and he could have done again, or even put it up my bottom. That didn't seem to be what he wanted, and I was his to command, so I sucked, pausing only to pull my top up over my breasts, something else men seem to like when a girl is down on them.

Vaguely I was aware that I was breaking every single promise I had made to myself in the past month; not to show a man my naked body again, not to let myself be spanked, not to suck cock, let alone suck cock kneeling near naked at the feet of a man who had just spanked me. I wasn't going to stop though, mouthing eagerly on his cock and teasing his balls, bottom and breasts on show for him, thoroughly wanton, thoroughly undignified, entirely submissive.

He took my head, moaning in ecstasy as he began to fuck my mouth, taking one extra element of control away from me, and almost immediately he had come, filling my mouth with thick, salty come. I swallowed it down as best I could, spurt after spurt as he ejaculated down my throat, spilling only a little onto the sac of his balls, which I dutifully licked up as soon as he was finished.

I had to come again, simply too high to think twice. The moment I had finished cleaning up his balls I rocked back, my mouth open, showing him what he'd done in it. That wasn't the best of what he'd done, though. I wanted to show him my spanked bottom and to come bare-bottom in front of him, every single detail on show, not even my most intimate secrets hidden. I twisted around, displaying my red cheeks to him, well parted, my little brown bottom hole on open show, my pussy too. I slipped my hands down, back and front, to rub my pussy and stroke my smacked cheeks, feeling the hot meat of my bottom, the ready mouth of my vagina, the tight, damp hole of my anus.

My fingers went in, up my bottom hole and pussy at the same time, thoroughly rude, penetrating myself as much to show off as for the physical pleasure of it. He gave a pleased sigh and I began to concentrate, probing my holes as I thought of how lewd I was being, how dirty, showing him every detail of my body, utterly uninhibited, utterly surrendered, all because he'd put me across his knee and spanked me, spanked me and spanked me and spanked me . . .

I came, crying out my ecstasy with my fingers pushed as deep into my body as they would go and my mind on the thought of how my smacked bottom would look from behind with both my holes penetrated and my cheeks rosy red. Then it was over and I was down on my knees, shaking with reaction, eyes closed, panting, bedraggled, too far gone even to think of covering myself. Duncan calmly placed a box of tissues beside me and I burst out giggling.

There was shame, but it didn't really hit me while I was in his company. He invited me over to the SCR dining-room and I went, enjoying the meal and the attention of the predominately male dons present. I got slightly drunk too, the college servants dispensing hock, claret and port with a liberal hand and Duncan insisting I take a shot of brandy in my coffee afterwards.

It was only afterwards that my feelings hit me, and I was filled with chagrin as I walked back across the quad. I'd been so determined, but in the end I'd just let myself get upended again, with no more dignity or protest than before, then sucked his cock.

That didn't stop me masturbating as I lay in my bed late that night. I had hoped to get to sleep without giving in, because I knew what it would be over. Unfortunately there seemed to be a never-ending stream of rowdies coming back into college and I couldn't get to sleep. Finally I was forced to do it. Even then I tried to focus on Jasmine and Caroline, imagining them side by side, naked, their bottoms raised for my caress or the kiss of my whip, as I chose. It didn't work, and before I'd even pulled my nightie up over my breasts I was thinking of how I had felt across Duncan's knee as my tights and panties were peeled slowly down off my bottom. I never even got to the spanking, reaching orgasm as I remembered how he'd inspected my anus.

It was plainly hopeless, and as I finally drifted towards sleep I made a resolution to separate my sex life into two distinct areas. With Jasmine and Caroline, and as far as Stan Tierney and Walter Jessop were concerned, I would be strictly dominant and lesbian. With Duncan I would be submissive and straight, thus getting the best of both worlds.

I hadn't had the opportunity to mention the Rattaners to Duncan after my tutorial, being too busy getting spanked and sucking his cock. In the end I didn't, reasoning that if I did manage to become a member then the fewer people who knew about it the better.

What I did do was begin my research. With a full week to complete my next essay I didn't feel under any particular need to work on the Friday afternoon, so spent it in the college library looking over the old records for St George's Hall before it had become an independent college. Had it not been for the wonders of modern technology and in particular computer indexing I might have spent several days there, and in the Bodleian too. As it was I had everything I needed in the course of two afternoons' intense work, one per library. It was quite something.

Dr Margaret Coln had indeed existed. She had held a Readership in English Literature at St George's Hall from when it was set up in the mid 30s until her retirement in 1964. She had also been Dean for most of that period, a leading light in local Conservative politics, the driving force behind several charitable organisations and a minor author. She had retired to King's Lynn and died in 1996, at the grand old age of 92, still active in half a dozen fields. Reading between the lines, that translated to her being a terrifying bluestocking and a consummate busybody. There was not the slightest hint of impropriety, but that did not surprise me. It was very easy indeed to imagine her spanking younger women.

Having identified Dr Coln, the real detective work began. If the Rattaners still existed, then no doubt there would be perfectly respectable links between their members. Therefore, and especially in view of what Tierney had hinted about 'little favours', it should be possible to trace the membership of the society down the years to the present. The first and most obvious link was the Oxford Ladies Choral Society, which had indeed existed, and boasted the redoubtable Dr Coln among its members.

Unfortunately it had been dissolved only two years after her retirement, in 1966. However, that fitted with it being a cover, as whoever her successor had been might well not have had the use of the Old Mill and would therefore have been obliged to make other arrangements. The Choral Society would thus have become a burden, although to judge by what Tierney had let slip the tradition of singing to cover up the victims' wails of anguish had persisted.

The Choral Society had been small, never with more than nine members. That again fitted well with what Tierney had said about eight older women being present at the punishment he had witnessed, making the chances that he was lying slimmer still. Of the members all but one had been from the Senior Common Rooms of one college or another, the exception being the wife of a local politician. The last woman to join, in '63, had been one Dr Elizabeth Hastings, the newly appointed lecturer in English Literature at St George's Hall, a woman who had gone on to be Dr Coln's successor.

That was too great a coincidence to be ignored. Sure enough, Dr Coln had been Elizabeth Hastings' tutor. I could just see it, the same way it had worked between Duncan Appledore and I. Margaret Coln would have spotted Elizabeth as promising material and in due course spanked her. Elizabeth would then have become the plaything for the society until she herself secured her Doctorate, a post doubtless well worth taking five or six years of ignominious spankings. Again like me, her natural taste would have been for dominance, and so she would have remained with the Rattaners, only no longer as their victim.

Following the dissolution of the Choral Society the thread became harder to follow. Aside from Elizabeth Hastings most of the members had been roughly of an age with Margaret Coln, and by 1970 all but two had retired, only one of these remaining in Oxford. That made four members at most unless they had recruited others, and there was no easily obtainable evidence of that. As I had surmised, it might be possible to go for years without finding a suitable candidate, and it seemed likely that the 70s had marked a decline in the Rattaners' activities, if not extinction.

Elizabeth Hastings had been a very different person from the formidable Margaret Coln, quiet, introspective and an expert on poetry. That caught my attention, and sure enough, she had written not one, but two books on Swinburne. Both were very detached and intellectual works, and yet here again was a link to her love of flagellation. Unfortunately she had been yet more discreet than Margaret Coln. There was no easily traced cover society, nor did she have any obvious protégés. There had been a Victorian literary salon in the 80s, but while it was tempting to see it as a successor to the Oxford Ladies Choral Society it had been open membership. She was also no longer in Oxford, but had accepted a chair in Cleveland, Ohio.

If I had been fascinated before, by the time I left the Bodleian on the Monday evening I was obsessed. The entire story had drawn me in, and had I simply been able to seek out Elizabeth Hastings I would have done so like a shot. She could have spanked me and had the entire society cane me, naked and in chains. Had it been asked of me I would gladly have accepted five years as their sexual plaything in return for a promise of eventual membership – anything.

As it was I couldn't, but my need to seek her out was so strong I almost jumped on a plane straight away. Unfortunately I could justify neither the time nor the expense, while I could just imagine my father's reaction if I suggested forking out for a trip to the Midwestern States in the middle of term.

I did have her address, including her departmental email, but I didn't feel it was sensible to use it. What I had to do needed face-to-face contact. A letter, let alone an email, could too easily be ignored, while for all I knew she had changed her attitudes, or just possibly never been a willing participant at all. The last thing I wanted to do was get so close and then make a complete mess of the actual contact.

Yet it was impossible to simply do nothing. All the other women I had identified as definite members of the Rattaners were long gone. While several of Elizabeth's colleagues were possibilities, I could hardly approach one and boldly demand to be admitted to membership of a secretive spanking society they had probably never even heard of. The most likely candidate was Professor Hope Ashdene, an extremely senior and respected academic. Elizabeth had been her tutor and they had published several papers together, including one on Swinburne, but that was not proof. Second favourite was Dr Jane Roberts, almost as senior and one of my lecturers, which made the prospect of accosting her seem yet more outrageous. Third was Lady Emmeline Young, not an academic but the wife of the Master of Bede College. The thought of approaching any of them was absolutely terrifying, and before making a move I needed to be one hundred per cent sure. To achieve that certainty I need to speak to Stan Tierney, and if it was not a road I wanted to take, then it was that or back down.

I have always been stubborn.

Three

I was very sure I could get the information I needed from Stan Tierney. However much he knew, the fact remained that my goodwill gave him access to Jasmine and Caroline. I kept him rationed, and while I could easily find another dirty old man to fulfil their need for erotic humiliation, he had no chance of finding another pair of pretty young girls to pay court to his grubby old cock. So I had plenty of bargaining power, while it was also amusing to think of Jasmine's reaction to being used as a tool in my search for the Rattaners, a search that when successful would inevitably lead to further pain and humiliation for her. Caroline's reaction would be different, as she was far more accepting of her submissive nature, yet she would still appreciate the situation.

Caroline was the more intelligent of the two, as well as being the one with the real ability, designing and making beautiful corsets, both modern and old-fashioned, with an enviable skill. She was also very different from Jasmine physically, and more appealing to me in that sense, for all that I found Jasmine's submission more satisfying for the very difficulty she had in giving it. Where Jasmine was willowy, Caroline was curvaceous, with a full bottom and ample breasts made to seem larger still by her tiny waist. She was shorter than Jasmine, yet several pounds heavier, with dark curls framing a pretty, vivacious face. She also had full lips, an upturned nose and large, lustrous brown eyes, which gave her a cheeky, somehow insolent look. It made her a delight to spank. Jasmine, by contrast, with her elfin face and pale blonde hair, always seemed sulky, a touch resentful, which was more delightful still.

Their corsetry business was going well, but barely brought in enough money to live on. While waiting for it to get off the ground they had taken to stripping, mainly at a working mens' club called the Red Ox. It was in Cowley, and just what you might expect, a sordid concrete shack full of coarse men and their equally coarse women. They still did it, neither of them suffering from my admittedly class based distaste for such things, because it made the difference between living in poverty and moderate comfort. I let them get on with it, not really approving but reluctant to interfere.

Tierney was a member at the Red Ox, and usually in the audience when they stripped. Being a male through and through, he preferred Caroline for her opulent figure, but was more than content to accept sexual favours from either. Generally I made Jasmine suck him, because she hated it so much more, which inevitably made him keener still on Caroline. Jasmine therefore became my first option, with Caroline in reserve if he proved stubborn and the two of them together if he proved really stubborn. The only thing I would not do was allow myself to benefit financially.

Despite the fact that he did my room every morning, I seldom saw Tierney. I was generally at lectures while he was working, although he did seem to have an unerring knack for knowing when the girls were visiting me. It was easy enough to see him anyway. I simply skipped a dull nine o'clock lecture on Prussian expansionism in the nineteenth century, never my thing. He was a little surprised to find me sitting at my desk, but greeted me with his usual over-familiar leer.

'You want me to come back later, love?' he asked, the standard question from scouts to students and delivered in the standard tone, expecting the answer 'no' and an apology for getting in the way of his work.

'No,' I answered him. 'Shut the door. I want a word with you.'

'Oh yeah?'

He sounded doubtful, belligerent even, probably thinking I was intent on putting a stop to the little sexual favours he was getting, which showed how little he understood the relationship between Jasmine, Caroline and myself. To the three of us he fulfilled a need, and our disgust at his body and behaviour was a positive thing within the context of our relationship. Inevitably he only thought of it as something we did to keep him quiet, and he was always ready to resist any attempt by us to wriggle out of the deal.

'Nothing bad, Stan,' I assured him. 'Do you remember what we were talking about the other day, when Jasmine was here? That society.'

'Sure,' he answered, more defensive still.

'I want to know, Stan,' I went on.

'Can't do it, love.'

'Yes you can, and you should. I'm not going to explain why you should, and we are going to strike a bargain. How would you like to have full sex with Jasmine?'

'I can't do it, love. Not for anything.'

'Yes you can. All I need is a name, the rest I can do myself. You have my word your own name will never come up. There, that's not much to give in return for Jasmine, is it?'

'No. Sorry, Isa, love. I would, but I can't.'

He had begun to do my room. I didn't answer immediately as he had turned the vacuum cleaner on, drowning out all possibility of conversation. It was intentional, making me raise my bid, because we both knew full well that he would accept in the end. Doubtless he was wondering just how far I would make them go, and so was I. Sucking his cock was one thing, but I didn't want him getting too intimate, while it definitely made sense to keep something in reserve.

'I'll have her perform a striptease for you,' I offered when he finally turned the vacuum cleaner off, 'a private show, with sex afterwards.'

'Can't do it.'

'I do mean full sex, Stan. On her knees if you like.'

'I already said. I can't do it.'

'Yes you can. Think of Jasmine, Stan, crawling naked on the floor, just for you, ready for you. You know she'll do it.'

'Sure, but I can't tell you what you want to know. I shouldn't've said nothing in the first place.'

'Well you did ... say something that is. So now could you please tell me? How about Caroline Greenwood instead of Jasmine?'

'No.'

'Oh come on, Stan. Think of the way she teases at the Red Ox. Think of those lovely big breasts, not just to look at, but to touch, to feel, to suck, to put your cock between them, to ...'

'Look, Isa, love, you're giving me a fucking big hard-on here, but I can't do it.'

'They don't need to know it was you, Stan! I'll make up some story ... I don't know, pretend I overheard a conversation or something.'

'No.'

'Oh come on, think of Caroline, naked and willing, yours to do as you please with. I'll tell her she has to do anything you say, suck you, take you in her pussy, anything.'

'Up the shitter?'

I hesitated, wondering if even Caroline might not rebel at being told to allow Tierney to sodomise her.

'If she will, yes, if that's what you want.'

'You are one dirty bitch, Isa, but I can't do it.'

I changed tack.

'I know who some of the members are, Stan, so you might as well tell me.'

'Who, then?'

'Well, for one thing I know that Dr Elizabeth Hastings took over the society when Margaret Coln retired. Yes?'

'No.'

He had winced visibly. I was right.

'Professor Hope Ashdene,' I went on, 'Dr Jane Roberts, Lady Emmeline Young.'

'No, none of them.'

'You're giving yourself away, Stan. You can say what you like but your face tells the truth. Now you may as well confirm it for me. All you have to do is say "yes", one little word, and you can have Caroline, maybe even up her bottom, and she does have the most beautiful bottom, doesn't she, Stan?'

He'd turned away, and I realised what he was doing an instant before he spoke and turned back towards me.

'Look what you've done, you fucking prick-tease.'

He had his cock out, balls and all, holding it up so that I could see how hard he was. I just shrugged, determined to hold my composure. He began to masturbate, his eyes on my stocking-clad legs.

'Put it away, Stan.'

'Why should I? You've turned me on with your dirty talk, you have. I didn't ask for that, so I reckon you owe me a blow-job.'

'You know that's out of the question, Stan, but just tell me what I need to know and I'll have Caroline and Jasmine do it together, on their knees in the nude, sucking your cock, licking your balls, touching each other to turn you on . . .'

He groaned.

'At least toss me off, you fucking little tease!'

'I said no, Stan.'

He had come closer, wanking furiously at his erection, which was pointed right at my face. I reached out to push him away but it was too late, as come erupted from the tip of his cock, full in my face an instant before I'd twisted away. It had gone in my eye, and all I could do was bat at him in a futile effort to make him stop as he milked himself down my neck and over my shoulder and chest, leaving me blinded and dripping sperm as he casually tidied himself up and left.

I could cheerfully have murdered Stan Tierney, but if he thought he was going to put me off simply by abusing me he had another thought coming. He was going to tell me, and that was all there was to it. It was just going to take a little more effort.

His reluctance was understandable, given that the women involved in the Rattaners were uniformly respectable and also influential. Yet none of my three possibilities were members of St George's, and so could not influence him directly, which set my mind on a new train of thought. If he wasn't prepared to give up his information even for the chance to sodomise Caroline, then he had to be pretty worried about the consequences. Therefore it was possible, even likely, that there was a Rattaner in college. Not only that, but she would have to be aware that he knew about the society.

With only four women in St George's SCR it had to be possible to work out who it was. Two were out of the question, both new appointments from outside the university and one of those a South African into the bargain. I felt I could also safely eliminate the bursar, a jolly, bustling woman who it was simply impossible to picture as sexually dominant, or really as sexual at all. She also had no connection whatsoever with any of my possibilities. The fourth was a different matter. Dr Antonia Cappaldi was a physicist and another outside appointment, but she had been a student at Oxford and, as I quickly discovered, at Lady Maud. She also looked the part, very tall, with striking black hair and a stern, Roman face, while her manner was very reserved and formal. There was no proof, but it seemed likely that I had my fourth Rattaner, which made maybe half or more of the society.

Other avenues of exploration were opening up with my growing knowledge, but Stan Tierney was still my best bet. I could see my mistake too. At work he was surly and defensive, very much aware of his low status and his job. At the Red Ox it was a different matter. He was in his element, among equals, much more assertive and, more importantly, frequently drunk.

Cowley is a place I do my very best to avoid. Jasmine and Caroline aside, I find myself very ill at ease in the town. My background is public school, finishing school and now university, while from earliest childhood I've been used to being apart from ... well, let's face it, common people. At home in Scotland I was always the landowner's daughter, and never really fitted it. Nor did I feel I wanted to, being something of a loner by nature. It was the same at college. Intellectuals were fine, and I did try not to be aloof, but at the end of the day the whole working class ethos embarrasses me.

The Red Ox on a Saturday night was about as bad as it gets, especially when the local Association Football team was playing at home. Inevitably they were, which meant it would be packed, noisy, smoky and generally about as unpleasant a place as I could imagine. To top it all, Jasmine and Caroline would be stripping and, however much I enjoyed having them show their bodies off when it was under my control, it was a very different matter when they weren't. Stan Tierney was going to be there, though, and so was I.

I met the girls at their house and we drove up together in Jasmine's car. They knew what I was up to, more or less, and were nervous at the prospect, Jasmine far more so than Caroline. Not that there was any question of them refusing. They wore my tattoos and that meant something to them.

The Red Ox was exactly as I had imagined it would be, packed to the doors, almost entirely with men, and many of those in football colours. Fortunately we were able to go around the back and were greeted by Mike, the manager. He knew me, but got the wrong idea immediately.

'All three of you, great, that's what we need. Believe me, you are going to go down a fucking storm tonight!'

'Just two,' I corrected him.

'On the rag?' he asked, sending the blood straight to my face. 'Don't worry about it, you can keep your panties and –'

'No, I'm not stripping, Mike. I just came along to keep Jasmine and Caroline company.'

'Why not? You know how they are about students. Nothing they like better than watching a posh bird get her kit off. You'd get two ... maybe three hundred with the crowd out there.'

'No, thank you.'

'Your loss. It'll be a good night. Three–two we won, some match ...'

He went on with a detailed account of the football game as he led us inside. There were no proper facilities for the girls to change, just a back room full of beer kegs and crates of bottles, but he did at least bring us large glasses of brandy, an inferior Cognac but welcome all the same. He seemed to have taken on extra stock and there was barely room to move in the back room, and I had to find Tierney anyway, so I left the girls to get changed and went out to the front, into a wall of stink: cigarettes, beer, cheap perfume, sweat.

I had tried to dress the part, in jeans and a bright red sweater, but it didn't work. A few of them had seen me before, but all of them seemed to know I was a student, and reacted with a disturbing mixture of hostility and lust. My bottom was pinched several times before I managed to reach a corner in which I could put my back to the wall. There was no sign of Tierney, so I settled down to watch Caroline's schoolgirl strip routine, trying not to feel too jealous about the ranks of ogling men.

Her uniform certainly wouldn't have passed muster at my school, a typical smutty pastiche designed only for men's pleasure. The skirt was red tartan, pleated and ludicrously short, not even covering her bottom properly at the back. The blouse was little better, several sizes too small so that the buttons were straining across her chest and left ample slices of creamy white flesh on show. Her underwear was

42

black, something else that had been frowned on at my school, and the same went for her five-inch spike heels in bright-red PVC. Personally I would far rather have watched her strip out of a real uniform, or just her ordinary clothes, but the crowd lapped it up, calling out for more and filling the beer glass Mike was passing around with coins and notes.

Going all the way was part of the deal, notwithstanding Mike's offer to allow me to keep my panties on if I had my period. To the first song she just danced, although with her body and the way she moved even that managed to be close to obscene. To the second she went down to her underwear, teasing with every garment and ending up flushed and dishevelled with her hair in disarray and most of her bum spilling out of her panties. To the third she made quick work of her bra and panties, the one flipped up over her big breasts, the other eased slowly down with her bottom stuck out to the crowd. She then danced nude but for her stockings, by the end crawling on the stage with every single detail of her pussy and bottom flaunted.

The entire performance had been aimed at me, and I was promising myself that whatever else happened she was going to get the spanking of her life before bed. Every single man in the place had noticed, the few women too, and as the music finally went down and she scampered off stage I caught a remark about dykes followed by coarse laughter. That left me blushing and wishing I was anywhere else in the entire world, preferably with Caroline's bare bottom across my knee and a riding crop in my hand.

Mike came out to announce Jasmine, which led to clapping and obscene remarks. She came out in her 20s-style outfit, her hair up and decorated with an ostrich feather, wearing a fringed dress in pale blue beneath which I knew she would have loose, split-seam knickers and no bra. It looked wonderful, but the reception from the crowd was lukewarm, at least until she began to dance. She was good, very elegant and sultry, managing to give the impression that she was reluctant, and yet always providing what was wanted.

It took her two songs to go naked and she spent the third dancing in the nude and showing absolutely everything. First it was cheeky and silly, doing the Charleston and the Black Bottom, then just plain dirty, modern-style, with her bottom stuck out and wiggling, her pussy and the little pink dimple of her anus on blatant show. She finished with an insolent wiggle of her bottom, her trademark, and went backstage. As the music died somebody spoke from right beside me – Stan Tierney.

'Fucking gorgeous, ain't she?'

'Yes,' I agreed, 'and a good dancer too.'

'You on next?' he asked.

'No I am not!'

'Don't get your knickers in a twist, love. I only asked. Why not, anyway? There's a good group, and they do love to see a stuck-up bird strip.'

'I've already had Mike on that subject, thank you.'

'Buy us a drink then?'

I restrained myself with an effort.

'Stan, the last time we met you ... you ... you know, in my face. Don't you think you should be offering me the drink?'

He chuckled.

'Yeah, all right. Guinness?'

He didn't give me a chance to answer, moving off through the crowd as the music started for Caroline's second number. She was in her Red Indian outfit, a microscopic skirt of raw leather with rough edges that once again failed to cover her ample bottom and a hopelessly inadequate bra to match. Stripes of red and white paint on her face and a swan's feather with the tip dyed pink completed the outfit, so she didn't really have much stripping to do. The crowd loved it anyway, egging her on as she went through the silly dance routine, until she was once more nude, and finished the act by pulling the feather from her hair and inserting it into her anus.

'Dirty bitch, your Caroline,' Tierney remarked as he returned to me.

'She could be yours, so easily,' I pointed out.

'Don't start that again,' he answered and buried his face in his pint of Guinness.

He had bought me two half pints. As there was nowhere to put our glasses down I assumed it was to keep my hands busy and so allow him to grope my bottom, until I realised that every other woman in the club was also drinking out of half-pint glasses, at least the ones with beer. They were also studiously ignoring the striptease, save for the occasional glance and catty remark, both at the girls and at me. I ignored them, wondering how best to deal with Tierney. Step one was clearly to get him drunk and aroused, which was not difficult.

Jasmine had come back on, in full football colours, complete with scarf and bobble hat, tiny nylon shorts, long socks and as usual, no bra. It was always a popular routine, and had the crowd singing rowdy songs and chanting the score of the recent game as she peeled down to just her socks. To the second song she gave a rude display with a football, sitting on it and rubbing her pussy and bottom on the leather, a sight that had Tierney mumbling lustfully under his breath.

As Caroline came back on, Tierney's hand found my bottom. I stiffened by instinct, but let him get on with it, feeling the shape of my cheeks within my jeans and giving me the occasional intimate little pat. Only when he tried to push his hand down the back of my panties did I tell him to stop, deciding that I had suffered enough. He went back to fondling me and watching Caroline, who had stripped quickly and was jiggling her breasts in people's faces in return for coins.

They were on for four strips each, by which time I was hoping Tierney would be fit to burst. Sacrificing my bottom to his fondling was well worth it, but it didn't give me much time to get him drunk. I couldn't get my own drink either, not being a member, but managed to press a five pound note onto him for a second round. He had just bought a third by the time Jasmine finished her final strip, and the moment I had taken my glasses his hand went back to my bottom. I let him grope for a while longer, then leaned down to whisper in his ear.

'I'm now going to take those two home, make them dress up in their striptease outfits, spank them both and have them perform together before they oblige me. You could be there, so easily . . .'

'You bitch.'

'No need to be vulgar. You choose. We'll be in the car park in a quarter of an hour.'

Mike had come out to announce the end of the stage show and many of the men were pushing towards the bar, allowing me to get to the stage and in at the back. Jasmine and Caroline were in the store-room, washing at the big sink more generally used for cleaning out equipment. Both turned as I came in, Jasmine with a bright smile and Caroline giggling.

'You have earned yourself a spanked bottom,' I told Caroline, 'probably more.'

She giggled again, clearly perfectly happy to be dealt with, just the mood I wanted her in.

'I've invited Stan Tierney back,' I told her, 'but only on condition he tells me about the Rattaners.'

Jasmine made a face. Caroline just shrugged.

'He wants to sodomise you,' I told her, determined to get a reaction.

It worked. Her mouth came open to refuse, but she had seen the look on my face and swallowed her words, turning her face to the ground instead.

'I might even let him,' I went on, 'so get into that ridiculous Red Indian costume and you had better behave!'

'The Red Indian costume? Isabelle . . . Mistress, it's freezing outside!'

'Good, it'll keep your nipples perky. Jasmine, you can dress normally, for not flaunting yourself at me on stage. Don't worry, I'll keep you firmly in role. Keys, please, I'll meet you outside.'

Caroline made to protest once more but thought better of it. I left, sure Tierney would be in the car park but not wanting to chance my arm by making him wait. Sure enough, he was there, looking sullen and more disreputable than ever in a heavy overcoat several sizes too large for him. Caroline was right: it was freezing, with the lights of the club showing a sheen of iridescent ice crystals on every surface and the windows of Jasmine's car patterned with frost.

I'd barely cleared the windscreen when Caroline appeared at the back door, attired as ordered and squeaking in shock as the cold air hit her. She scurried over and ducked into the car, presenting Tierney with the target of her ample bottom just long enough for him to plant a heavy smack on it. He made to follow her, but I pushed the seat back, forcing him to get into the front.

'Uh, uh, no you don't, Stan, not so much as another slap until you've told me what I want to know.'

'I'm not falling for that one, love,' he answered me. 'You'll fuck off home and leave me standing.'

'I keep my word,' I assured him, but he merely grunted.

I climbed in beside Caroline. She was shivering, and looked extremely vulnerable in her ridiculous little costume, while the cold had certainly had the right effect on her nipples, both sticking up taut through the thin leather of her crude bra. I cuddled her to me as Jasmine arrived, sliding quickly into the driver's seat and taking the keys from me.

'Home,' I ordered.

She set off, through the yellow-lit, frosty streets of East Oxford. There were only a few people about, hurrying back to the warmth of their homes with their coats pulled close about them, each busy with their own affairs. Tierney was talking, a loud and drunken monologue about how much he had appreciated each of the striptease acts. I wasn't listening, instead thinking of what a strange group we made, a student, a college servant and two girls from the town, united only by our taste for unconventional sex. It would have been the same for the Rattaners, on the very streets I walked and cycled along every day, for perhaps half a century now, their wonderful secret hidden behind a cloak of respectability, of normality.

I didn't try to bargain with Tierney until we had arrived at Jasmine's and she had turned a couple of fires on. We gravitated naturally to the kitchen, the warmest place, and also the best. Upstairs was their playroom, customised for the most elaborate of erotic torments, but it was inappropriate. This was going to be a crude, domestic buggery, sordid really. How else could it be with Stan Tierney involved?

As the dominant I simply sat down, allowing Jasmine to serve me by pouring me a glass of heavy red wine before coming to kneel at my feet. Caroline came to me too, to stand behind my chair. Tierney made himself comfortable, taking a beer from the fridge and sitting down splay-legged, with a big bulge showing in the crotch of his shabby trousers. I took a sip of wine, composing myself.

'So, Stanley, the name?'

'Not yet, you don't. First I want to watch you spank Carrie's big arse, bare.'

'Very well, to show good faith, but first, am I on the right track, with the names I told you?'

'Not too far off.'

He was looking very shifty indeed, and I was sure I was closer than he implied. I pushed my chair back and beckoned to Caroline, who came around the chair, biting her lip as she laid herself down across my lap, bottom high, the ridiculous little skirt rising up to leave more than half her cheeks showing. I turned it up, completing her exposure. There were no panties, just the full, glorious globe of her bottom, so ripe and so feminine, making me wish Tierney wasn't there so that I could concentrate on her rather than giving him a show.

'Turn her round a bit,' he instructed. 'I like to see a bit of cunt, and pull her tits out.'

I obliged, shifting my chair to bring Caroline's bottom more directly into his line of sight. He responded by unzipping himself and pulling out his cock, still flaccid but heavy with blood, and the skin already glossy with a sheen of sweat. Carrie was trembling a little, and I spent a moment stroking her hair to soothe her, then hooked my thumb into her foolish little bra and tugged it up, spilling out her breasts. Tierney grunted and leaned out a little to let himself see them. He had begun to masturbate. He was drooling too, spittle running out at one side of his mouth, a truly disgusting sight.

'Better get you spanked,' I told Caroline, and set to work.

She always does like to make a fuss, and was kicking and squealing in no time, as well as wriggling madly, to make the fat globe of her bottom quiver and spread, showing off her anus between slaps, and her pussy. Tierney just stared, his eyes glued to her bouncing cheeks as he caressed his cock and balls, quickly bringing himself to full erection. She is adorable, so sweet and so voluptuous, and so good to spank. Even the little Red Indian costume seemed appropriate, playful and somewhat silly, especially disarranged to show off every rude detail of her body. Tierney or no Tierney, I was enjoying myself, and getting more and more turned on as her big bottom warmed beneath my fingers and the scent of excited female grew slowly thicker in the air.

I wasn't going to stop, delighting in her pained reaction and wanting to get her as warm as possible before she was sodomised – if Tierney didn't come in his hand first. He was about to, jerking hard at his erection with his face red and sweaty, but he stopped himself, sitting back with a sigh, bubbles of pre-come already showing around the bloated tip of his cock.

'Stop that or I'll spunk,' he gasped. 'Fuck me but you've got a gorgeous arse, Carrie. I love 'em fat.'

'She's not fat, just curvaceous,' I answered him.

'Fat,' he answered, gloating. 'Fat and pink and round like a little fucking piglet. Now spread her cunt, I'm going to fuck her.'

I didn't need to. Her plump little thighs were already well parted, her pussy on show, wet and ready for his cock. He was fit to burst, and pretty drunk. He had to give in.

'Now tell me,' I demanded, 'and she's all yours.'

He shook his head.

'No way. This is the deal. I get to fuck Carrie, in her cunt and up her shitter. Then I give you what you want.'

'No. I don't trust you. You tell me first.'

'No.'

'Then . . . then you can have her pussy, but you tell me before you sodomise her.'

'No chance. I want it up that fat arse of hers.'

'What about me?' Caroline wailed suddenly, twisting around.

'Shut up,' Tierney and I answered in unison.

Jasmine giggled. Tierney stood up, cock in hand. I nodded and took hold of Caroline's bottom, spreading her anus and pussy hole wide. She had depilated to do her strip, both her pussy and the skin between her bottom cheeks smooth and pink, making the view more revealing still. She gave a low groan at being readied, but stuck it up, her smacked cheeks warm against my skin as Tierney came down, knees wide, cock stuck out, in a truly obscene position, then aimed at her hole and pushed into it, sliding up with a wet sound and groan of ecstasy.

Carrie moaned as her pussy was filled, and began to sigh and whimper as the fucking started, Tierney moving in her with long, slow pushes, each one driving his erection down into her vagina. His hands went to her cheeks, replacing mine to hold the chubby balls of reddened flesh wide, spreading her tight brown anus to his view and also displaying the junction between his cock and her body.

Again I thought he would come, overwhelmed by the sheer pleasure of fucking such a beautiful young woman, and again he held back, pulling out to leave her pussy agape and his cock shiny with her juices.

He pushed it towards me, offering a chance to suck, but I pulled back, denying my own urge to take the horrible thing in my mouth and swallow down my lover's juices.

'Suit yourself,' he growled, and spread her cheeks again, dipping to put his cock head to her straining anus.

'Let her get ready,' I ordered. 'Jasmine, quick.'

Jasmine rose to fetch lubricant, not bothering to go upstairs but simply opening the fridge to pull out a big tub of margarine.

'Nice,' Tierney grated. 'Stick some up her.'

He had her cheeks as wide as they would go, the brown ring of her anus stretched open to show bright pink flesh at the centre. I dipped my finger into the margarine as Jasmine held the pot for me, scooping out plenty to make sure she was well lubricated. Tierney was big, and I knew it was going to hurt, but it would hurt as little as I could possibly make it.

Putting the blob of margarine to her bottom hole, I began to smear it around, letting her open slowly. She relaxed and I pushed in as much of the margarine as would go, to leave her anus open around a blob of slowly melting yellow fat. Tierney was gaping, his mouth wide, and his eyes stared from their sockets, fixed on her bottom hole as the margarine dribbled slowly from her ring and down into the open hole of her pussy. I took his cock, gripping it hard.

'Get off, you mad bitch!' he gasped, trying to pull back.

'Now tell, Stan, now!'

'I . . . fuck that hurts . . .'

'Tell me!'

'It's Emmy Young . . . Lady Emmeline fucking Young, she's the one you want . . . now let go of my cock, you fucking psycho.'

'Certainly.'

I let go, grinning as I transferred my attention back to Caroline's bottom hole, sliding a finger up into her greasy passage and probing. She twisted, looking back, her face wild with shock.

'You . . . you're not, Isabelle . . . are you?'

'Of course,' I answered, probing deeper in the hot, moist cavity of her rectum. 'I keep my word.'

Her answer was a low sob, which broke as I pulled my finger out, sticky and yellow with margarine, to leave her anus a star of puffy, greasy, pink flesh at the centre of a brown corona. Tierney dipped down again as I took hold of her bottom, her big cheeks quivering. I just could not resist watching her being penetrated, and spread her wide, stretching her anus to make an easy target for Tierney's cock. Her sphincter tightened as the big, round cock head touched it, then spread, Caroline pushing out to accept him. A ring of margarine squeezed from her hole as he pushed, and her anus was accommodating the full bulbous head. She gasped in pain and he pulled back a little, leaving a yellow tidemark around the neck of his cock. Again he pushed, forcing his head in again, and more, right up to the fleshy collar of his foreskin.

Caroline gasped again as her anus pushed in too far and I quickly scooped up some more margarine, smearing it on Tierney's cock. He pushed again, harder now, and up it went, the full length of his erection forced into Caroline's back passage to leave her sobbing and gasping in reaction. I watched, glorying in having her sodomised and in my triumph, but with deeper feelings too, my own bottom hole twitching at the thought of penetration, my pussy aching to be touched and filled. Jasmine was watching too, her face working with emotion.

'I'm not going to rush this, no way,' Tierney grated and began to row her, slowly, her taut bottom hole pulling in and out on the shaft of his penis.

Carrie began to grunt immediately, lost in the overwhelming sensation of being buggered. She was whimpering a little too, and I let go of her bottom to take hold of her shoulders, cuddling her to me as the big cock worked in her rectum. Jasmine got down to hold Carrie's head, stroking her hair and kissing her, then taking her dangling breasts in hand. I was shaking, struggling to hold my poise as my girlfriend was sodomised over my lap, in the same position I'd held her to spank her, wishing I could just push down my jeans and panties and have the two of them lick me to ecstasy.

Tierney kept on, his face slack with pleasure as he worked his cock in her ring, kneading her bottom as he buggered her, spittle running down his chin, his face red and wet with sweat. He lost control suddenly, speeding up, grunting with effort as Caroline began to squeal in pain and shock, jamming himself deep, harder and harder, his front slapping her quivering bottom cheeks. I held on to her, tight, feeling every shudder pass through her body as his cock was pumped in and out, and then it had stopped and I knew he had given her the final humiliation and come in her rectum.

He began to pull out immediately, panting and running sweat as his cock eased from her hole. She gave a soft whimper as it came free, and then he had collapsed back onto a chair, his big, dirty cock sticking up from his fly, steaming from the heat of her insides. Caroline got down from my lap, to kneel at my feet and look up at me, big, moist eyes pleading. Jasmine crawled in too, her lower lip trembling. Tierney or no Tierney, I could not refuse. I nodded, undid my jeans as coolly as I could manage and pushed them down around my ankles, my panties with them.

Caroline came straight to me, pressing her face between my thighs, first her lips finding my pussy, then her tongue, licking me eagerly but with her face half turned to watch the man I had allowed to bugger her. Jasmine waited her turn at my feet, stroking the crotch of her jeans, wide-eyed with submissive pleasure. Caroline began to masturbate, rubbing herself firmly between her legs, her big bottom stuck well out, a mixture of sperm and margarine dribbling from her anus to make a ready lubricant for her fingers.

She came in just moments, as I was still trying to block the presence of Tierney from my mind. Jasmine replaced her, pushing down her jeans and panties to get at herself as she came between my thighs and immediately bega to lick. I closed my eyes, sacrificing the beautiful sight of my Jasmine at work on my pussy to rid myself of Tierney's leering crimson face.

It worked, the sheer joy of what I'd done to Caroline rising up in my head. For me she had dressed in a lewd parody of a Red Indian costume. For me she had allowed herself to be spanked in front of an audience. For me she had allowed a dirty old man's cock up her bottom. She was mine, so lovely, and Jasmine too, my dirty little playmates, my slave girls, my pride and joy, and as I came I was imagining how it would feel to show the pair of them off to Lady Emmeline Young.

Four

It was one thing to know that Lady Emmeline Young was a Rattaner and therefore shared my sexual tastes, but it was another thing altogether to approach her. For a start she was a formidable woman, as tall as me and a touch heavier-set, with blonde hair worn in a severe bun and a permanent no-nonsense expression. It took no stretch of the imagination at all to think of her holding down some squalling brat as she administered a thorough spanking, and that did not make my task easier.

She was also an important social figure in the university, heavily involved in fund-raising, charity work and Liberal politics, habits not dissimilar to Margaret Coln before her. Simply to walk up to her and ask to join the society was out of the question. First I needed to be introduced, and that meant finding an excuse unrelated to our mutual love of inflicting corporal punishment on other women.

Tierney had not been particularly forthcoming. Having come up Caroline's bottom he had closed up again, refusing to part with further information and doing his best to persuade me not to use what I had. That was out of the question, but I had promised him I would not get him involved in any way, and I intended to keep my word even if doing so made my task considerably harder. Emmeline Young was sure to want to know how I had found out about her. So I needed a convincing cover story as well as an introduction.

My first task was clearly to find out as much as I could about her. That was not difficult, a simple matter of checking a few college records and the funding publicity for her college. Bede is one of those colleges with a claim to being the oldest in the university, but is not particularly rich and had to have an astronomical maintenance bill for its medieval buildings. Much of Emmeline's time was therefore spent persuading romantically inclined intellectuals, mainly Americans, to part with large sums of money in order to prevent the entire place falling in on itself.

As I was a poverty-stricken student and not a member of Bede's, I had no excuse for getting involved. Joining any of her political campaigns was also out of the question. It would have given my father a heart attack for one thing, and it was going to look somewhat peculiar if I suddenly came out as a union hack halfway through Hilary term. Her charity work was a different matter, very commendable from a CV point of view and easy to get involved in. She supported various organisations, but her pet project involved drying out alcoholics: hardly tasteful, but worthy. I could put up with Stan Tierney, so I reckoned I could cope with a few drunks.

My cover story was harder to establish, and I rejected several options before settling on one. Emmeline had been at St George's Hall shortly before it became independent and was now in her forties. Elizabeth Hastings had been her tutor and they had published one paper together, an offshoot of Emmeline's MA degree. It therefore seemed likely that she had been a Rattaner for twenty years or so, and had presumably taken over the society on Elizabeth Hastings' departure. That assumed she was the head, but it seemed likely from what little Tierney had said.

The knack, it seemed to me, was not to claim an intimate and obviously well-researched knowledge of the Rattaners, but simply a mutual interest in spanking. That way she could remain in control, which went against my nature but was clearly necessary. She could then get to know me and would doubtless in due course invite me to become a member. Possibly it might involve having my own bottom attended to a few times, but so long as Jasmine and Caroline didn't find out I could accept that.

As a long-standing member of the Rattaners she had undoubtedly spanked a good many girls, but if I claimed that we had shared anybody she would quickly be able to disprove it. Nor could I claim to know Elizabeth or any other surviving members, nor their victims, nor to have been a victim myself. It had to be anonymous and, as I knew nothing whatsoever about the internal workings of the Rattaners, it also had to be simple. The best bet was to claim that her name had been dropped into a conversation in an internet chatroom by somebody using a nickname. It would therefore be untraceable. Alternatively I could just hint and hope that she approached me herself.

Signing myself up for two evenings a week voluntary work with her charity was easy. They were crying out for people to help and I was accepted after no more than a few cursory questions. I attended my first evening with a smacked bottom after my Thursday post-tutorial session across Duncan Appledore's knee, which added to the delicious sense of conspiracy I'd built up, so that afterwards the supervisor, David Anthony, commented that he had never known anyone to go about her work so cheerfully.

Emmeline wasn't there that evening, but I steeled myself to be patient and took my excitement out on Jasmine's bottom with a hairbrush on the way back to college.

With three weeks of term to go I knew I was going to be lucky to get my invitation to join the Rattaners before the Easter break, yet I was determined not to wreck my chances by doing anything impatient. They were sure to be very careful about new members, wary of snoops from the press and keen not to invite anyone inappropriate. I would need not only to prove that I was genuine, but that I was discreet and could fit in. I knew I was right for them, but proving that to Emmeline Young was a different matter.

I met her on the Monday evening, although there was no time for more than a brief introduction. She was very brisk, with a stern, no-nonsense manner, just as I had imagined her. The volunteers she treated with a mixture of kindliness and impatience, the ex-alcoholics with sympathy but more than a little condescension. I was fascinated, recognising so much of myself in her, and also noting those characteristics that seemed to run through the members of the Rattaners, from Margaret Coln onwards.

She commended me at the end of the evening, with a kind word and a gentle squeeze of my hand, leaving me feeling ridiculously flattered in a way I hadn't experienced since being complimented by my favourite Mistress at school. That wasn't the worst of it either, because it was far too easy to see myself not as her fellow dominant but her plaything. I could just picture it, her laying me gently across her knee, adjusting my clothing to bare my bottom, spanking me until I absolutely howled, stroking my hair to soothe me and finally putting me on my knees and between her thighs.

The image would not go away, but stayed with me while I shared a glass of beer with my fellow volunteers, on the bus back into central Oxford and in my room as I sat sipping Port and trying to feel dominant. It didn't work, any more than it had after Duncan Appledore had taken me to task. I knew the result would be the same. I could not hold back and so it was best to get it over and done with.

My lips were pursed in resignation as I made sure the door was locked and the curtains properly closed. I was going to masturbate, and I was going to masturbate over the thought of her spanking me, so it made sense to do it in style and hopefully get rid of the disturbing submissive thoughts. So I knelt on my bed, my eyes closed, imagining myself being put through a routine, perhaps to test if I was eligible to be a Rattaner, perhaps just to punish me for my arrogance, or just for the hell of it.

It was easy to see how it would happen. Once she had realised that I was genuine she would invite me back to the Master's Lodge at Bede College, choosing a night when her husband was out. I would be taken up to a spare room, perhaps in the attic space, a place she had set aside to beat her girls, bare, austere, with a plain bed on which I would be made to kneel.

She would order me to tuck my skirt up, but she would take my panties down herself, tugging them low around my thighs with the same brisk, irritable manner I had seen her use that evening, as if the task were a mere nuisance. I would then be left, my bottom and pussy bare, kneeling in that cold, empty room as she went to fetch something to thrash me with.

I suited action to thought, imagining her calm, imperious commands as I hoisted my skirt up and tucked it in, pushed down my tights and lastly my panties, thinking of her doing it, stripping me for punishment, a quick, perfunctory exposure. My hands went up, folded on top of my head, the way she would order me to stay.

When she came back it would be with a cane, a long, vicious rattan, the society's emblem, stained dark with the sweat of all the girls whose naked bottoms it had been laid across down the years. She would give one sharp order, expecting immediate obedience, for me to get down on all fours and lift my bottom. I would obey, instantly, assuming the rude, vulnerable position, my pussy showing from the rear, my cheeks flared to let the cool air to my bottom hole. She would give a cluck of disgust at how rude I looked, tell me I was to get forty strokes . . . no, sixty, and that I had to take them well to stand a chance of membership. Then she'd thrash me.

It would be hard, merciless, each stroke delivered with the full power of her great bony arm, the rattan whistling down onto my poor, naked bottom. I'd be screaming at the first stroke, whimpering in pain after the second, crying after the third. In no time at all I would be reduced to a blubbering, tear-streaked mess, face down on the bed, my bottom humped up over a pillow, in an agony of humiliation and hurt as cut after cut lashed down on my defenceless bottom . . .

I laid myself down, pulling a pillow quickly under my tummy to leave my bare bottom well up, everything showing. The pain of the cuts seemed almost real, and if I had my hand down between my thighs then that was just me. I began to rub, and after a moment I reached back to stroke my bottom, imagining the hurt of the cane cuts and how she would soothe me afterwards, whispering into my ears as I sobbed my heart out into the bedcover, shortly before she sat on my head.

That would be the perfect climax. Sixty strokes would leave me in an awful state, my bottom a ball of fire, sweat starting from every pore, my face as red as my bum and streaked with tears. She would sit down beside me, suddenly soft and sweet and soothing, to cream my smacked bottom, rubbing plenty in, over my cheeks and between them, exploring my anus, my pussy, as she explained that she understood my feelings. She would masturbate me, really quite casually, bringing me off with her expert fingers down between my thighs from behind, all the while murmuring to me, stroking my beaten bottom, teasing my anus . . .

I came, a long, tight orgasm with my mouth wide against the sheets of my bed and my bottom pushed up as I rubbed firmly at my clitoris. It was good, glorious, but it wasn't enough, and I was still rubbing as it died, and focusing on the supreme moment of my fantasy, me pleasuring her.

Once I'd come she would explain quite casually that I had to return the favour. There would be no choice, no polite request, just a bald statement of fact. I would be unable to refuse, and over I'd go, onto my back. She would climb onto the bed, to straddle my head, throwing one long leg over me as she hitched up her skirt. Her tights and panties would come down, pushed low to leaving her bottom and pussy bare, bare and ready for my mouth, bare to have her cheeks spread in my face, bare to have her musky bottom hole put to my lips for a kiss of utter, grovelling submission . . .

I screamed as the second orgasm hit me, unable to hold it back, just too high to care who knew or who heard. Then it was over, my body limp on the bed, my head burning with shame and self-accusation.

I had really thought I had brought the submissive side of my sexuality under control when I had decided to express my desire to be spanked purely with Duncan Appledore. It hadn't worked, but at least I had the satisfaction of knowing that if there was some sort of apprentice period or initiation ceremony for the Rattaners, then I would be able to cope with it.

That only went so far to soothe my ruffled feelings. On the Tuesday evening I took my ire out on Jasmine and Caroline, putting them across my knee one after the other to spank them both rosy. After they had licked me I made them clean the entire house, nude with carrots in their bottom holes, the foliage protruding from between their cheeks like absurd tails. It did them the world of good, leaving both bright-eyed and cheerful, so high on submission that I was forced to make them eat their carrots and spank them again before having each bring the other off, head to tail.

It was four in the morning by the time I got back to my rooms, and I watched dawn break over the spires of Oxford while desperately trying to finish my essay on the Hanoverian succession. I went to hall for breakfast, intending to bully through the day, but I just couldn't face it and collapsed onto the bed as soon as I was back in my room, waking several hours later to the sound of a vacuum cleaner. It was Stan Tierney.

Normal etiquette when a scout finds a student still asleep is either to skip the room or to clatter around outside until she gets the message. With Stan Tierney this was not the case, at least not with me. He was whistling tunelessly and loud enough to be heard over the vacuum cleaner, and greeted me with a dirty leer when I finally found the strength to prop myself up on my pillows.

'Heavy night, love?' he demanded, as the whine of the vacuum cleaner died away. 'Over at Jas's, was we?'

I nodded, seeing no reason to try and deny it. His leer grew dirtier still.

'Good, was it? What'd you do, spanky stuff?'

'It's none of your business. What I did do, not with them of course, was to meet Lady Emmeline Young.'

He started as if he'd had an electric shock, then gave me the most peculiar look.

'D'you speak to her?'

'Not about the Rattaners, no. I'm helping out at her charity, the one for rehabilitation of alcoholics. As you should know by now, Stan, I keep my word. So don't worry. I'm taking it carefully.'

'Don't take it at all, that's my advice.'

'Why not? I can cope, and if it turns out I can't I can always walk away. This isn't the Mafia, you know.'

He just shrugged and pointedly turned on the vacuum cleaner, despite having done the entire room. I watched as he redid it, wondering why he was being so diffident. It wasn't like him. He was shifty, yes, and sly, and a gobshite, but he was usually bold. Certainly he'd been bold enough in demanding sexual favours, which in the circumstances was only one step away from blackmail.

Not that he was going to tell me, ignoring my questions and leaving as soon as he had finished. Our exchange left me feeling ill at ease, and I stayed that way all day, wondering what was going on in his horrible little mind and why he was quite so determined that I should not contact the Rattaners.

I still wasn't quite myself the next day, and certainly not in the mood for a spanking. Duncan was, and I submitted anyway, with as much grace as I could muster. He put me over his knee as usual, and had me take my panties in my mouth, but it wasn't until I was warm that I began to respond, ending up bent over his desk as he gave me a leisurely fucking and came over my reddened bottom.

What with starting off in the wrong frame of mind, I hadn't come myself, but by the time I'd finished dinner I was feeling both aroused and submissive. Half a bottle of college claret had also made me feel bolder, and I was wondering if I wasn't being over-cautious with Emmeline Young. After all, she was a spanker. If I offered to go over her knee but made it clear that I was usually dominant, how could she refuse? I didn't even need to mention the Rattaners.

I was in the mood for it, and might even have done it had she been there, and had the Centre not been quite so busy. She was supposed to be coming later, so David Anthony told me, and I was on edge all evening, wondering if I really dared do it and thinking of just how exquisitely humiliating the spanking would be. That was until Stan Tierney turned up, asking to come into a counselling session, which put me on the edge of panic.

Tierney drank, certainly, and sometimes to excess, but he was no alcoholic. There had to be an ulterior motive for his presence, and it could only be that he wanted to prevent me from talking to Emmeline Young. It was a pretty stupid move. Obviously she knew he was aware of the Rattaners or he need not have worried, and his presence at the same time as mine could only look suspicious. If I approached her she was bound to realise that he had been the one who had told me, which would ruin everything for me, and incidentally precipitate whatever fate he dreaded right on top of his great ugly head. I had to get rid of him before she turned up, and to do that I needed to explain what an idiot he was being. The instant the counselling session was over I cornered him in the tea room, speaking in an urgent whisper to avoid being overheard.

'What are you doing, Stan? You know you shouldn't be here!'

'Why not? I've got a right.'

'You know perfectly well why not!'

'Nah, free tea and choccy biscuits, that's why I'm here.'

'Don't talk such nonsense! You're here to prevent me from speaking to Emmeline Young, aren't you? Well it doesn't work that way, does it? If she sees us together and I ask about the Rattaners she'll guess, won't she?'

'Don't ask, then.'

'No. You're not manipulating me, Stan Tierney. If you don't go right this minute I will ask her, and you can take the consequences.'

'Fuck it up for you, though, wouldn't it?'

'For both of us! What's at stake? Your job? That's it, isn't it? Dr Cappaldi is a Rattaner, isn't she?'

For a moment he looked genuinely puzzled, then spoke again.

'Don't go asking her, for fuck's sake!'

'So she's not?'

'I'm not saying anything.'

'OK, never mind that. Just leave, will you, please?'

'Nah. I like it here.'

'Yes, but –'

'Do you know what I could do with? A nice, slow blow-job.'

'Fine. Jasmine or Caroline, take your pick, just so long as you leave now. I'll have –'

'No, not them. You.'

'Me!? Absolutely not!'

'Suit yourself.'

He moved to the tea machine, concentrating on the little ritual of making it work as I stood there with my mouth working in outrage and indecision. He knew that I didn't give sexual favours, and he knew I would make one of the girls do it, and that they'd enjoy it. He wanted to humiliate me, specifically me, because they do and I don't, and it was just such an unspeakably dirty, vulgar, sneaky, foul thing to do.

'Want a tea?' he asked.

'No I do not!'

'Coffee? Chicken soup?'

'No! Look, please, Stan, will you just go?'

'What, and waste this lovely tea?'

He winked at me. There were other people close by, far too close to speak openly. I heard the outside door go and my heart leapt, expecting to hear Emmeline's cut-glass voice at any instant. It wasn't her, but it would be soon, and I was left with my stomach fluttering. Again the door banged, and I nearly wet myself as a female voice spoke from the passage. Again it wasn't her, but the loo beckoned. There was one upstairs for female staff, which in the circumstances meant me and me alone. I was at the top of the stairs before I realised Tierney was following me.

'What are you doing? This is a staff area.'

'You're going to give me that blow-job, aren't you?'

'No I am not!'

'Then why'd you come up here?'

'For a . . . for a pee, of course!'

'Come on, love, I know you better than you know yourself, I reckon. What you want is a nice big cock to play with. It's what all women want.'

'No it is not, especially yours, you filthy old pervert!'

'Temper, temper, any more of that and I might just have to spank that little botty.'

'You can try, Stan Tierney!'

'Hey, keep your knickers on . . . no, better take 'em down, as it goes, or you'll piss in them!'

He laughed, but he was right. I badly needed the loo. He opened the door and stepped inside.

'Stan! That's the Ladies!'

'Yeah, I know, it says on the door. "Female Staff Only" it says, and as you're the only female staff here tonight I can't think of a better place for you to suck me off. You can piss in front of me too, if you like?'

I couldn't find an answer, simply too outraged by the appalling suggestion, and by the awful desires he was triggering in me. Stepping quickly into the loo, I caught him by the shoulders, twisted him around and was about to throw him out by main force when I heard footsteps on the stairs. Another volunteer was coming up, maybe David, maybe Emmeline Young. I let go of Tierney, pushed the door shut and slid the bolt into place, not a moment too soon as a board on the landing creaked.

'I knew you'd be up for it, you dirty bitch.' Tierney chuckled. 'Squat over the bowl, backwards – I'd like to watch it squirt, and see the way your arsehole pokes out like you're going to take a shit.'

'Shut up, you . . . you . . . there's somebody out-side!' I answered him in a furious hiss even as I imagined my anus pouting as the pee squirted from between the lips of my pussy, with him watching. 'I am not up for anything!'

He didn't answer, but his hand went to the bolt. I clamped mine over it. Whoever had come up had turned the other way, to the storeroom, but that meant they would have a clear view of the loo door.

'What are you doing?' I whispered, crushing his fingers onto the bolt.

'Oi! Let go, you mad bitch! You don't know your own strength, you!'

'Yes I do. Now stay here and shut up!'

'Get your knicks down then. Come on, love, it's just a bit of fun.'

Not for me it wasn't, but I had a straight choice: let go of his hand or wet my panties. My long coat was downstairs, locked up in the staff cupboard, which meant walking through the common room with a wet patch on my bottom, my pussy, down between my legs . . .

The discussion group was in full swing, 27 alcoholics and ex-alcoholics discussing their experiences and I was going to have to walk through them in pee-soaked jeans. They'd see, they could hardly miss it. They'd smell me too. Even Stan Tierney was better.

'OK!' I snapped. 'You are a filthy, dirty old pervert, Stan Tierney!'

'Look who's talking,' he answered as I struggled to open my jeans. 'Come on, backwards, I want to see that little arsehole stick out. I love the way girls' arseholes do that, I –'

'Shut up!'

'Aw, come on, Isa, it's not like I ain't seen what you got.'

'Sh! Somebody will hear!'

'Be a sport and I'll shut up.'

I could have slapped him, but what I did was take my panties down and turn my back to him. He was right, he had seen me, just about every detail, but not like that, not peeing. If I hadn't been spanked earlier I'd never have done it. If I'd reached orgasm with Duncan I'd never have done it. As it was I used his offer of silence as an excuse to deliberately humiliate myself, squatting over the lavatory bowl in the painfully revealing pose he had suggested, my jeans and panties taut against the stand, my bottom stuck out, my tight brown bottom hole pouting just the way he wanted to see, my pee squirting out from between my pussy lips as I let go . . .

Stan gave a pleased grunt and sank down, to let himself see up between my legs, at every rude detail. I was sobbing as I did it, my eyes tight shut, wishing my bladder hadn't been quite so full, wishing it would end, wishing the splash and gurgle of my stream in the water beneath me wasn't quite so loud, wishing I didn't smell so rich and hormonal.

None of my wishes came true. I had to hold my pose, my humiliation rising with every second, and it seemed to go on forever, my pee spurting out in a thick, fast and apparently inexhaustible stream. Tierney said nothing, but I knew he was watching, staring, his dirty eyes fixed to my open pee-hole and the distended ring of my anus, leering, imagining his cock inside me, maybe even up my bottom the way he had handled Caroline, the way I had let him handle her.

As my stream finally died I heard the tread of footsteps as whoever had come up went back, but it was too late. I'd done it, peed in front of Stan Tierney with my pussy spread and my bottom hole pouting. I turned and sat down, feeling mentally drained as I tore off a piece of loo paper to dab my pussy dry. He had his cock out, which was no surprise, a fat pink erection sticking up obscenely from his open fly. I was too broken to resist, and I did it, burning with shame and consternation as I accepted him in my mouth. He took my head as I began to suck, holding me by my hair and mumbling, loud enough for me to hear.

'That was fucking gorgeous, Isa, you have the sweetest little cunt, you do, the sweetest. The sweetest arse too, nice and round . . . girlie . . . real girlie . . . and your arsehole, even that's pretty, so neat, like your cunt's neat, neat and young and fuckable ... yeah, that's right, down your throat you dirty fucking bitch you!'

He grunted and he had come, full in my mouth, only to whip it out and jerk the rest of his sperm into my face and hair. Some went in my eye, on purpose I was sure, and I was left coughing and snatching at my face as he stood back against the door, panting with the effort he had made to do it standing.

I tidied myself up as best I could, spitting out his sperm and cleaning my face with loo paper before pulling my jeans and panties up. Tierney had lit a cigarette, and watched, his face set in an amused grin between puffs. At last I felt I could face the world, physically restored but burning inside. I drew the bolt and peered cautiously out of the door. Nobody was visible, and there was only the faint drone of someone's voice from the group session downstairs. Tierney followed me onto the landing.

'Now go,' I snapped, 'before Emmeline Young turns up!'

'No fear of that, love. She's not coming tonight.'

'Yes she is, she'll be here any minute! She might already be here, in fact.'

'Nah. She was going to come, but changed her mind. I asked your boss when I came in.'

With that he left, simply turning, walking down the stairs and out of the front door, pausing only long enough to flick the ash from his cigarette onto the carpet.

Five

Lady Emmeline Young didn't turn up on the Thursday evening, just as Stan Tierney had said. I was left to go back on the bus with my mouth full of the taste of male cock, which even three cups of strong tea hadn't managed to entirely eradicate. My head was whirling with emotion, bitter shame at having been tricked into peeing in front of him and sucking his cock, as well as self-recrimination for letting it happen and because I felt so aroused and so, so submissive. I needed spanking, hard, to really punish myself, then a good fucking, or to masturbate as I licked some dominant woman's pussy and bottom hole.

All I got was a shame-filled rub at my pussy in the darkness of my room, with my mind focused on the disgustingly intrusive remarks he had made about the way my bottom hole pouted as I peed. Afterwards I felt angry and used, and worried about Jasmine finding out, and even Caroline a little, for all that I knew she would just giggle. There was Emmeline Young too, who was certainly not going to be well disposed towards me if she found out I'd been sucking men off in the staff loo.

Sleep took a while to come, and I seemed to pass from lying there worrying with my hand still down the front of my panties to waking in a tangle of sheets within no time at all. All morning I was playing the events of the evening before over in my head, from my spanking to my final orgasm, and it was next to impossible to concentrate on my lectures.

I put in some time in the library during the afternoon, although it was largely wasted, and when I finally got back to college it was to find Jasmine and Caroline outside my room, with a third person, Walter Jessop. I was pleased to see them, if only to take my mind off Tierney, at least once I'd realised that he hadn't sought them out to sneak on me for my dirty behaviour. I invited them in and made coffee, Walter speaking as soon as I'd propped myself by the window.

'Jasmine mentioned that you were seeking out some society of dominant women?'

'Yes, I am, although I could wish you hadn't said anything, Jasmine. I was trying to keep it as quiet as possible.'

'Sorry, Isabelle . . . Mistress.'

'Ah, well, no matter, you know you can rely on my discretion.'

'Well now you know, is there anything you can tell me? I don't think they have any particular taste in Victorian clothing, or not that I know of, but it's possible.'

'I don't recall anything as regards clothing, no, but there was one incident that came to mind, which is why I came down to tell you.'

'Yes?'

'Yes. It was last year. Two women came into the shop, one a student, one older, mother and daughter I assumed, and there seemed to be something odd about them from the start. The young girl couldn't stop giggling and seemed extremely nervous. Then, when I had gone out to the back to look for hairbrushes . . .'

'Hairbrushes?'

'Yes, hairbrushes. They wanted to buy hairbrushes, something the student seemed to find endlessly amusing and not a little embarrassing. I strongly suspect I know what they were intended for as well, spanking the younger one's behind.'

'It certainly sounds like it.'

'They bought seven in the end, I remember, two quite fine pieces in silver, both late Victorian, one ivory, one mahogany and three very ordinary wooden ones.'

'Seven hairbrushes?' Caroline queried.

'One for each member of the society, I suspect,' I answered her. 'Doubtless the girl had earned herself some elaborate ritual punishment.'

'Ouch!' Caroline squeaked.

'Do you know their names, Walter?' I asked. 'And what did they look like?'

'I have the older woman's name,' he replied, 'because she also asked me to call her if I ever got any old-fashioned horsehair fly whisks in. She was very particular that they had to be horsehair. I looked it up for you.'

'Horsehair whisks, for whipping the girl's breasts?' Jasmine queried.

'Double ouch!' Caroline added, immediately putting her hands across her chest in a protective gesture.

'She was Sarah Finch,' Walter finished. 'I have her number here. As for looks, I don't remember clearly, except that both were dark-haired and could have passed for mother and daughter. Quite tall too, I think, above average anyway. The older one had quite a stern expression, the younger seemed very delicate.'

He passed the number to me. It looked as if I'd found another Rattaner, or at least a woman who enjoyed giving out corporal punishment, and presumably her slave girl with any luck. That went a long way to improving my mood, and I gave Walter a kiss on the tip of his nose, promising myself that he only had to ask and he would get Jasmine or Caroline over his knee, even down on his cock. Not that it might not have happened in any case, as the three of them went back several years before I had arrived on the scene.

It did. Walter spanked Caroline, panties down, with her plump bottom bouncing to the smacks as Jasmine waited at my feet for her own punishment. With Caroline standing in the corner with her hands on her head and her big red bottom showing to the room I spanked Jasmine, also bare, and sent her into the corner to join Caroline. We left them there while we finished our coffee and I tossed a coin for who had to suck Walter's cock. Jasmine lost and down she went, wearing her normal expression of resentful misery as she brought him to erection and orgasm, then swallowed his sperm.

I did enjoy myself, but my heart wasn't really in it. Even after I'd sent Walter out of the room so that the girls could lick my pussy I was finding it hard to concentrate on anything other than getting my own comeuppance. Had Walter been alone I might have asked for it, but even then I could not have been sure he would not have told the girls. So I contented myself with imagining that Jasmine, Caroline and I were being made to perform together for the amusement of the Rattaners, all three of us with pink bottoms.

It was the same over the weekend, although I did my best. I stayed with them overnight, very much Mistress of the house in the beautiful black silk corset

Caroline had made for me, spike-heeled boots that lifted me to six foot four, black panties and stockings, and nothing else. I made them both go nude about the house, kneeling or crawling unless they had a job to do such as serving me dinner, spanked them both, whipped Jasmine for showing reluctance to eat the slops I had made them prepare themselves and generally abused them.

Even at best, with Jasmine naked, whipped and with her hands and ankles tied while Caroline licked my anus as I sipped a leisurely after-dinner Armagnac, I was still imagining myself putting on the same show for the Rattaners. At worst, late at night with the two of them cuddled onto my chest in bed, I was imagining myself being put through the same cruelties and degradations by Lady Emmeline Young.

I had to speak to her on the Monday, there was simply no choice. We got on well enough, and all it needed was a hint, a word, and I would have made my craving reality. I'd made the decision, and I found myself with butterflies in my stomach and completely unable to concentrate on work. Having daydreamed my way through the morning lectures I gave up and went to the library instead, knowing that to continue my research into the Rattaners was the only way I could possibly keep my mind sensibly occupied.

It took several hours at the computer to identify Sarah Finch, but only because she wasn't a don at all. She was head of catering at Erasmus Darwin, one of the redbrick colleges in North Oxford. That didn't necessarily mean she wasn't a Rattaner, and she was certainly worth further investigation. I had no leads at all as to who her girlfriend might be, or if they were still together, but that was a minor thing.

My main fear that evening, as I made my way out towards the Centre on the bus, was that Tierney, having successfully squeezed one blow-job out of me, might be back for more. If he was I was just going to have to do it, there was really no choice. The thought made my butterflies worse still, and really brought out that odd contradiction which is inherent in the submissive side of my sexuality. On the one hand I was genuinely scared of what the evening might bring, first having to suck off a dirty old man, then to reveal my most intimate secret to a comparative stranger, and lastly to have to accept physical discipline from her if it was demanded. On the other hand I found the same possible chain of events extraordinarily arousing.

One way or the other I was going through with it, and when I saw Tierney in the tea room I was nearly sick. Come what might, I was not going to reveal the embarrassing side of my feelings, or give in to them without a fight. It was early and nobody else was in the room, so I could at least talk and hopefully get rid of him quickly. He came over to me immediately, his dirty leer spread wide on his face as he greeted me.

'Hi Isa, just the girl. Look, I've got something . . .'

'No. It's not going to happen, Stan, not again.'

'I ain't even said what it is yet.'

'I can guess.'

'Yeah?'

'Yes. You want me to take you up to the staff toilet, make some sort of dirty display for you and do what I did the other night . . . suck you.'

'I wouldn't mind a bit of that, sure, if you fancy it, but that's not it . . .'

'I do not fancy it! What is it, then?'

'Jesus, Isa, don't get your knickers in a twist. You coming up on the rag soon or something?'

'Stan!'

'You're so touchy, that's all. Anyway, Mike's set up a game at the Ox. It's a thousand to buy in and –'

'Game? What game?'

'Poker.'

'Oh, I'd been expecting something dirty. What about it? I can't lend you any money, Stan. I have an enormous overdraft as it is.'

'No, no, not money. I want you to lend me Jas and Carrie, as my stake.'

'To gamble with? You mean to prostitute them to cover your losses!? Absolutely not! That's ... that's outrageous! Sex play is one thing, Stan, but I will not –'

'Leave the lecture, Isa, you know they'll be well into it, and anyway, I ain't going to lose.'

'That's what all gamblers say, Stan, especially the losers.'

'I'm no loser, Isa, believe me, I am no loser. That lot up at the Ox are, though, a right of bunch of wide boys. I'll wipe the floor with them, but I just need my stake.'

'I really don't think ...'

'Come on, Isa, be a pal. You know Jas and Carrie'll do it if you say so, and love it too. Anyway, it's not whoring, not if they don't take any of the money.'

I laughed, unable to ognore the way his weasel-like little mind worked, immediately turning my objection to having the girls prostitute themselves to his financial advantage. He didn't seem to see the humour in it and went on.

'This is serious stuff, Isa. Big money, and they will love it, they will ...'

David passed the door and Stan trailed off, looking shiftier than ever as he buried his face in his mug of tea. I had been going to put in a flat refusal, but I paused, imagining it as a piece of submissive play, making the girls stand as poker stakes in a game, obliged to suck men's cocks on the luck of the cards, and maybe worse. He was right, it would appeal to them, just so long as I remained in control. He went on before I could reply, abruptly changing tack.

'Come on, Isa. If I don't come through I'm going to get my head kicked in!'

'Why?'

''Cause I said I'm doing it.'

'That was foolish, but I hardly think your friends are going to resort to violence if you don't keep your promise.'

He just looked shifty, briefly making me wonder if there wasn't a protection racket or something equally sordid going on at the Red Ox, before deciding it was just more of his aimless blather.

'I'll do it,' I offered, 'but only on two conditions. First, I come, to watch and give the orders to the girls, nothing more, do you understand? Second, you leave here now.'

'I thought you were after giving me a blow-job.'

'No I am not! Now get out!'

'Yeah, right. It's Sunday afternoon, be there at one.'

He left. What I'd said was at least half a lie and I was left with an odd sense of disappointment beneath my relief at not having to debase myself once again. It was just as well, though, because Emmeline Young arrived no more than ten minutes after he'd gone. By then quite a few people had come in, all of them to attend a session with Dr Erskine, a psychiatrist from Brookes who was using our facility for research purposes. David was sitting in to keep an eye on things, which left Emmeline and me alone. I was on the desk, but she was in the office directly behind me. Suddenly there was no excuse. It had to be done, then and there. I stood up, walked into the office, every ounce of courage screwed up as I braced myself to ask the carefully prepared question, which was not what came out . . .

'Would you like a cup of coffee, Lady Young?'

'No, thank you, Isabelle, dear,' she answered, looking up from the paperwork she was busy with.

Behind me the front door banged. One voice sounded, urgent, stressed, and another, slurred and whining. All my elaborate conversational gambits were swept aside as I spoke quickly and clearly.

'I suspect that you and I have something in common, Lady Young, something we also share with Dr Elizabeth Hastings. If you would be willing, I was hoping to explore . . .'

I broke off at a loud demand for attention from the desk, but I had done enough. Her response was a smile, a gentle, knowing smile, brief, but that was all I needed.

The rest of the evening passed in a blur. I had to deal with the crisis, a drunken boyfriend who should have been taken to the Radcliffe and not to us, but whose aggressive and highly strung girlfriend wouldn't take no for an answer. By the time I had that under control the meeting had come out and I was busy from then on, but all the while with a little flame of wild imagination burning in the back of my head. Twice more Emmeline gave me her quiet, knowing smile, and by the time we had finished my crush on her had grown to a painful intensity, something I had never imagined I would feel again: not love, but a slavish devotion I really thought I had left behind at school.

Clearly I hadn't. She could have asked me to do anything, however dirty, however submissive, even something completely irrelevant to our shared sexuality, and I would have done it, gratefully. I was even hoping she might ask me to come with her afterwards, but of course it was impossible. She had a husband to go to and an image to keep up, but she did give my hand a little squeeze again, and spoke, very quietly.

'Do you have an outfit? If not, I recommend Bronco Billy's in Coventry. I'll put in a word for you.'

I was left in raptures. It was nearly midnight, but I knew I was not going to be getting a great deal of sleep. On the bus back I was imagining all sorts of scenarios, both with me as submissive and as dominant, undergoing some painful and degrading initiation ceremony and showing off my control of Jasmine and Caroline respectively. All of them involved the 'outfit'. Bronco Billy's didn't sound like a sex shop, and was presumably not even a shop in which fetishistic clothing and equipment was sold, or at least not as such. It seemed much more likely to be a specialist in Western-style jeans, maybe hats and so forth as well, but almost certainly leather. Possibly they did a sideline in erotic leatherwear.

She was going to put in a word for me, so the shop owner would be expecting my arrival. That might mean being fully kitted out as a leather-clad dominatrix, and if it was going to put an even worse strain on my overdraft then I would just have to subsist on economy bread and cheap beans for the rest of the year. I didn't mind, it would be worth it.

Alternatively the 'outfit' might be something very different, some humiliating little ensemble like Caroline's Red Indian costume, in which I would be soundly punished in front of the entire society. Whatever it was, I had to find out, and buy it to show willing although Caroline and Jasmine could have made me anything I needed.

* * *

Back in my room I locked the door, pulled the curtains, lifted my top, dropped my jeans and panties and lay down to masturbate. At first I warmed my pussy gently, imagining myself dressed head to toe in leather, spike heels, tight trousers, a studded corset, long gloves, maybe even a helmet to give me an Amazonian look. I'd put Jasmine and Caroline in collars, nothing else, and bring them in crawling behind me on their leashes, a pair of obedient little puppies. I would give them as a present to Emmeline for the evening, securing my place in the favour of the Rattaners.

That was if I was allowed to express my dominance. If I wasn't, then it would be a very different matter. I wouldn't bring the girls, but go alone, in nothing but minuscule leather panties, maybe a leather bra if they were feeling generous or wanted to delay my complete exposure. Then I would be the one on the lead, I would be the one crawling at their feet, I would be the one given to Emmeline, to be spanked and humiliated and tied and tortured and . . . and . . .

I came, imagining myself grovelling naked in a circle of leather-clad women, my beaten bottom on fire, my hands strapped up painfully tight behind my back, my pussy and anus penetrated, my breasts bound, and my tongue wedged firmly up Lady Emmeline Young's bottom hole.

Come hell or high water, I was going to Coventry. Nothing else mattered. I'd put Stan Tierney aside for the irritating little oik that he was, and everything else was a mere distraction. It was an effort to work, but I did it by promising myself I could take Wednesday off to go to Coventry if I finished my essay on Tuesday night. I succeeded by drinking black coffee until four in the morning, but I knew it was a good effort and went to sleep content, catching up on the train.

I had never been to Coventry before, and it was not somewhere I would have considered glamorous. Yet in the circumstances every street and every building was invested with an almost sinister mystique, much like that I had come to associate with all those places linked to the Rattaners.

Bronco Billy's proved to be one of a line of shops well away from the city centre. It was more or less as I had expected it to be, small, rather pokey and garish, but considerably more specialist. Everything was centred on the American Midwest in a style highly exaggerated and somewhat outdated. There was certainly leather: hats, jackets, waistcoats, chaps, boots, much of it fringed and tooled, generally brown but with some red, some blue and some in a Stars and Stripes pattern, which quite simply had to be the most vulgar thing I had ever seen. There was also denim in abundance, figure-hugging jeans and loose jackets, again mostly decorated.

There was a music department, which I ignored as completely beyond the pale, and various books, videos, posters and collectibles about cowboys, line dancing and a dozen related subjects, not one of which I knew the least little bit about. Only one area really did pique my interest, the accessories, which included a selection of truly evil-looking whips, spurs, lassoes, leather harnesses and even branding-irons. Evidently there was a kinky aspect to it, but the more raunchy clothes would either be custom made or kept carefully hidden, or so I thought until I introduced myself to the owner.

He was about as far removed from the muscular young men and well-built women on the posters and advertising material about the place as it was possible to be and still be thought of as human. For a start he was barely five feet tall, about fifty and had a soft, pear-shaped body supported on spindly legs. He was also balding, but rather than having the grace to age naturally or the sense to shave his head he had grown one side long and wore it combed over his balding dome and held down with some heavy and foul smelling grease.

Unappealing he might have been, but he was certainly friendly, greeting me with embarrassing bonhomie and a sort of cheer which was presumably a normal greeting among cowboys, or at least among British cowboy fans. When I had told him who I was he became more effusive still, speaking rapidly in a mix of native Coventry and anything-but-native American Midwest.

'So you're Emmy's new find? Great to meet you! She's told me all about you, of course, and she says to put it on the account seeing as how you're a student. Isn't she just the best?'

'Yes,' I agreed earnestly as I realised that he knew considerably more than I had anticipated.

'I'll fix you right up,' he went on, pushing out from behind the counter. 'Just leave it to Billy. You're a tall girl, but I have your size, I sure do.'

He began to whistle, and to gather up various garments from around the shop. I watched in mounting horror as my fate slowly sank in. In return for membership of the Rattaners I was to be utterly, comprehensively humiliated. I had expected to be made to go nude or near nude, perhaps obliged to dress as a maid or a schoolgirl, the sort of costume men like girls to wear for striptease. I'd been naîve, simplistic. The Rattaners were far more subtle. The way I was to dress for my initiation made Caroline's most vulgar, most foolish outfit look positively sensible.

84

First, and least offensive, were the jeans, flares with tassels down the outside of each leg and the back pockets done as the Stars and Stripes. The flag motif was repeated with the blouse, which was well tailored but actually appeared to have been made from a US flag. The boots were the same, vertical red and white stripes with the toes and the big square heels blue with white stars. The hat was the same, the brim red and white stripes, the crown blue with stars. The little denim waistcoat was not the same, fortunately, in just a reserved blue with a flag on the single breast pocket although it did have tassels and little metal horse-shoes sewn on. The chaps were also plain, at least in colour, but elaborately tooled and fringed. Last was the belt, a great heavy thing ideal for taking to girls' bottoms, buckled with a six-inch-wide boss showing yet another US flag.

He made a pile, whistling to himself all the while and clearly having immense fun. I stood staring at the clothes I was supposed to get into for my punishment and thinking of just how completely ridiculous I was going to look, let alone once I was across someone's knee with the jeans and my panties pulled well down. Panties were something I expected him to add to the pile, along with a bra, but he didn't, only socks in the inevitable pattern, a pair of spurs and a sheriff's badge. There was no whip or lasso, which would have been inappropriate when they were likely to be used on me and not by me.

'Put 'em on, be my guest,' he drawled, gesturing towards a bead curtain closing off a tiny alcove.

I swallowed hard, telling myself that it made perfect sense for me to ensure everything fitted, and that Emmeline would not have been so cruel as to set up some hideously demeaning test for me with Bronco Billy. My insides were doing somersaults as I picked the pile of clothing up and pushed through the curtain. There was no doubt in my mind whatever that within the Rattaners unquestioning obedience would be expected of new members, particularly those who had yet to pass initiation. Once I was in, or formally knew about them even, then if I erred I could be punished. Until then my behaviour had to be immaculate, and I had to be on the lookout for tests.

To my great relief Billy did not follow me into the changing space. It was still embarrassing, with the ancient bead curtain providing a less than perfect screen and with barely room to move within the tiny mirrored cubicle. I was getting ever more flustered as I stripped to my bra and panties, and hot, despite the cold weather and the inadequate electric fire he used to heat the place. He was watching too, glancing towards the curtain every now and then and asking if I was ready or making facile remarks about how good I would look, until my fingers were shaking so hard I could barely do up the buttons on my idiotic blouse.

I made it, though, all the way, jeans, shirt, waistcoat, boots, chaps and hat, even the spurs and badge. A glance in the mirror had me close to tears, showing just how truly foolish I looked. I would barely have recognised the girl staring back, a big, brash, vulgar Midwest cowgirl in party costume, utterly silly, not me at all, and so, so appropriate for spanking. For a start the jeans and chaps made my bottom look simply enormous, a plump ball of denim sticking out from the leather surround and made to seem bigger and rounder still by the patterned stitching and the flags on each back pocket. Then there was the combination of hat, waistcoat, spurs, and most of all the little plastic badge, all things designed to make a girl look soft and vulnerable, a ridiculous parody of male machismo. I looked as if I ought to be spanked, and worse, and giggle and squeak and pout my way through it as if grateful even for the attention.

By the time I had finished I was desperately in need of a spanked bottom across Emmeline's lap. I was also profoundly grateful I hadn't brought Jasmine and Caroline along, as the way I was being treated had brought me to a new depth of submission. The Rattaners were so clever, so experienced, exploiting feelings I barely understood myself, and without even being there.

As I stepped out from the curtain Bronco Billy gave another loud cheer and began to fuss around me with drooling enthusiasm, pouring out oily compliments on my appearance and the fit of the clothes. He meant it, I was sure, so obviously he didn't know all that much, but the fact that he did genuinely think I looked good was far, far more humiliating than any other response could possibly have been. It was almost as if I'd been on stage in the Red Ox, dressed as I was but obliged to strip naked, or in one of Caroline's girlie striptease outfits. Then the bombshell dropped.

'That's just swell,' he said for about the twentieth time, 'and like I said, it goes right on the club account. So, how's about Billy's little treat, then?'

For a long moment I simply could not answer. It was my test, it had to be, and I had to go through with it. I couldn't, though, my pride rebelling against it despite my overwhelming feelings of submission. Yet Emmeline would know how I felt, just as doubtless she herself had felt so many years before at the time of her own initiation. She would know, and she would know that if I was worthy I would do it. At last I forced myself to swallow the lump in my throat and answer him.

'Yes . . . yes, sir. What would you like?'

'Anything you'd care to do would be a privilege, but how about the Watermelon Crawl? That's a favourite of mine.'

I hesitated, wondering what a Watermelon Crawl involved. Was it some strange perversion? A euphemism for spanking, for buggery? The watermelon had to refer to my bottom, no question, and the crawling part was obvious. What else I was supposed to do I had no idea whatever.

'Yes, all right . . .' I managed, blushing furiously. 'I'll try, but you may have to show me. Come into the back.'

'In the back?'

'Well I'm not doing it here!'

'Hey, hey!'

He chuckled and rubbed his fat little hands together, then took my hand. I was burning with humiliation as he led me into a little shabby room, piled with boxes of stock around a table topped with chipped red Formica. There was a single chair, a badly stained sink, a kettle, a tray with the apparatus for making instant coffee set out on it, linoleum on the floor, and that was it.

'You all right?' he asked. 'There ain't a lot of room.'

There was floor space, about enough to allow me to get down on my knees. I nodded. He put some music on, awful folk stuff with an American flavour, and entirely appropriate.

'I'll lock the door,' he said suddenly. 'Be right back.'

He was gone for maybe thirty seconds, while I stood with my stomach churning and wondered what I should do and how much of it would go back to Emmeline Young. I had to show I was obedient, that much was clear, as was the fact that Bronco Billy knew that Emmeline belonged to some sort of erotic club, if he didn't know the details. After all, they seemed to have an account. All I could think of was to put on as good a show as I could and hope he didn't actually fuck me.

I was wishing he'd be like Tierney and make me do it, pull out his cock, order me to get my panties down or to adopt some obscene pose. Not Billy – he just settled himself onto the single ancient chair and folded his arms above his paunch, waiting and watching. I turned to face him, my hands on my hips, deliberately insolent, the way Caroline sometimes does before starting a striptease, just to make the fall from grace further still, from haughty young woman right down to naked little slut.

His smile grew broader, then changed to lust-filled delight as my fingers went to the buckle of my belt, as if he hadn't really expected me to go through with it. I pulled it open, my eyes never leaving him, popped the button of my jeans and slowly peeled down my fly. He swallowed, said something incomprehensible, and abruptly adjusted his cock.

I took my heart in my mouth as I turned around, praying that the Watermelon Crawl simply involved him masturbating as I showed off my bottom. I stuck it out, making myself as round and full as possible, trying not to think how rude and silly my rear view would look and struggling to find the courage to bare myself. My thumbs went into the waistband of my jeans, and under the chaps, then I pushed and I was peeling my tight blue jeans down over the out-thrust peach of my bottom. The top of my panties came on show, then the seat, taut across my cheeks, and the tuck, bare and meaty, curving down to where my pussy was covered by a hopelessly inadequate scrap of cotton, and that soon to be taken away.

'Oh boy!' he breathed as I gave him a little wiggle, doing my best to imitate Caroline.

A backward glance showed him just as he had been before, his cock a rigid bar in his trousers but still covered. I gave him a wink, settled my jeans into the top of my chaps and took hold of my panties, my heart hammering as I prepared to expose myself. He squeezed his cock and I gave him another wink and a smile, keen to show willing, then began to strip myself behind, easing down my panties, inch by inch, exposing the little V where my crease begins, the top of my cheeks, more . . .

I paused as he put his hand to his fly and gave me one brief and doubtful glance before jerking it wide to pull out a stubby and slightly bent erection. Suddenly I knew that him fucking me was no part of the deal, not even me touching him, but his cock was out and my panties had to come down anyway. Again I began to push, and down they came, spilling the full weight of my bottom out, my anus now on show, my pussy too, my sex lips pouting out from between my thighs. I was sobbing with humiliation as I stuck it right out. He gave a long sigh and began to mastur-bate, then spoke.

'Whee doggie! A nudie one. That I ain't never seen!'

All I could manage was a weak smile as I adjusted my panties at half-mast. I had my watermelon showing and he hadn't objected, so all I had to do was crawl. I went down, knock-kneed, another of Caroline's little tricks as it makes a girl look extreme-ly vulnerable and gives a fuller show of bottom hole and pussy lips. On the floor I began to crawl, making sure he got a good view, my naked bottom framed in the chaps and my lowered clothes, everything show-ing, rude and submissive and foolish, just as I was supposed to look, just as I ought to look before being spanked pink and sent to stand in the corner with my red bottom showing and my hands folded on top of my stupid hat . . .

Suddenly I could hold back no longer. I felt so dirty, so lewd, such a little slut, flaunting myself, by Emmeline's orders, but for a dirty old man I had met only moments before. What I wanted didn't matter, only what she did, and therefore whatever she had said he could do. Even if he hadn't expected to get his cock out I had to make the offer, to show willing, for Emmeline.

'Go on, do whatever you have to do.'

'Oh boy!'

He moved, fast, and the next moment his stubby, bent little cock was between my bottom cheeks, rubbing, his balls slithering in the damp crease between my cheeks, grunting and puffing as he rutted on me, and just came. I heard his grunt of pleasure and felt the sperm splash on my back, then down between my cheeks as he went lower, over my bottom hole, and up again, over my shirt and in my hair. More came out as he took himself in hand, squeezed into my crease and over my bottom hole, and at the last moment, just when I thought I had got away without a fucking, he stuffed himself to the hilt in my sopping pussy.

Six

On the way back from Coventry my only regret was that Bronco Billy hadn't made a proper job of me, with a good, hard, panties-down spanking followed by a proper fucking, or even sodomy. I was high on submission, and with an hour to kill before my train I had added a few touches of my own, just in the mood to deliberately humiliate myself after what he had done to me. I'd managed to find a truly awful Stars and Stripes bra and panties set in a tacky lingerie shop near the station, as well as a plastic gun from a toy shop, quite obviously fake, along with a holster.

Emmeline would be pleased, I was sure, not only with my obedience but also that I was prepared to really get into the spirit of things. She wanted a comic cowgirl and she was going to get one. I thought about it on the train, wondering what other details I could add and thinking about the moment my jeans came down to expose the ridiculous panties. The train was an old diesel, non-stop but pretty well empty, it being mid-afternoon on a winter weekday. I had a group of seats to myself and could admire my purchases, including the new blouse Billy had provided in exchange for the one he had come all over.

I knew I would masturbate over my experience, but I had been intending to keep it for that evening, in the safety and privacy of my room. At the thought of how he'd come over my bottom and back I knew it couldn't wait. All it needed was a few minutes in the train loo and I'd be there, the ache in my pussy relieved, my lewd fantasies brought to the conclusion Emmeline would expect.

It was right to do it in the train loo anyway, appropriate in that to do so added to my lack of control over my own lust and therefore to the overwhelming humiliation of the whole situation. So in I went, feeling thoroughly embarrassed as I slid the lock home and pushed down my jeans and panties to the floor. I sat down and pulled up my jumper and bra, baring my breasts to the warm, humid air as I closed my eyes.

There was something wonderfully smutty about the idea of the Watermelon Crawl, a rude name for a rude act, an act in which I had made a deliberate mockery of myself, dressed as a cowgirl, exposing my bottom striptease-style, offering my crease for Bronco Billy to rut in. To think of my bottom as fat and round like a watermelon was bad enough, but the idea of my crease like a pink slit of melon flesh made it cruder still. It was as if Billy might have fucked me with no more personal consideration than if he'd stuck his cock in a hole he'd carved in a melon.

It hadn't been true. He had been all over me afterwards, babbling compliments and apologising for making a mess of my shirt and hair. Another thing he'd said was that he 'still respected me', which showed quite clearly that he didn't. Whatever he did or didn't understand about the Rattaners and Emmeline Young, he clearly had no idea about submission. To him I was a slut, a bad girl, the sort of girl who would let her panties down simply because she was told to do it, because she enjoyed showing her naked bottom off.

I spread my thighs and slid a finger into my pussy, letting the fantasy develop in my head. It would have been better if he hadn't been so pathetically grateful for what I'd done, and if I'd had my Stars and Stripes bra and panties set on. Then I would have been fully dressed, a complete cowgirl, humiliated in every detail. Only he wouldn't have asked for a favour, he would have punished me, simply for being me, for being pliable, a slut.

That was perfect, and I made myself as comfortable as possible, slid a finger lower to tickle my bottom hole, took hold of one breast and began to masturbate in earnest, moving my hand between my thighs to touch the way I needed it. In no time my feelings were rising towards orgasm, and as my rubbing matched the rhythm of the train I began to let the fantasy run one more time.

I would have been told to offer him something, something minor, like being allowed to watch me change. He would have accepted, and stood in the opening of the cubicle, the bead curtain held aside as I stripped, not to my underwear but all the way, naked in front of him. I'd have had my silly bra and panties set, and I'd have put them on, giggling and flaunting my bottom for him, deliberately teasing. He'd have let me do it, a reverse striptease, until I was in full cowgirl gear, my bottom taut in my jeans, every contour picked out in blue denim. I would have wiggled it at him and made a cheeky comment, telling him he could look but not touch or some other deliberate put-down.

He would have snapped. I'd have been taken by the ear, pulled squealing into the back room, and thrown down over his lap. Pleading, begging for mercy, I'd have had my tight blue jeans hauled down again, panties and all, exposing my bottom ... my watermelon, fat and pink for spanking. He'd have pulled my breasts out too, then set to work, calling me a slut and a tease as I writhed and yelled in my pain, my bottom bouncing wildly, my knees cocked wide to show off my tight brown anus and already juicy pussy.

Only when I'd had my bottom well and truly roasted would he put me on the floor, ordering me to crawl, to do the Watermelon Crawl, flaunting my plump, naked bottom in the frame of dropped blue-jeans, Uncle Sam panties and blouse and my leather chaps. I'd have been in tears, snivelling pathetically as he pulled out his cock. He'd have groped my breasts as I was made to suck him erect, maybe slapped them a little, my face too. Then it would have been back down on my knees, big fat watermelon up in the air, his cock stuffed up my pussy, pumped hard into me and whipped out at the last moment to come all over my ridiculous clothes, on my hat, my shirt, in my hair, in the crease of my bottom, over my anus and in the pouch of my Uncle Sam panties . . .

I came, a long, glorious orgasm with my back tight and my whole body bouncing to the thumps of the train moving on the track. It lasted a long, long time, with my thoughts held firmly on being spanked and fucked as a cowgirl until the end, when they switched to Emmeline Young, imagining her delight and amusement at what I had done.

My mood lasted until bedtime, but in the morning I felt very differently. I had been sure I'd done the right thing, but now I wasn't. Emmeline clearly saw me as a submissive, and in my effort to please her I had reacted as one, letting her skilful manipulation bring out my feelings. Yet those feelings were secondary to me, and if I was willing to suffer a little to gain full membership of the Rattaners, then I was not prepared to be merely their victim.

Possibly the test had not been what I thought it was at all. Possibly the entire Bronco Billy episode had been to see if I was truly dominant. Possibly I should have rejected him, or at least rejected doing his awful Watermelon Crawl. Possibly . . .

A dozen other possibilities were going through my head, and in every case I simply did not have enough facts to be sure of an answer. All I could do was hang on and hope for the best. Meanwhile I at least had some new facts to play with. The account name Bronco Billy had put my new clothes down to was 'Line Ladies', evidently a cover name, and clever, outwardly innocent yet suggestive of caned bottoms to anyone in the know. The Rattaners also had some unexpected influence and at least reasonable funds, given that my outfit would have cost nearly three hundred pounds, a sum well beyond my normal reach.

I was still in a flap at breakfast, and stayed that way until I went to the porters' lodge to check my post. There was a letter in my pigeonhole, an envelope of heavy-laid paper with the Bede College crest as a watermark. There was no stamp and it was addressed to me in an elegant, flowing handwriting. It could only be from Emmeline Young, and it was clearly an invitation. I was in.

As I walked back to my room my heart was pounding and my imagination was running at full speed, as I asked myself all the same questions over and over. Would they simply accept me on my own terms? Would there be a period of probation, or some gruelling initiation ceremony, perhaps worse even than what I had been made to do with Bronco Billy?

Would they perhaps want me as their victim, nothing more, so that I would never be accepted in my true place?

All there was inside the envelope was a hand written invitation, from the Line Ladies, to attend their next event on the Sunday evening coming. It was exactly what I should have expected, very discreet, with nothing untoward so much as hinted at, let alone plainly stated. The venue was given as Fieldfare Hall, near a town called Thame, which proved to be some ten miles east of Oxford.

I could just imagine it, some fine old manor tucked away in one of the shallow English valleys. Undoubtedly it would be the home of a Rattaner, and had probably been in use for years, maybe ever since Margaret Coln had retired. It would be set in its own grounds, shielded from prying eyes and far enough from the neighbours to allow the Rattaners' victims to scream just as loud as they pleased. There might even be servants, an old family retainer or two, moving quietly and deferentially among the members while some poor girl squirmed and pleaded on the floor as her naked bottom was thrashed.

Sunday seemed an age away, and I was extremely glad I'd made the effort to finish my essay, as it was harder than ever to think of anything beside the Rattaners. Thursday passed in a haze until my tutorial, after which Duncan gave me a thorough spanking, panties down and across his knee as usual, but even as I sucked his cock in heartfelt gratitude I was imagining myself down between Emmeline Young's thighs. That was where I would end up on the Sunday, I was sure. I had to assert myself, it was true, but that would come in time.

I had hoped to speak to Emmeline in more detail in the evening, but she wasn't at the Centre.

Doubtless there was good reason, but her absence made me paranoid, spoiling my spanking high as I fretted over the possibility of my having done something wrong with Bronco Billy or of Stan Tierney having somehow ruined things.

It was the same on Friday, my mood swinging from elation to trepidation, from the certainty that I had found my ideal place to equal certainty that everything would go wrong, or already had. I simply had to do something connected with the Rattaners, so continued my researches into Sarah Finch, despite the fact that I would be meeting her on Sunday evening.

Given her job, it was easy to predict her whereabouts, and equally easy to find an excuse to lunch in hall at Erasmus Darwin, where two of my friends from my normal university life were at college. They went off to lectures afterwards, but I stayed on the pretext of a visit to the college library, a modern concrete and glass building from which it was possible to look down into the delivery bay for the kitchens.

I actually got quite a lot of work done, over half the reading Duncan had set me for the following week's essay, sparing only the occasional glance when one person or another came out into the bay. By late afternoon I had a pretty well comprehensive knowledge of the Erasmus Darwin College catering staff, but none answered Walter Jessop's description of Sarah Finch, until a delivery van arrived and a tall, dark-haired woman in a neatly cut skirt suit emerged from the buildings.

It had to be Sarah. She was perhaps five feet nine or ten, of average build, very precise in her manner. I could easily imagine her as a spanker, and my admiration grew as I watched her deal with the lorry driver, a garrulous, over-familiar man who reminded me not a little of Stan Tierney. While I couldn't hear what they were saying it was plain that there was some problem with the delivery and that he was trying to talk her into signing for it anyway. She wouldn't, and sent him on his way with a flea in his ear.

I turned back to my book as Sarah went inside again, and was smiling quietly to myself as I once more turned my attention to the complexities of eighteenth-century European politics. Sarah Finch was evidently a fine woman and deserving of her place in the Rattaners. She was attractive too, and for all that she was maybe twice my age the idea of getting her across my knee appealed, especially imagining her chagrin at being spanked by a student. Meeting her was an enticing prospect.

The time was approaching five before I came up from my book. I was beginning to think of tea, and perhaps treating myself to a slice of cake in one of the coffee shops along St Giles on the way back to college. Having seen Sarah it was hard to see what else I could do, but my little bit of spying had provided me with a pleasantly naughty feeling.

I left the library and went to collect my bicycle from the sheds, which were a hundred yards or so down the road from the delivery bay. A girl was passing as I wheeled my machine out onto the pavement, and we swapped a smile and an apology for getting in each others' way as she passed. She was very pretty, with tight dark curls and freckles, her face full of pert insolence and her jeans much the same. I took a moment to adjust my front light and surreptitiously admired the sweet rotation of her bottom, imagining how it would feel to spank her, when to my surprise she stopped at the delivery bay.

Sarah Finch stepped out into the road. They spoke, casual, friendly, obviously very much at ease with each other. I watched, certain that the pretty young girl was the very same who had giggled over having to choose hairbrushes for use on her own bottom in Walter's shop. They began to walk south, and I just had to follow, wheeling the bicycle and occasionally ducking down to pretend to look at an imaginary problem with the chain.

They were laughing happily together, oblivious to everyone and everything around them. As they reached Keble they linked arms, with an unmistakable intimacy that gave me a jolt of envy despite my own wonderful situation with Jasmine and Caroline. Yet I knew that if I was right then the younger girl was regularly spanked by a group of women, a group that would shortly include me. It was an exciting thought to say the least, and I found myself wondering if she would be there on Sunday, and whether I would be allowed to join in when she was punished.

I wanted to, badly. She was very fine, with a desirable sweetness, innocence even, and a deliciously rounded bottom, very cheeky and midway in size between Jasmine's pertness and Caroline's opulence. She bounced as she walked too, almost skipping, which projected both insolence and a wonderful naîvety for the effect her body had on other people. It was quite a bit of an effect too, most men turning to take a sneaky glance at her rear view as they passed.

She was ripe for spanking in every way, and it was so easy to picture her in the ridiculous cowgirl outfit, or something equally humiliating, deeply embarrassed by the way she looked and then bursting into tears the moment her panties came down. I was projecting my own concepts onto her, as for all I knew she would revel in the look, just as Caroline did in her striptease outfits. Yet it was a wonderful fantasy, and I had every intention of making the best of it once I got back to college.

They went into one of the small shops at the top of St Giles and I decided that it was pushing my luck to follow, so I made for the Twistleton and a large slice of lemon cake to reward myself for my sleuthing, before heading for college. Caroline and Jasmine were due to have dinner ready for me at seven. That just gave me time for a leisurely bath, as well as an orgasm over the thought of Sarah's girlfriend in the cowgirl outfit, trussed up like a chicken with her jeans and panties down while she was leathered with her own belt.

Coming did nothing to dilute my good mood as I cycled down the Cowley Road to their house. They were ready, as ordered, Jasmine as cook, naked except for a pinny and high heels, and Caroline as maid, in a corset of peach-coloured satin with stockings and gloves to match. They knew nothing about Bronco Billy, aware only that I was invited to the Rattaners' meeting on the Sunday. Without actually telling any lies I had hinted that I would be one of the dominants and apologised for being unable to invite them.

'Your time will come,' I assured them as I made myself comfortable at the table. 'Quite soon, in fact. I saw Sarah Finch today, and her girlfriend. Once I've got to know them, I think I'll swap you for an evening, one of you anyway.'

'Is she cute, this Sarah?' Caroline asked.

'Yes,' I told her, 'not that it matters. You go to whosoever I tell you to, and if you do go to her I expect immaculate behaviour. What's for dinner?'

'Sausages and mash, with peas.'

'Good, you can have your bowl in the kitchen. Caroline will eat later.'

'Yes, Mistress.'

She disappeared into the kitchen, her neat little bottom wiggling behind her. Caroline poured me a glass of wine and stood to attention as I took a sip.

'Not bad,' I remarked, 'and suitable, I dare say. Which butcher did Jasmine go to for the sausages?'

'We didn't have time to go into town, I'm afraid, Mistress. She just nipped round the corner to Pound-saver.'

'Poundsaver?'

'Yes, Mistress.'

She skipped quickly out of the room. It was deliberate, it had to be, because Jasmine did know how to cook. I sighed, wishing they'd chosen some way of getting punished that allowed me to have a decent meal first. After a while Caroline came back, holding a plate piled high with mashed potato stuck with sausages and ringed with a soggy green mass I took to be the peas. It was set in front of me.

'Bring her in,' I ordered.

Jasmine appeared without having to be called, looking nervously at her bare feet.

'I thought you were cooking me dinner?' I asked.

'Yes, Mistress.'

'Frozen pork and beef sausages, instant mashed potato and mushy peas from a can does not consti-tute dinner, Jasmine. Why didn't you go to the market?'

'Sorry, Mistress, I didn't have time!'

'You had all day, Jasmine. You are lazy, that's all. Now come here.'

She came, reluctantly, pouting, yet obedient, know-ing full well she was in trouble. As she came up to me I took her by the hair and pulled her down. Her expression changed briefly to sharp consternation an instant before her face met the surface of the mashed

102

potato, under which it disappeared with a soft squelch.

I held her down until she began to struggle, then pulled her back, waiting until she had stopped spluttering and gasping for breath before speaking. Her face was a mask of the watery white mash, with more in her hair, along with several bits of pea. Behind me Caroline suppressed a giggle.

'Eat it,' I ordered, 'all of it except for two of the sausages. You have five minutes, with a stroke of the cane for every one minute over.'

She began to eat immediately, mouthing down the slimy green and white mess like a pig at a trough, as fast as she could. I watched, still holding her hair and occasionally dipping her face in the mess just to keep her on her toes. To my disappointment she made it, swallowing the final mouthful in just over four minutes and doing her best to lick the plate clean. A lot of it was on her face and in her hair, but I decided to allow her to get away with that, or at least think she had. Only the two sausages remained. Both she and I knew where they were going.

'Turn around, hands on your knees, bottom out,' I ordered.

There was no hesitation. She just turned, stuck her little bottom up and rested her hands on her knees, which were together, flaunting her pussy and anus, both already glistening with juice.

'Slut,' I remarked, and took a careful hold of one of the sausages, to slide it deep into the hole of her vagina.

I left just the end sticking out, a truly ludicrous sight that made me giggle as I picked up the second sausage. Half of its fat brown length was liberally coated with instant mash, which I was sure would be an adequate lubricant for her bottom hole. She didn't even need to spread herself, her neat little cheeks so firm and her position so revealing that I had easy access to the tight pink star of her anus. She gave a sob of pure misery as I touched the sausage to her hole, but she relaxed her muscle, letting it spread as I pushed the sausage in, and up. I was grinning to myself as I watched the thick brown sausage slide up into her body, a collar of mash forming as it went up, just as the collar of margarine had formed on Tierney's cock as he penetrated Caroline's anus. As with her pussy, I left the end sticking out, so that she had about a half-inch of sausage protruding from each hole as a fat brown dome of meat.

'You're done,' I told her and landed a firm swat across her bottom. 'Now get me some real food.'

'Yes, Mistress.'

She walked away, waddling a little, with the tip of the sausage in her rectum still just visible between her cheeks, a truly obscene sight. I sat back and took another sip of wine, well pleased with myself and feeling both dominant and mischievous. As I finished my glass Caroline poured me another, one plump breast lolling forwards against my shoulder as she moved. I caught the smell of frying onions from the kitchen.

'What is she actually cooking?' I asked.

'Rib-eye steak, Mistress,' Caroline answered, 'with red onions, mushrooms, green peas and new potatoes.'

'Better, much better. We might be able to improve the atmosphere, though, don't you think? Candlelight would be pleasant, just right for a romantic dinner, don't you think? Up on the table.'

'Why me? It was me last time!'

I snatched out, catching her by the hair to turn her whining protest into a squeak of shock as she was pulled abruptly down across my knee. Jasmine had come to the door and gave a pleased snigger as her girlfriend's bottom came up and open, and another as I laid in, spanking the big, wobbling cheeks with all my force and entirely ignoring the stream of apologies, squeaks and gasps pouring from Caroline's mouth. Only when the whole plump globe of her bottom was an even pink did I let go, depositing her on the floor with a bump. She stared ruefully up at me from big, moist eyes.

'Don't let the onions burn, Jasmine,' I instructed, 'but the moment you've given them a stir fetch me a candle, one of the pink ones. Why aren't you on the table, Caroline?'

Caroline climbed up, her face set in a sullen pout as she got into position, her bottom towards me, lifted high, the red cheeks spread to show off the rear purse of her pussy, her anus at the vertical.

'Wouldn't it have been easier to obey in the first place?' I queried. 'You would be in the same position, after all, but without a smacked bottom. It should be obvious that Jasmine can't be the candlestick. She has a sausage up her bottom. She is also cooking. Don't be so selfish.'

Jasmine came back, holding a pink candle a good inch thick at the base and a foot long, as well as matches and a pat of margarine on a teaspoon.

'I hope you're not cooking with this?' I asked, taking the spoon to smear the margarine onto Caroline's anus.

'No, Mistress, butter.'

'Good, you're learning.'

Butter is for eating, margarine for greasing slave girls' bottoms, at least in my books. I waited a little, until the margarine had melted, making a little yellow pool in the cavity of Caroline's anus, then put the candle to her. Her ring spread as she relaxed it. She was as experienced in accepting anal penetration as Jasmine, and the candle slid up, tight in her hole but easily enough. I put about four inches up, just to make sure it stayed firmly in, and lit it.

Jasmine scampered back to the kitchen, turning the main light out on the way. I was left to my wine, and my view, the glorious full moon of Caroline's bottom, the cheeks flared, the long stem of the candle protruding upright from her anus. It was quivering slightly from her trembling, to make the flame flicker and fill the room with dancing shadows.

There is something fascinating about wax. I could watch a candle burn for hours, just to see the way the beads form and run down, hardening as they cool, to make fantastic shapes. In this case there was the added pleasure of wondering whether or not any particular drop was going to catch Caroline's anal skin. It was low-temperature wax, but it was still going to sting, badly, and I was grinning in sadistic glee between sips of my wine as I watched.

The first two drips cooled on the shaft, leaving a little blob of wax sticking out at one side of the candle, about halfway down. The third took a different path, and went lower, stopping just a couple of inches from the taut ring of her hole. By then a little bowl shape had formed at the top, and rather than run down, the wax began to build, forming a little hump, the flame light flickering on the meniscus, swelling, larger and larger.

It broke, hot wax running down the side of the candle to catch the hard bead formed earlier and fall free, splashing onto the soft curve of Caroline's inner bottom cheek. She gave a little pained cry and her shaking grew abruptly worse, dislodging another drop, which this time ran all the way down, right onto her straining anal skin. I laughed as her high-pitched squeal rang out, high on the cruel joy of torturing her.

The wax hardened quickly, sealing the candle into her anus. I continued to watch and to drink, her trembling growing ever more pronounced, her breathing deeper and less controlled. She had depilated, fortunately for her, and there was no hair to get clogged, allowing the wax to form a round plug over her anus as more and more ran down. Soon her bottom hole had begun to resemble the mouth of one of those Chianti fiascos you get in cheap Italian restaurants. She had shaken quite a few drops free too, to make splashes of pink in her bottom crease and on the plump curves where her cheeks rose to either side.

She was getting wet, her pussy juicing slowly as her pain and the humiliation of being used as a candlestick got to her. I wasn't immune myself either, my arousal rising slowly until by the time Jasmine brought my dinner I was ready. As she put the plate down I lifted my hips, to pull up my skirt and ease my tights and panties down, all the way to the floor. It was hardly a dignified pose, but as Duncan had pointed out when explaining why he should spank me, a true dominant does as she pleases.

'Under the table,' I ordered as I pulled my chair in. 'Lick slowly and gently until I tell you otherwise.'

'Yes, Mistress.'

She got down, crawling under the table to give me a brief flash of the sausages in her vagina and anus. I spread my thighs wide, allowing her to lick me as I ate. She began with a kiss, low down, right over my bottom hole, then began to lick. My position was a little awkward, but it felt good, good enough to come. I began to eat, taking my time, savouring each mouthful and every drop of wax as Jasmine licked and Caroline's pained excitement grew slowly greater.

Only when I'd finished did I sit back, allowing Jasmine full access to my sex. She immediately went lower, her tongue tip tickling my anus then burrowing a little way in. I stretched, feeling thoroughly content as she cleaned my bottom, licking my anal ring and as far into the hole as she could get, until I felt open and moist. Caroline's candle was halfway down, a pink stub protruding from a plug of wax that entirely hid her anus. It was time to come.

'Do it now,' I told Jasmine, 'and then you can get your tongue back up my bottom while you come yourself.'

She immediately transferred her attention to my pussy, licking right on my clitoris, firm and even, a technique I knew would have me there in seconds.

'You I'll deal with later,' I told Caroline, 'with that plug still in your bottom hole, maybe burning. Does it hurt? How hot is your skin? Are you scared of the flame? It's just inches from your skin, Caroline, just inches from that beautiful smooth bottom, and it's not going out, not until I've come, Caroline, not . . .'

I broke off, overwhelmed by the touch of Jasmine's tongue on my sex and the thought of their pain and degradation as they served me, near naked, their bottoms penetrated, maid and human candlestick, cook and pussy licker . . .

My hands went to my breasts, cupping them. My back arched. My pussy and bottom hole began to pulse and I was coming, calling out in ecstasy, completely in love with both of them as they brought me to climax, long and tight and wonderful. At the very peak Jasmine slid her fingers into me, both vagina and anus, giving me a glorious sensation of being filled right at the top of my pleasure. She kept them in too, deep up inside me, even when my contractions had died, only then pulling both free and popping them straight into my mouth.

The candle was getting dangerously low, and I took a moment to blow it out, then settled back, leaving the wick on top of the mound of wax over Caroline's anus smoking like a miniature volcano. As I eased my body forwards on the chair once more Jasmine's tongue went back up my bottom, probing deep as the wet, fleshy noises of her masturbation began. I relaxed, enjoying the feel of her tongue in my anus and the utter submission it represented. Caroline was ready, her pussy juicy and wet, her bottom squeezing to make the mass of wax between her cheeks move slowly up and down.

'Dinner time, slut,' I told her, 'just as soon as your girlfriend has finished licking my bottom. You may start to masturbate.'

Caroline turned a little, to look back, her face flushed, her eyes half-lidded. She reached back to find her pussy, briefly touching the plug of wax in her anus before she began to rub herself. Jasmine came, her tongue wedged as deep as it would go up my bottom, and the moment she was done I reached down, to pull her out by the hair. She came, crawling, and I turned her about with a couple of well aimed slaps.

She had been masturbating with the sausage in her vagina, which was still in her hole but had split down the middle, revealing the lumpy interior, smeared with pussy cream. I pulled it free, lifted it to show Caroline what she had for dinner, and as her mouth came wide open I put it in. Immediately she began to eat, chewing on the sausage with her eyes closed as the rhythm of her masturbation picked up.

I laughed to see the sheer height of submission I had brought her to, reaching down to fondle

Jasmine's bottom and, as Caroline's body began to tighten in the approach to climax, I drew out the second of the fat brown sausages from her girlfriend's anus. She swallowed her mouthful as she started to come, only to find the second sausage right in front of her mouth as her eyes came open.

My timing was perfect. She gave one hollow groan of abandonment and it was in her mouth, sucked on, and eaten as she came, her whole body in spasm, her bottom cheeks clutching on the plug of wax in between, her fingers working furiously among the plump folds of her pussy, her jaws working on her mouthful, her face set in ecstasy and disgust.

It had been a good dinner. I felt well served, and I allowed them to have a glass of brandy each afterwards. That put us in a mellow mood and we went to bed, to talk and drink and tease until the early hours of the morning. I was just drifting to sleep when Caroline mentioned that they were planning to go into London on Sunday coming, where there was a special exhibition of Edwardian clothing at the Victoria and Albert Museum. I declined, knowing I would never forgive myself if I missed the Rattaners.

Seven

While it was a shame not to see the exhibition in London, I knew I could not possibly afford to go. I needed to be fresh for the evening, and did not want to do anything that risked me not being at Fieldfare Hall for six-thirty.

I spent Saturday with Jasmine and Caroline, my every need looked after, and once again stayed the night. It was only on the Sunday morning, when I was already back at college, that I remembered Stan Tierney's poker game. It didn't really interest me, but I had promised and felt the least I could do was drop in at the Red Ox and apologise. It was a beautiful day, cool but clear and bright, and I had already decided to take a picnic lunch up to the Chilterns and spend a very easy day in the hills, just to make absolutely sure I was in time for the Rattaners' meeting. Given how far it was to go and that it was in a private house I could be sure of facilities to wash and change, allowing me to present myself in tip-top condition, ready for whatever the evening might bring. Taking a bus up the hill to Cowley and catching another for Thame was only a minor diversion.

For the best part of a week my head had been full of fantasies about what might happen on the Sunday, and at last the time had come. Playing with Jasmine and Caroline as their Mistress for almost two days had left me feeling confident in my essential dominance, and sure I could assert myself whatever I might be in for. But that didn't stop me thinking about what might happen, and I was feeling both excited and aroused as I sat on the bus up to Cowley with my cowgirl outfit stowed in a travelling bag beside me.

Closed and supposedly empty, the Red Ox looked more squalid than ever, the peeling paintwork and bits of decaying poster on the walls somehow more prominent in the silence. I knocked on the door and a man I didn't know opened it, immediately locking it behind me and pulling the drape to as I came in. He was not one of the regulars, or not one that I'd noticed, but looked much like many of them, big, burly and rough-cut, with a coarse face and ill-kempt black hair around a small bald patch.

'I'm not staying,' I explained as Mike popped up from behind the bar. 'I just dropped in to explain to Stan that Jasmine and Caroline can't make it.'

'You're joking.' Tierney's voice sounded from the area where the girls usually stripped.

'Sorry,' I answered as he appeared. 'They've gone to London.'

'Don't worry, ducks, you'll do,' the big man said and a large hand closed on my bottom.

'I can't stay, as I said,' I answered firmly as I moved quickly out of his reach.

'You promised me!' Stan exclaimed. 'Jesus, Isa, this is no fucking joke!'

I shrugged. He came forwards, to take me by the arm and lead me quickly to one side. The big man gave us a somewhat worried look and stepped out of sight as Stan began to talk in an urgent whisper.

'You can't let me down, Isa, you've got to do it!'

'No I haven't, Stan. I never said I would.'

'Yeah, but you promised me Jas and Carrie.'

'I told you, they're in London.'

'What are they doing in fucking London!? You said they'd be here!'

'I know, Stan, but . . . look, I forgot. I'm sorry.'

'You're sorry? You're not half as fucking sorry as I'm going to be if I don't come through. Dave, him who let you in, he doesn't take kindly to blokes who back out on what they owe, and nor do the others.'

'So don't play.'

'I've got to fucking play, haven't I. I owe money!'

'To them?'

'Of course to them, you daft cow! Jesus, Isa, you have well dropped me in it. I thought I could rely on you?'

'Look, I'm sorry, what else can I say?'

'You can say you'll do it, that's what you can say, 'cause if you don't I'm dead!'

He was genuinely scared, his face white, his hands shaking. I felt really bad, because I had promised, and the man called Dave looked quite capable of violence.

'Who are they, gangsters?'

'Gangsters?' Stan demanded. 'What are you fucking talking about, gangsters? Dave drives a truck, Mo's on the line at Rover, so's Big Dave. Jack's a pro, sort of.'

'Pro? A professional gambler, and you expect to beat him?'

'Well, he reckons he's a pro. It's all crap really, 'cause he's still on the social. I just had a bad run last time, that's all.'

'So you lost money to him last time, and to the others. How much?'

'Seven hundred.'

'Seven hundred pounds!

'Yeah. I can make it back in a couple of hands, but only with you. You've got to help me, Isa. I helped you!'

'Couldn't you postpone it? I can bring the girls up another time.'

'No! It has to be today, or they're going to do me, Isa. They're going to . . .'

'I don't want to know.'

I drew a deep sigh. I had promised, and more importantly he had told me about the Rattaners – reluctantly, but he had, probably at the risk of his job. It meant a lot to me, and there is such a thing as gratitude.

'OK, OK,' I told him. 'I'll stand as stake, but you had better win, that's all!'

'Count on it, love.'

His manner had changed in a second, from real fear to his usual over-friendly garrulity, and he steered me towards the main bar with a pat on my bottom. I went, my lips pursed, wondering exactly what I had let myself in for. The others were already around the table – Dave, who'd let me in, and three others who were quickly introduced to me. Mo was Chinese, or maybe half-Chinese, with a heavy, fleshy body and a large round head. Big Dave earned his name, well over six foot and fat as well, a truly massive man, stark bald with faded tattoos showing on both arms where they emerged from a string vest. Jack was not that much smaller, with none of the slickness I'd expected, just a beer belly and the balding remnants of a teddy-boy haircut.

'So what's the scale for your tart, Stan, my man?' Dave asked as I pulled up a chair behind Tierney.

I didn't bother to remonstrate about the insult,

hoping to get the whole thing over and done with as quickly as possible.

'I reckon a blow-job's twenty,' Jack suggested, 'ten in the hand, a fifty a fuck.'

'No way!' Tierney protested. 'A posh bird like Isa would charge a ton just to look at your dirty little dick! Fifty a hand-job, and that's generous, a ton and it's in her mouth, two for a fuck.'

'No, no, nothing like that,' I put in hastily. 'Stan can play for my clothes, ten pounds an article, and . . . I suppose I'll take you in my hand if I have to, at . . . I don't know, fifty pounds, and that's only if I end up naked.'

'Oh, you'll end up naked!' Dave laughed. 'Bare baby naked!'

'Student, aren't you?' Jack asked.

'Yes,' I admitted.

'Good, I've never fucked a student.'

'I've told you –'

'Cool down, Isa,' Tierney interrupted me. 'Are we playing or what?'

'When we know how much your tart is worth, sure we are,' Dave answered him.

'Let Mike set the stake,' Mo suggested.

Big Dave gave a single ponderous nod and that seemed to settle the matter. I gave Mike a pleading look, wishing I'd been a bit less formal towards him. He considered for a moment, then gave his verdict.

'Stan's right, she's not cheap. I reckon a tenner for each piece of her clothing, thirty for hand-jobs, fifty for blows . . .'

'I am not sucking,' I insisted.

'You'll suck,' Big Dave growled.

I shut up, not at all happy about the situation but seemingly with very little choice. Whatever I thought of Stan Tierney, I had broken my promise, and could not allow myself to be responsible for him getting beaten up. If I had to suck cock I had to suck cock, but I could feel the tears of frustration building in my eyes at the prospect of doing it.

'What're you having, Isabelle?' Mike asked. 'On the house.'

There was sympathy in his voice, immediately making me warm towards him.

'Cognac please, Mike,' I answered as Jack dealt the cards with a fluttering agility that filled me with dismay.

I have little idea how poker is played, and less when it's for money, but when Tierney lifted his cards to reveal a pair of threes, a jack, a ten and a five my heart sank. The others were making very sure they gave nothing away, but I was certain somebody would be able to do better. Feeling very small and very vulnerable I sat back, trying not to look or to think of having to strip in front of them, let alone taking one in my hand or my mouth.

'Put your stake out then, Stan,' Dave said suddenly, with a dirty leer in my direction.

I took off my college scarf, which fortunately none of them objected to, and laid it across the back of a chair. All six of them were smoking, filling the air with a bluish haze and making my nostrils twitch in revulsion. They had drinks too and, while both Tierney and Jack were taking it easy, the other three had nearly finished what might well not have been their first pints. Stan changed his cards twice, and to my relief secured a third three. Mo threw his hand down with a grunt of disgust, as did Big Dave. Jack pushed a ten pound note forwards. Dave followed suit.

'Her coat,' Stan offered, only for Jack to immediately push a twenty onto the pile.

116

Dave added his own twenty, but Stan shook his head, presumably alarmed by their confidence. I took off my coat and laid it on top of my scarf, a trivial act of exposure which still made me feel more vulnerable than ever. Stan reached back to ruffle my hair, which I answered with a dirty look as Dave and Jack finished the hand. Dave had won, with a full house of three tens and two sevens, and he pulled the chair with my coat and scarf on it a little closer to himself.

'Tenner each, yeah?' he queried.

'Course it's a fucking tenner each,' Tierney answered him.

I hadn't realised my clothes would continue to act as stakes after they were off, but there was nothing I could do about it. Even pointing out that my coat had cost nearly two hundred pounds seemed pointless.

The cards were dealt again, and I had to put a shoe aside as Tierney's stake. To my delight and relief he was dealt three kings straight away. I hid my reaction behind my brandy glass, swallowing about half the contents. Stan changed, but failed to improve his hand, calling out immediately he was ready.

'Her other shoe, both socks, thirty quid.'

My relief changed to trepidation as I realised he was going to play the hand as it stood. Both Daves matched him, Jack withdrew, but Mo raised the bid.

'Sixty sees me,' he stated.

'I'm out,' Dave replied, Big Dave merely throwing his cards down.

'Sixty,' Stan stated. 'One sock, jumper, jeans and a hand-job.'

'I want her stripped!' Dave sneered.

'You get what comes,' Tierney answered him. 'Well, Mo?'

117

Mo paused, then put his cards down, showing three twos and two aces.

'Shit!' Tierney swore as my heart sank. 'I was so fucking sure you was bluffing!'

Mo just grinned. Slowly, my hands like lead, I began to undress, peeling off my footwear and my jumper, then hesitating. I had a top on, but to take my jeans off meant showing my panties, and all six of them were grinning at me like so many wolves. It had to done, though, because I did not want to give them an excuse to do it for me. So down they came, and off, to leave me in my top, bra and panties. I gave it all to Mo, who piled everything up, grinning out of his big moon face all the while, then reached out his hand for mine. I accepted it, realising I was to be taken into the lavatory to do my business.

'Don't hang about,' Jack advised. 'Get the drinks in, Dave.'

Their talk was lost to my hearing as Mo led me into the Gents toilet. I winced as a smell of antiseptic and stale urine hit me, but I felt strangely numb, as if with matters no longer within my control it was all rather detached. Mo went into a cubicle, sat down and calmly took his cock out, then patted his knee. I perched myself on his lap, his hand immediately finding my panty-clad bottom, to knead my cheek as I took hold of him, feeling his cock squirm to my touch within its thick sheaf of skin.

I began to tug, letting him have a good time with my bottom because it was sure to make things quicker. After a moment he took out his balls, to play with them as I masturbated him. He'd been a bit swollen in the first place, and I soon had a little stubby erection in my hand, the glossy tip popping in and out of the heavy foreskin as I tugged. He began to breathe more deeply, his groping firmer and more intrusive, pushing my panties into the crease of my bottom, and suddenly he had come, thick white sperm erupting over my hand and across his shirt front. He sighed, gave me a slap on my panty seat and I was done.

Back in the main room they were ready to get on with the game. I took my seat again and peeled off my top as the next stake. To my shame my pussy was a little wet and my nipples stiff, showing through my top to betray my reaction and the feelings of submissive arousal that were beginning to replace my fear and disgust. I had just masturbated a man I barely knew, as a bet in a game of cards, which has to be about as humiliating as it gets, if hardly as heavy.

To my surprise and delight Tierney actually won, saving me the exposure of my breasts as my top remained his stake. It went on the next hand, though, and I was forced to undo my bra and put it on the table, to the tune of their whistles and catcalls. Topless, my stomach fluttering, I sat back down, only for Tierney to fail to make anything whatsoever of his hand.

Off came my panties, as simple as that. I was nude, my body exposed in front of six men, six coarse men who saw me only as a receptacle for their sperm, something to be used. Tierney was not going to win, and I was going to get well and truly used, in my mouth, in my pussy, maybe even up my bottom before the afternoon was through.

Sure enough, he lost my panties and into the loo I went, first to toss Big Dave off, then to suck Mike's cock for a fifty-pound advance from the till for Tierney. Big Dave made me pose, in a variety of dirty positions that put my breasts and bottom and pussy on show, which I suspected he had taken from a pornographic magazine. He got himself hard while I did it, then like Mo he had me sit on his lap and felt me up while I pulled him off.

For Mike it was down on my knees in the lavatory cubicle, his cock growing slowly in my mouth as I sucked. He hadn't bothered to close the door, and my bare bottom was sticking out to the wash area with my pussy showing so that all the while I was expecting one of the others to come in behind and just fuck me. None did, but for all my chagrin I was wet and ready, easy to penetrate.

We went back to the game, and I was confidently expecting Tierney to lose the fifty pounds and for me to be back on my knees in minutes. To my amazement he didn't, but began to win, slowly but surely building up the pile of money in front of him. Big Dave and Mo had come, and Jack was intent on the game; only Dave was paying attention to me, but luck was against him.

It began to get serious, tempers rising, until first Dave and then Mo had been cleaned out. Tierney was several hundred pounds up, and paid off his debt to each to allow them to continue the game, as well as paying back Big Dave. That left him and Jack playing seriously, Big Dave backing out while he was ahead, and I found myself ignored, the two of them head to head, deadly earnest.

Dave wanted me on his lap, but while I was prepared to accept their right to use me as winnings I was not going to show willing. I went to Mike instead, because I knew him best, and also because he'd come, but it didn't stop him stroking my bottom and breasts as I perched naked on his lap, bringing my arousal and sense of submission higher still. I wanted spanking, maybe even fucking, but either way to be given it because they had won the right to do it. It was going to happen as well, because Tierney and

Jack were piling everything they had into the middle of the table, neither prepared to back down. I heard Tierney put me up for fucking, and I simply didn't have the will power to contradict him.

'Read 'em and weep,' Jack drawled, spreading his cards out with me already imagining myself on my back on the lavatory floor with him inside me.

He had four jacks and an ace. I felt my pussy tighten in anticipation. I hadn't seen Tierney's hand, but as he put it down my feelings changed abruptly, to relief but also a shameful regret. He had four kings, taking the hand and every penny of what was on the table, including my discarded panties.

'Want to play on?' Tierney queried as he began to count notes over to Jack.

'Nah,' Jack answered, 'it's not my day.'

'Told you I could do it,' Tierney boasted as he sauntered over to the bar with his handful of money, maybe two hundred pounds over what he had paid back. Jack spoke again.

'I want to fuck your tart, that's what I want. How much?'

'Not like that,' I answered, 'not ever.'

'Snotty bitch, ain't you?' he answered. 'How about a quick toss in the lav anyway? You done Mo and Big Dave, you can do a handsome lad like me.'

'No,' I answered, 'certainly not if you're going to call me names. Can I have my clothes back now, please?'

'Sure,' Tierney answered, and tossed me my panties, which I quickly struggled into.

Dave had my bra, and I reached out for it, only to have him pull it away.

'No chance, darling. This is worth ten quid, this is.'

'Yes, maybe,' I answered, 'but it's no use to you, is it, not unless you're a secret transvestite.'

The others laughed and he went red, but stood his ground.

'No way. You want it back, you pay for it, and the price just went up, to a blow-job.'

'Yeah, right,' Jack added. 'You want your clothes back, you pay for them. How's that suit you?'

'Yeah, you lost your clothes, you lost your clothes, simple as that.' Mo laughed. 'A bet's a bet.'

'Don't be ridiculous, I have to get to Thame!'

'You can have your socks back,' Big Dave offered.

'Thank you,' I answered him. 'At least one of you is a gentleman. Now come on, please?'

'You want to cover those titties, you put out,' Dave said.

'How about if Stan buys them back?' I suggested as I pulled my socks on.

'No way,' Tierney answered quickly. 'Come on, Isa, you did it for Mo and Big Dave, Mike and all, and it's just for a laugh. Be a sport.'

'Just for a laugh?' I echoed, wondering how he could possibly view the use of my body so casually.

'Yeah, a laugh,' Dave agreed. 'Stop being so fucking stuck-up.'

'I like 'em stuck-up, I do,' Mike put in. 'Nothing like seeing a really posh bird get down and dirty.'

'Yeah, well, you've had her, ain't you?' Jack answered him. 'I want mine. Come on, your fucking high and mighty Ladyship, you want your kit, suck my cock.'

'No, not you,' I answered, angry at his attitude, 'but I'll help Dave with my hand. Come on, Dave.'

It was stupid, an ill-thought-out move brought on by anger. He had my jeans, top and jumper, which had changed hands several times during the first part of their game. I had to get them back or go in bra and panties, with my coat and shoes, assuming Mo was nice to me in the end. I wanted to make Jack angry, though, and my determination rose higher still as he followed us into the loos, the others coming behind.

'I'll suck,' I offered. 'You can watch, Mo, if you give me back my stuff, and you, Big Dave, for being kind.'

'We're all going to fucking watch,' Jack sneered.

'I ain't doing it in front of you, you bunch of poofs!' Dave responded, but he was already seated on the loo, his legs wide, his cock a sizeable bulge in his jeans.

I went down on the floor, between his knees, my panty seat taut behind me, the others crowding around the door to get a good view. Dave was going to say something else, but merely groaned as I squeezed his cock through his trousers. It felt big, and sure enough, as soon as I'd got his fly down it sprang out, already close to erection, thick and long and smelling of man.

By then I wanted to be watched, to be made his plaything because I was angry at Jack, and because for all my resistance the idea of being made to buy my bra back by sucking his cock did appeal. It came within an inch of prostituting myself, but I was too turned on to care, and took him in my mouth, sucking eagerly to draw cries of delight from my audience.

It felt so good, so utterly humiliating and so dirty, down on my knees in a men's lavatory, in nothing but panties and socks, sucking cock as I was watched. All of them were dressed, only Dave's cock exposed, and that because it had to be. I was near nude, and I had been nude, my clothing stripped off me to pay the stakes in their poker game, my body used too, made to masturbate them, made to take them in my mouth.

I was going to have to go further too, because I had to pay off the obnoxious Jack. If I didn't I'd be going to the Rattaners in just my panties and bra under my coat, something I also wanted to be made to do.

They made the decision for me. I was lost in my fantasy, mouthing on Dave's cock with my eyes closed, when suddenly my panties had been pulled down at the back, my bottom was nude and the next instant something hard and hot had been pressed between my cheeks. I did try and pull away, one instant of automatic objection to being so summarily fucked breaking my dirty mood. Then he was up me and it didn't matter any more. I'd been done.

It was Jack, the others cheering and clapping as he took a firm grip of my panties and began to pump into me, hard, forcing me to grip onto the lavatory bowl or lose Dave's cock. I wanted to rub myself, but I couldn't, my whole body shaking to the hard thrusts, Jack's front slapping hard on my bottom, my breasts jiggling wildly beneath me. Dave took me by the ears, hard, and began to fuck my head, robbing me of the last vestige of control, so that all I could do was cling on and take it.

The men began to clap in rhythm, the rhythm of my fucking, my body rocking back and forth on the cocks, Dave and Jack using me like a big saw, my pussy and mouth nothing more than toys for their amusement. Both were laughing at my helpless plight, then Dave was grunting and Jack mumbling obscenities, and I realised they were going to come an instant before their sperm exploded up my pussy and in my mouth at the same instant. It burst from my holes, too full to hold it, spurting out around my penetrated vagina and all down my chin, then from my nostrils as I started to choke. They didn't care, both holding their cocks deep in until they were spent, with me jerking in helpless spasms, retching and clutching at Dave's legs, but to no avail.

He just laughed, the moment he'd come down from his orgasm, with me still gagging on his erection and Jack's sperm squashing in my pussy as he finished me off with a last few pumps. Dave pulled out, moving quickly aside to leave me spitting my filthy mouthful out down the lavatory, with long streamers of it hanging from my nose and chin. Jack was still up me, no longer pumping but holding himself in as his cock went slowly soft in my hole, and as he finally left my body I heard Mike speak.

'Go on, Stan, she's your tart and you the only one who ain't had her!'

'Yeah, fuck her, Stan!' Mo added. 'You can see she wants it. Look at that cunt, as slick as a greaser boy!'

'I ain't fucking in Jack's load,' Stan growled.

I half turned, to offer to suck him, because I just had to come before it was over. He was behind me, erect cock in his hand, but it was only as he squatted down that I realised what he meant by not fucking in Jack's load. He'd put his cock head to my bottom hole, and my gasp of protest was ignored, my attempt to keep him out useless as my slimy ring came open to the pressure, and he was up me.

All I could do was moan as my bottom hole was filled in one firm shove and I was being sodomised, in front of an audience, my anus agape, my rectum full of hard penis and five men watching it done to me. I reached back to find my pussy, struggling to make my mood match my filthy circumstances as Stan began to pump. The others were laughing and crowding in, Jack and Mo actually in the cubicle, their bodies trapping mine at either side, staring at my buggered ring as I masturbated.

'She's wanking her cunt!' Mo called in delight and disgust. 'The dirty tart!'

'I told you she was a filthy bitch,' Stan grunted.

'Posh tarts always are, underneath,' Mike put in.

'Imagine, taking it up the shitter from old Stan!' Dave crowed.

'She needs a wash, that's what she needs,' Jack added.

It all sank in, every humiliation, every insult, and all of it bringing me higher, except the last, which made no sense until Mo took a tight grip in my hair and shoved my head firmly down into the lavatory bowl. Suddenly it was too much. I just went wild, kicking and struggling in their grip, begging for it not to happen as calls rose up to flush my head, writhing against the hard china of the bowl, all the while as my bottom hole pulled in and out on Stan Tierney's cock.

They just did it, totally ignoring me. I heard the grate of the lever and the rush of water in the pipes in one ghastly moment when I realised it was truly going to happen, and then it had, freezing water swirling up around my head, filling my eyes, my ears, my nose, my mouth, choking me. I was fighting desperately, but Mo just held my head down, so easily, Stan and Jack gripping my body too, to render me utterly helpless, buggered and bog-washed, and still masturbating because they had robbed me of every last scrap of decency.

It was not too much. It was just right, exactly what should be done to me, my head flushed down a lavatory as I was sodomised, the final degradation for being such a slut. The water went down, but they kept my head in, my hair dangling wet into the bowl, soiled with bits of green loo paper and Dave's sperm, my face too. One of them spat on my back, then another, others jeering and egging Stan on to bugger me harder, and my orgasm was rising up, my bottom hole tightening on the fat cock inside, and it all came together in my head.

I'd been well and truly used, as something for crude, vulgar men to bet with. I'd been stripped of my clothes and of my dignity, used as a sex toy, made to suck, fucked, spitted on cocks, laughed at, spat on, and finally sodomised and bog-washed with Stan Tierney's cock in my anus. I was screaming my head off as I started to come, cursing them, calling them every filthy name I could think of, and myself as I clutched at my pussy over and over. Then Stan had come and I knew my rectum was full of his sperm. The lever grated once more and again my head was swamped in lavatory water, sperm and bits of paper, but I was coming and both were just extra touches to my utter submission, my mind focusing on what they had called me as the orgasm finally broke – Tierney's Tart.

Of course I could have gone to Thame dressed as a cowgirl, a humiliating fate but scarcely comparable with what the poker players had done to me. I had wanted it though, ultimately, even if he had pushed me further than I'd expected, much further. On the bus I was telling myself that it was for the best, that I had been given what I needed, my control taken away from me completely, as it should be for really good submissive sex. Unfortunately I knew it wasn't submissive sex at all, not from their point of view. To them I was simply a dirty college girl, Tierney's Tart.

There was half an hour to spare by the time I got to Thame, and the third person I asked knew the way to Fieldfare Hall. As I had expected it was a fair way out of town, but what I had not expected was for it to be a large wooden hut with a board outside declaring it to be the headquarters of some sort of youth organisation. The discovery dampened my expectations slightly, but I could see the choice made sense. There were no other buildings within over a hundred yards, and the closest were both offices, while there were fields on the far side of the road and a screen of pine trees hiding it almost completely.

I could hear music, much like the stuff Bronco Billy had played for me to show off to, which put a wry smile on my face as I knocked at the door. It was opened by Emmeline herself, looking very different from how I had expected. She was in fringed leathers, buckskins I think they're called, complete with a hat – a bit silly, but nothing like as bad as what I was about to get into. Her manner was also very different, and I was greeted with a kiss and a smile, which was far more encouraging.

'Welcome to Line Ladies, Isabelle,' she said. 'Do come in. You'll want to get changed and made up, of course, but let me make a few introductions first.'

'Thank you, yes.'

It was all I could manage, completely taken aback by my surroundings. The entire hall had been decorated in a way of which Bronco Billy would have thoroughly approved, with US flags, Country and Western posters, red, white and blue tinsel and pennons, even a mechanical horse complete with saddle. I could just imagine what the horse was for, and immediately wondered if I would be put on it. Certainly enough of the women there had lassoes and whips, and I could imagine being given a serious punishment, perhaps not as humiliating as my recent bog-washing, but a great deal more painful.

I had to admire them. It was perfect, a cover so wonderfully eccentric that nobody would ever think it was not genuine, a cover that allowed them to have rope and whips and even a spanking horse without the slightest hint of impropriety. Whoever had thought it up, presumably Elizabeth Hastings, was a genius. In fact so perfect was it that there was the

128

tiniest seed of doubt in my mind, until I saw that Professor Ashdene was also there, and I knew for certain I was with the Rattaners.

Emmeline introduced her to me, very informally, as Hope, and took me round to meet several other women, all much older than me save for one, Katie, who looked about the right age to be a postgrad, and was clearly going to be on the receiving end once the spanking started. She was small and blonde, very pretty in a soft sort of way, with freckles around her nose and a bob haircut. Her outfit made her role very clear, over-tight white jeans encasing a chubby little bottom, a Stars and Stripes shirt exactly like my own, tooled leather boots and a wide brimmed cowboy hat in white leather. I instantly wanted to spank her myself, and once more found myself hoping that some flexibility had been introduced to the Rattaners' rules since the 50s.

Jane Roberts wasn't there, nor Antonia Cappaldi, nor Sarah Finch and her girlfriend, although it was early and it seemed likely they would be in due course. Emmeline excused herself, leaving me to talk to Hope Ashdene, who had immediately struck me as deliciously strict in look, despite her open friendliness. Just the thought of being put across her knee had me shaking like a leaf, and I was forced to make my own excuses and go to the changing room, certain that I would wet myself in sheer anxiety.

Putting on the cowgirl outfit really brought my feelings home. By the time I was fully dressed I didn't just want to be spanked, I needed to be spanked. It also needed to be public, panties down, and hard, hard enough to make me cry. Then I would come, in front of all of them, to show them what they had done to me, before demonstrating my gratitude with my tongue. The horse would be ideal, with me tied in the saddle in a thoroughly rude pose, well down so that as I was stripped my pussy and bottom hole showed, then I would be whipped with the thing turned on, bucking madly as the Ladies demonstrated their skill on my naked flesh.

Once ready I stood back to admire myself in the mirror. A sassy, over-made-up American slut looked back at me, silly, openly sexual and extraordinarily vulgar. To be spanked in the outfit was going to take me to the limit of what I could bear, perhaps beyond even how I had felt with my head down the toilet and Stan Tierney's cock up my bottom at the Red Ox. There I had actually had very little choice in what was done to me. Now I did, my humiliation self-inflicted.

Several of the women there turned to look at me as I stepped out of the changing rooms, giving me appreciative smiles. They understood, they were the same, and suddenly I realised that the older, less flamboyant outfits did work, as the dominant counterpoint to mine, and to Katie's. To make us look so absurdly cute and then punish us without maintaining the same role could never be as strong as it was going to be, and besides, there was the Line Ladies cover to maintain.

'You look wonderful, Isabelle!' Emmeline enthused as she stepped up to me with a glass of mulled wine. 'But Hope and I have been wondering, and you must tell me. However did you find out about us? You must have been frightfully clever.'

'Not really,' I answered, blushing, 'and it was extremely generous of you to put my outfit on the account.'

'Don't mention it. I know how it is, believe me. I do hope it was right?'

'It was . . . it was perfect, as if you'd read my mind.'

'And I do hope Billy behaved himself. He can be rather over-enthusiastic at times.'

'He . . . he had me do the Watermelon Crawl for him.'

'Oh dear, well, he will have his little games, and no harm done I dare say. Is the Watermelon Crawl a favourite of yours? We could do it this evening if you like, properly, forty count and four wall.'

'Whatever you like, Lady Young. I was . . . um . . . thinking of going on the horse . . . if . . . if that's OK?'

'Of course you may go on the horse, darling, and we'll do the Watermelon Crawl too. How's that for a first night?'

She gave me a pleased smile and a gentle pat on my shoulder, then excused herself, leaving me shaking so hard the drink in my glass was quivering. I was going to be made to do the Watermelon Crawl and put on the horse. I'd be whipped and probably belted too, forty strokes, which I'd have to count, a task so, so hard under the pain of a severe punishment. I'd have to crawl as I took it, down on my knees with my bottom stuck up for punishment, maybe from wall to wall, counting as I was beaten, probably with my breasts pulled out, undoubtedly panties down, showing everything. Then it would be the horse, mounted up and tied in place, my naked bottom flaunted for whipping, really hard as it bucked beneath me, as I squirmed and screamed in my pain. The tears would be running down my face, my pussy rubbing on the hard saddle, until I came in a helpless, submissive ecstasy beyond even what I had experienced at the Red Ox.

Katie was across the room, examining the horse, doubtless with not dissimilar thoughts running through her head. I went to her, drawn as one victim to another and intent on learning more about her. She smiled as I approached, and patted the saddle.

'This is great! Have you been on it?'

'No, it's my first time. Have you?'

'No, but I'm going to. Rachel went on last time, and it was so funny. When she got off she couldn't even stand!'

She was so full of enthusiasm, a bit like Caroline, bubbly and uninhibited, only a lot braver considering what was going to happen once they'd got her on the horse. I didn't know who Rachel was, but if she hadn't been able to stand then it had to have been a serious punishment, a true flogging. Katie thought it was funny, but she had a right to. She was going to get put in the same state herself.

The music had stopped, and a sudden buzz of anticipation went through the room. Emmeline started over towards us, smiling happily.

'Patience, girls, all in good time. We're going to do the Watermelon Crawl now, Isabelle, if you're ready?'

I nodded, the lump in my throat far, far too big to let me speak. It was time, at last, my stomach churning horribly and my pussy twitching as my hands went to the button of my jeans, only to stop. I wanted Emmeline to take charge of me, from the start, to be my Mistress as I was for Jasmine and Caroline, as I was praying she wanted to be. Also I needed my bottom warmed, to make me ready for the whip.

'Will ... will you warm me up first, please, Emmeline?' I asked. 'A good spanking, panties down, and ... and in front of everyone if ... if you would, please?'

For a long moment she said nothing, as if she wasn't sure she had heard me correctly, and I wondered if I had made some error of Rattaners' etiquette.

'Sorry, Mistress Emmeline,' I tried, hanging my head in submission, 'do as you want with me, of course, it was wrong of me to be impertinent.'

She found her voice.

'I'm sorry, Isabelle, I don't quite think I understand you? Did you say a . . . a spanking?'

'Please, yes,' I managed.

'I . . . I don't . . . I don't really understand. Why ever would you want me to do such an awful thing to you? We . . . we were going to dance, weren't we?'

There was no irony in her voice, no teasing lilt, only shock and confusion. I looked up, to find every single woman in the hall staring at me in horror, not one with the slightest hint of amusement or sexual sadism, and every one expecting an explanation.

I just ran, in an agony of embarrassment, the tears exploding from my eyes the moment I reached the street.

Eight

I was going to kill Stan Tierney. It was the only thing I could do that would even begin to soothe my feelings.

All the way back from Thame I was in tears, and I walked the full ten miles. Thanks to Tierney I had just propositioned a senior and highly respected woman, the wife of a college Master, perversely, and in front of a dozen other people, all because the dirty little bastard wanted to get into my panties. He'd succeeded too. I had given in to him completely and utterly, been played for a complete idiot, my inexperience taken advantage of, my sexuality taken advantage of.

It hurt so badly, and if I had met him on the road I really think I would have tried to strangle him. All I could do was play the day over and over in my head, the afternoon at the Red Ox and the evening in Thame. My most intimate feelings had been grossly abused by him and his horrible friends, then exposed in front of the Line Ladies, who were quite obviously a genuine dance club. Then there was the stripping, the hand masturbation, the cock-sucking, the fucking, the sodomy, the bog-washing . . .

All of it was Tierney's fault, every single detail, including Bronco Billy, who must have thought I was both insane and a nymphomaniac for offering sex when all he wanted were a few steps from a country dance. Probably the Rattaners had never existed at all, or if they had they were long gone. Yet I had wanted them to exist, desperately, something Tierney had all too evidently realised. I'd thought he was stupid, but it was me who was stupid, naïve as well, and completely out of control.

It was nearly midnight by the time I got back to college, and even then I couldn't sleep, but just lay in the darkness cursing myself and Tierney and also the fact that beneath all my anguish I was still desperately turned on. I was in far too bad a state to masturbate, but that didn't stop me thinking about what a wonderful castle I had built in the air, and how simply perfect it would have been had it only been real.

At some point in the early hours I managed to cry myself to sleep, and woke the next morning with sore eyes and sore legs. My ridiculous cowgirl outfit was strewn on the floor where I'd left it, and I quickly put it away, unable to look at the thing. My other clothes were still in Thame, as well as my purse with all my money and cards in it, while I was expected at the Centre that evening.

The Centre was right out. I knew I could never ever look Emmeline Young in the face again. I had to go to Thame, though, and could only hope that whoever was in charge of Fieldfare Hall during the day was not a member of the Line Ladies. It was something to do, anyway, because I couldn't face lectures, especially as it was quite obvious that I'd been crying, while if I stayed in my room Tierney was due to arrive within a couple of hours.

It was not my day. My clothes weren't at the hut, and the uncommunicative old man who was the only person there had no idea what had happened to them. That meant either one of the Line Ladies had taken them back to Oxford or they'd been stolen, and I wasn't sure which option I preferred. To make it worse I ran into Mike on my way back. After the long and frankly scary bicycle ride in from Thame to East Oxford I'd stopped to fill up my water bottle and met him coming out of the shop. He was perfectly friendly, and casually asked if I would like to strip on Saturday night to earn some extra money. I had to ride off before I burst into tears again.

The rest of term was little better. Katie brought my clothes back on the Wednesday, another hideously embarrassing moment, although she did at least give me an embarrassed smile, which was better than the reaction of uncomprehending shock I had imagined. There was nothing from the Centre, Emmeline Young evidently having decided that the less said about my transgression the better. I kept expecting a bill for the cowgirl outfit, but it never came.

I was too upset even to accept my remaining Thursday afternoon spankings, although Duncan was very good about it and didn't press the point. Jasmine and Caroline did at least provide some solace, both understanding something of how I felt, emotions that every sadomasochistic bold enough to express their sexuality must I suppose face at one time or another. Tierney I avoided completely, although just the knowledge that he had been in my room tidying up was often enough to bring my feelings back to the boil. He wanted to talk to me, I knew from Jasmine and Caroline, who had told him roughly what had happened in Thame. I did not want to talk to him, and managed it, until the very last day of term.

My sole revenge, and it felt both petty and inadequate, had been to deny him the sexual favours he had been getting from Jasmine and Caroline. I knew he wasn't happy about it, and had expected some fresh bit of unctuous blarney from him, so was ready when it came. He had actually been waiting for me on my stairs, and was wearing his most obstinate and crafty expression.

'I wanted to talk to you before the term's over, Isabelle,' he opened. 'You've got me wrong.'

I sighed, and was about to tell him to get lost when I caught a clatter of feet lower down the stairs, one of my neighbours, who I did not want to see me in heated conversation with my scout. Quickly pushing open my door, I tried to close it in Tierney's face, only to have him push past me as I was trying to get the key out of the lock. I took a deep breath, trying to hold myself back and not let my feelings show, so he spoke first.

'It's your own fault, you know.'

'My fault!?' I demanded, my attempt at calm instantly shattered by the sheer outrage of what he was saying.

'Yeah, your fault,' he went on. 'I tried to tell you. You wouldn't listen.'

'Wouldn't listen? Yes, Tierney, you tried to put me off, but only to string me along, only because you knew it would just make me keener, you . . . you . . .'

'Nah, that's not true, it's not true. I told you stuff I shouldn't have done, but you wouldn't leave it would you? So you've only got yourself to blame, ain't you?'

'What!? Well . . . maybe . . . partly . . . for being stupid enough to believe you and going along to the line-dancing club, but what about what you made me do at the alcoholics centre, and as for at the Red Ox!'

'What you talking about? You wanted a bit of dirty stuff and you got it, both times, and don't give me no bullshit. You could've had Jas and Carrie come up to the Ox, same as you'd said you would, but oh no, you came up yourself, didn't you? We both know what you wanted, don't we, Isa, and you got it, so don't give me any crap.'

I couldn't answer him, speechless with indignation for the way he was justifying what he'd done, yet knowing that there was some truth in it. I had enjoyed what I'd done, no question, but that did not in any way excuse his behaviour. He went on before I could find the words to express my outrage.

'So that's the way it is, eh? Sorry about Emmy and that, but they were never going to take you, no way.'

'What do you mean not take me? You sent me to a line-dancing club, Tierney, pretending it was a secret society for lesbian dominants!'

He gave a single gruff laugh.

'Don't lie to me, Tierney, I'm not falling for it any more. How much was true, anything?'

'All of it. I never told you no lies.'

'Rubbish! You were lying from start to finish.'

'Nah, you just can't take it, can you? They rejected you, that's all.'

'Rejected me! Rubbish, Tierney, absolute utter rubbish!'

'It's God's honest truth, it is. They gave you a fair trial and all, but they rejected you.'

'Why then? What's wrong with me? I should be ideal!'

'Nah. They're not like you, up on your high horse one minute and stuck on some bloke's cock the next. The way they see it, you got to be one thing or the other, a mistressy type or a slut, cane and cushion, they call it. You, you ain't one thing nor the other. So when you stepped in there in your sassy little tart outfit, you were out.'

'But . . . but why? I hadn't said anything! Emmeline Young couldn't have known I'm dominant, not possibly. Oh, you are so full of rubbish, Stan Tierney . . .'

'Emmy knew, love, 'cause I told her.'

The beginning of the Easter holiday was a strange time for me. I'd become so involved with Oxford that home seemed strange, and the open moors and high bens of Scotland the alien environment rather than the gentle Thames Valley countryside. I also felt I was in the wrong place. For all the bad feelings since my disastrous Sunday, I wanted to be in Oxford, where I at least had a chance of sorting things out. I also couldn't stop thinking about it.

My interview with Tierney had ended with me throwing him bodily out of my room, and I'd been wishing it was the window. Yet the more I thought about it the more what he had said seemed to make sense, as it did with the more research I did on the subject. I did plenty too, often online until the early hours of the morning and reading everything I could get on the subject of sadomasochism.

It did make sense. Many people writing on the subject held that sadomasochists, or even everybody, was inherently submissive or dominant in nature. The viewpoint was especially common among the earlier commentators and novelists, as well as the older people. Those who did change roles, and I was coming to realise that I was one of them, were frequently dismissed either as mere dabblers or even denied altogether. I could easily see that in a small community of practitioners in the 50s the dichotomy between the two might have been taken as read. That any such society might well have stuck to its rules over the years was not all that surprising either.

Yet if it was true, then Emmeline Young and the other Line Ladies were very good actors indeed. Their response to my request for a spanking had seemed entirely genuine, and Tierney, of course, had not been there to see it. He had also implied that the decision to reject me hadn't been made until the moment I stepped out of the changing room in my cowgirl outfit, which again seemed odd.

Yet what choice had they had? Tierney might only have told Emmeline Young about me after my visit to Bronco Billy, and they were hardly going to cancel the whole evening just to get rid of one inappropriate applicant. Better surely to have given me the spanking I had asked for, a caning and the horse, and then to have denied me full membership when the time came. Except that it would then have risked bad feeling and even exposure.

Nor was it possible to see what Tierney hoped to gain from admitting he'd told Emmeline Young. It was hardly going to endear him to me, or to her. Judging by his initial reaction to the prospect of me contacting the Rattaners, the last thing he'd have done was admit he knew about me. That supported the idea of him having made it all up, and yet it didn't ring true. Surely what I had found out about the club was too complex to be mere chance? Nor could I see Tierney spending the hours on computers it would have needed to put together such an elaborate scheme. On the other hand, Tierney had tried to dissuade me from the start. I had assumed it was because he was worried for himself, but just possibly it was because he knew I would be rejected and didn't want me to get my feelings hurt. That put a very different complexion on things, if it was true, but again, it was hard to imagine such sensitivity in a man who enjoyed flushing a woman's head in a lavatory while he buggered her.

There were endless ifs and buts, with no clear solution. Nobody was going to tell me anything either, or if they did I would never be able to be sure it was the truth. I was determined to get as near to the bottom of it as I could, anyway. A few days after coming home I took a picnic up onto the side of the ben, well away from the frequented paths, and spent the entire day trying to make logical sense of it all. At one extreme there was the possibility of Tierney having made the entire thing up simply in order to get into my panties. At the other was the possibility that he had been entirely honest with me, and basically friendly, but was ultimately loyal to Emmeline Young. Somewhere in between the two lay the truth.

I had taken up a notepad, and solemnly wrote down all the pieces of evidence for and against the existence of the Rattaners. Both cases were strong, which seemed to make it most likely that there had been such a club, and that Tierney had known about it, but that it no longer existed. That left only two anomalies. First was Tierney's pretending to spank to a modern tune, which could easily have been done out of pure mischief on the spur of the moment. Second were the links I had found between Margaret Coln, Elizabeth Hastings and Emmeline Young, which could just about be put down to coincidence.

Despite having solved nothing and changed nothing my little piece of deduction made me feel considerably better. I was also sure that I did not want to abandon my sexual choices, and that they were something too deeply ingrained in my personality to be removed by any such setback. On the way home I stopped at a little hidden gully, a private place of mine for as long as I'd been coming up onto the moors alone. I stripped naked, spent a pleasant ten minutes bathing in a stream and another less pleasant ten trying to get warm, then took myself up to a slow, gentle orgasm.

I thought of Jasmine and Caroline, as we'd been the last time we had played before my disastrous weekend, and for once managed to stop my imagination from slipping off on inappropriate tracks. It felt very good indeed, far better than the handful of guilt ridden and awkward sessions I'd given myself in the previous weeks, and afterwards I felt more content and at ease with myself than I had since the fateful day.

The rest of the holidays were less fraught, and I divided my time between walking, often for miles, amusing myself among the old Victorian and Edwardian clothes in the attic, reading and spending time on the net. My researches had led me to a number of sites I would otherwise never have visited, including internet communities dedicated to sadomasochism. My first thought had been to attempt to trace the efforts at recruiting victims by the possibly non-existent Rattaners. I drew a blank, and there was so much back-biting and general unpleasantness among the groups that it put me off exploring further.

Only two days before I was due to go back up to Oxford did my by then desultory research produce any results. I was struck by the profile of one woman, simply because she was so wonderfully bold about her tastes. Her profile described her as a dominant but willing to switch on the grounds that she felt it morally right to be prepared to take what she dished out. She also stated a preference for old-fashioned military uniforms and formal punishments, both things I could appreciate. There was even a photograph of her, showing a solidly built, middle-aged woman in a very masculine get-up which I imagined as being First World War cavalry. She called herself

Major Soames, although it was presumably not her real name, and she lived in Witney, which was temptingly close to Oxford.

Too temptingly, as it turned out. Given the fiasco with the Rattaners, I had still never had a chance to speak to a mature dominant woman. Jasmine was older than me and had taught me a great deal before accepting her place as my slave girl, but really she was on the same path of development as I. Major Soames seemed ideal, and also very much in control of herself. After just a few hours of prevarication I emailed her, saying who I was and asking to chat. Her response was to ask for a photo of me holding an orange with some recognisable Scottish landmark in the background, in return for which she would do the same with the fruit of my choice. I could see it made sense and the next day borrowed my father's digital camera and took the bus up to Loch Ness. A picture of me, orange in hand, beside the monster at Castle Urquhart did the trick, one of her beside the A40 with an apple was returned, and by ten o'clock I was online to her.

It went well, my plea to learn more about myself immediately understood, and when I finally signed off at nearly three in the morning I had arranged to meet her on the Saturday of next week. The next day I went up on the train with Rory, my cousin's boyfriend and a fellow student. He was good company, despite a slight awkwardness over our brief fling in the Michaelmas term, and by the time we reached Glasgow we were chatting away happily in a way I find possible with only a handful of people. By Carlisle it was only my loyalty to Sammy that was preventing me from suggesting attempting a knee-trembler in the train loo, but I was a good girl and held back.

I felt ready for Oxford, just about, telling myself it was a big university and I was unlikely to bump into any of the Line Ladies. They also seemed to be pretty discreet, presumably feeling that their hobby didn't fit particularly well with their college lives. With Tierney I had decided to adopt an attitude of cold formality, while I felt it was actually an important part of reasserting my sexuality to allow myself to be put across Duncan Appledore's knee.

Not all that many people were about, giving St George's a curious air, almost as if it were a medieval ruin rather than a working college. I called in briefly at Jasmine's for a kiss and a cuddle, spanked them both and had them pose their red bottoms as I came, then retired to college and bed, determined to get a decent night's sleep.

I had considered taking one or both the girls to meet Major Soames, but in the end had decided against it. She was genuine, or at least I had every reason to believe she was, but there still seemed to be plenty of room for disaster. Besides, Caroline was such a slut she was bound to start something within five minutes of our arrival, and I really wanted to talk. What I did take was a picture, of the two of them side by side in their corsets and stockings with their hands tied across their tummies.

It was as easy to get to Witney as it had been to Thame, and much the same distance but, unlike Fieldfare Hall, it was not easy to find her house. I had directions, but they led me down one footpath and then another before I realised I'd gone wrong completely and had to double back. Finally I realised that the disreputable looking corrugated iron stack I'd passed twice was actually the house. Telling myself it was a romantic and eccentric hideaway and not a decaying fleapit, I pushed in through the ancient wooden gate, to discover that I was right.

She, or somebody, had built an extension onto an old railway carriage. Not only that, but it was still standing on rusting tracks that extended twenty yards or so to either side along what I had taken for a long, narrow strip of wasteland, but was in fact a disused railway cutting. The hedge and the corrugated iron front hid it almost completely, while fields or rough pasture to either side and a steep, wooded bank behind made it one of the most wonderfully secluded spots I had ever seen. I was captivated immediately, and was still gaping vacantly when the door swung open, Major Soames herself stepping out in full uniform, right down to the crowns on her epaulettes.

'Isabelle?' she queried, with just a touch of surprise, probably at realising I was considerably taller than her.

'Yes,' I answered. 'This is wonderful! What a place to live!'

'It has its charms,' she admitted. 'Privacy first and foremost. Come inside.'

She led me through the door, and into a big, cluttered room that clearly served as kitchen and bedroom as well as being the main living space. Cooker, sink, cupboards and other essentials were at one end, leaving the rest for books, a workstation, books, two wardrobes, a bed, more books and all sorts of junk. At three places steps led up to the doors of the carriage, which was unaltered save for where the extension walls joined on and a long wooden skirting to hide the undercarriage and sleepers. Nothing suggested her sexual tastes.

'Coffee?' she offered. 'Tea?'

'Please, yes, coffee,' I answered, and we went into the precise and very British little ritual of hot-drink making.

Despite having spent so long talking to her online I still felt a trace of embarrassment, but it faded as she made coffee. By the time I had the mug in my hand I felt able to talk, which I suppose is the true function of the ritual, that and being able to choose one's words while sipping the drink. She seemed to have no such qualms, but introduced herself as Laura and cleared me a space on the skirting, which was topped with cushions for part of its length.

We had swapped a lot of intimate detail online, and she already knew a lot about my recent history, certainly more than I had told Rory on the train. I had even told her about my failed attempt to contact the Rattaners, and what had happened at the Red Ox, leaving out only the dirtiest details. It had been easy, with the anonymity of a computer, and now that it was out, it was easy enough face to face. Within half an hour I had explained in depth about my background, how I felt it was appropriate to spank women, how to me physical punishment seemed inextricably linked with sex, and about my relationship with Jasmine and Caroline.

She gave fairly, in much greater detail than she had online, and without a trace of embarrassment. Now in her late forties, she had been pretty much in denial of her sexuality for most of her life. As a teenager in the late 60s she had been into hippie culture, and while free love and lesbianism had been reasonably acceptable, spanking very definitely had not. For years she had repressed the urge, telling herself it was a hangover from her upbringing.

In her late twenties she had begun to come to terms with her own sexuality. At first she had only allowed herself to indulge her taste for uniform and formality, by joining a re-enactment society in which the members would dress up in full period dress and play act elaborate battle scenes from history. She had enjoyed it, and fitted in well with the masculine atmosphere, being treated as one of the boys. That in turn had led to a shy and nervous lesbian approaching her in the hope of finding a butch partner.

The relationship had lasted five years, on and off, every minute of it stormy. Her girlfriend had been no better at coping with her desires than had Laura, and had never really accepted her need to be dominated, let alone spanked. Instead of simply asking, she would make a nuisance of herself until it was done, and never once had the two of them discussed their real feelings. Only after the relationship was over had Laura made an attempt to explore more fully. She had begun reading, keeping an open mind yet always questioning, and over the next ten years she had come to develop the philosophy of life with which I had been so impressed.

All of this had been in Bristol, London, and later Cheltenham, which she had found stifling. The railway-carriage home had come up in a property auction and she had bought it, extending herself to the point where she was now working sixty hours a week to cope with the mortgage. Her job in administration involved endlessly sitting in front of a computer, hence her high profile on the internet. She had no regular girlfriend, but two playmates, both married women who came to her for discipline and a taste of lesbian sex, one with her husband's knowledge, one without.

It was all a little more mundane than I had been imagining, but the carriage and her personality more than made up for it. She was open and friendly, yet with a strict tone, and it was easy to imagine her dishing out a severe spanking and making the punished girl stand in the corner with her hands on her head afterwards. As we went into the railway carriage for me to be shown around I was already wondering if I would end up across her knee.

The carriage was the old-fashioned sort, which I'd only seen in films, with a corridor at one side and compartments opening off it, six in all, and each with six seats. She took me to one end, pointed out that she had converted the original loo, and opened the first of the doors. The blinds were down, and for a moment everything was too dim to really see, but as she flicked a light on it revealed twin rows of garments hung from the baggage racks at either side of the compartment – uniforms.

'My collection,' she explained, reaching out to touch a brilliant scarlet jacket hung with braid and shiny with brass buttons. "All genuine. This is a guards' mess jacket, in perfect condition but unfortunately a little big for me. Most of them are.'

It was also going to be big on me, I could see, but not by so very much. I kept quiet, feeling it would be impolite to suggest I put anything on unless she offered. She went on, showing me each one, an extraordinary variety from several different nations and stretching back for nearly a century. Most bore majors' insignia, a few that of other officers, and nearly half no rank at all.

'Are these for your girlfriends to wear?' I asked, fingering a set of neatly tailored battle dress, relatively small and cut for a woman. 'I see they're all privates'.'

'Yes,' she answered. 'I prefer a submissive woman to have no authority at all, even if it is purely symbolic.'

'Oh, I don't know. Wouldn't it be fun to have a girl as, say . . . a sergeant, then strip her of her rank before she was beaten? Surely it's stronger to come down from on high than start at the bottom?'

'There speaks a dominant,' she answered. 'A true submissive would want to be at the bottom of the pile in the first place.'

I flushed with pleasure at her recognition of my nature. Only Jasmine had ever really understood, and she tended to be instinctive about it.

'Fifty-three at present,' she stated. 'I really should stop, and I definitely can't afford it, but it's compulsive.'

'I'm the same about corsets,' I admitted, 'and any Victorian underwear. Fortunately my girlfriends make them. That's how we got together.'

'You lucky thing. All mine make is trouble.'

She laughed as she moved out of the compartment and went on as she came to the second door.

'I seem to attract brats, I don't know why. What I really want is a girl who takes pleasure specifically in being obedient. Still, shock treatment has its virtues, and I suppose it is more spontaneous.'

'Shock treatment?'

'Pippa's favourite technique,' she said, switching a light on. 'She's the one whose husband does know. This is where I keep my implements.'

I'd been going to ask for a better explanation of 'shock treatment', but stopped as she opened the compartment door. On both sides the baggage racks were hung with objects designed specifically to inflict pain on female bottoms: canes, crops, tawses, paddles, a whole variety of whips and even kitchen spoons. She was right about being compulsive, and it wasn't just with uniforms. No one woman could possibly have needed so many implements.

'No two are exactly the same,' she explained, taking a cane down. 'This, for instance, is a seven-millimetre kooboo cane, thick but light and relatively flexible. Here.'

She passed it to me and I gave it a swish through the air, feeling the familiar satisfaction of holding a punishment implement. It was thicker than Jasmine's favourite, but no heavier. I took another, slim and dark, more to my taste.

'A five-millimetre dragon,' Laura explained, 'for precision work.'

'I can imagine.'

I could happily have spent an hour in the compartment, just looking, never mind experimenting, but she moved on and I followed. The next compartment was entirely bare and had the blinds up, no different in any way than had we been in a genuine railway carriage at a station.

'My small playroom,' she told me. 'As I have a railway carriage it makes sense to be able to play out railway fantasies. Unfortunately I've never been able to get several people together, you know, to play out the fantasy of spanking a girl in front of other passengers.'

'That's a nice idea. Spankings ought to be public, really, shouldn't they? That is, if a girl has to be punished, why should it matter who sees?'

'I wish.'

'Me too.'

We shared a smile and she ushered me from the compartment and down to the next. Again there was a moment of dimness, then illumination, this time of a long and fully furnished playroom. She had knocked the remaining three compartments together, producing a room somewhat like a dining car save that in place of seats and tables there was equipment designed for the torture or correction of her girls. There was a pillory, a cage, a padded trestle and a thing like an upright St Andrew's cross, all made of dark and highly polished wood and all hung with chains and cuffs.

'The room was like this when I moved in,' she explained as if in apology, 'in shape, that is. The fixtures are all mine.'

It was not unlike Jasmine and Caroline's own playroom, unsurprisingly as there are only so many ways the human form can be restrained and the bottom and breasts still kept available for punishment. The main difference was that with Jasmine the emphasis was on restraint and penetration, and with Laura on beating bottoms.

'You do your slave girls proud,' I told her. 'Did you make all this yourself?'

'Everything,' she confirmed, 'and most of the wood salvaged from skips. So, would you like to play out a scene?'

It was the question I'd been expecting from the start, and prepared to accept since halfway through my welcoming mug of coffee. I nodded in response, content to let her lead as it was her house, and fairly sure what I wanted. She was a lot older, and everything about her suggested dominance and control. There was very little softness to her, and none of those subtle touches of personality and body language that make me want to spank another woman. Dominating her seemed wildly inappropriate.

'As we both prefer to dominate,' she said, 'I would be quite happy to toss a coin.'

'It's good of you to offer,' I answered, with a catch in my voice despite being sure my decision was right, 'but I really think it would be more suitable if you were to do me.'

'If you prefer?'

'I do.'

'I will, then. I can just see you in uniform, you have the height and the bearing, so much so it seems almost a shame to whip you.'

'I think I'd rather be spanked, if you wouldn't mind. Jasmine prefers that I don't submit, or at least that if I do she doesn't know about it. Welts are a bit of a giveaway.'

'So you want to be spanked? Hmm . . .'

She snatched out, suddenly, to take me by the ear, hard. I squealed in pain, too surprised to react as I was pulled smartly out into the corridor, into the neighbouring compartment and down across her lap. An instant later my skirt was up over my back, my panties had been wrenched down my legs and she had set to work on me, spanking me with furious, unrelenting slaps that sent me straight into a wild, kicking frenzy. It was such a shock, one second talking to her as an equal, the next bare-bottom across her knee, squealing and wriggling as I was given a thoroughly undignified spanking.

After a moment she paused to catch my arm up into the small of my back and pull off my panties completely, leaving me free to kick about properly as the spanking started again. I was making a full show of my pussy and bottom hole as I thrashed and squirmed and howled, and I knew it. What she'd said came back to me too, about spanking girls in public, and how suitable it would be. Now it felt very different, with me the one across a woman's lap, me the one whose panties had been pulled down, me the one squalling pathetically under the slaps, me the one stripped of every vestige of my dignity and modesty . . .

It was right. It was the thing to do to naughty girls, to take their panties down in public and spank them, and I was being spanked now, my bare bottom on fire, helpless in her grip, my head full of humiliation and pain. As I burst into tears I knew she had me, with a vengeance, hers to do with as she pleased, taking me down in the space of a few seconds. Even as she spanked me I was babbling my gratitude between my gasps and squeals, soaking up the awful pain because it was what I needed – punishment, then sex.

I got it, pushed to the floor the instant she had finished with my bottom. Her uniform skirt came up, exposing stocking tops, soft white thighs and the crotch of a pair of big cream-coloured panties bulging with pussy. She tugged them aside, one-handed, even as she took me by the hair, and I was pulled in, no questions, no chance to compose myself, just put to her sex with my spanked bottom stuck out behind me. I began to lick, immediately, right on her clitoris. I wanted to masturbate too, but I wanted to serve her more. After all, she had spanked my bottom.

She held me in, her hand twisted painfully tight in my hair, making not the slightest sound as I lapped at her. Only when her pussy began to contract in my face did I realise she was coming, but even then she gave no more than a gentle sigh. The instant she had let go of my hair I rocked back, intent on masturbating in front of her to show her what she'd done to me, but got a finger wagged in my face for my effort. She beckoned me and I came forwards, trembling slightly and wondering if I was to be spanked again, perhaps as she masturbated me to orgasm. Sure enough, she took me by the arm, pulling me close, only not across her lap but onto it, cradling me. I was going to be made to suckle.

I was held in, my head to the fullness of her chest as she quickly opened the front of her uniform jacket, then the blouse beneath, to lift her bra and spill one big, heavy breast into my face, her nipple long and brown and stiff, ready for my mouth. Immediately I took her in, sucking as she pulled my legs up and eased them gently apart. I let it happen, my pussy spread wide, suckling on her breast with my spanked bottom on her leg and my thighs apart, completely vulnerable, completely surrendered. Her fingers found my sex and began to rub, clinically, bringing me up towards orgasm, soothing me as much as exciting me.

It all came together in moments, the glorious combination of spanking and suckling, being punished, so swiftly and so severely, then put to her breast, a punished girl comforted by the very woman who had just spanked her bare bottom ...

Suddenly I was crying again, still suckling, my legs cocked as wide as they would go. My body began to jerk and I went into orgasm. The tears were streaming down my face even as I came, squirming in ecstasy on her lap, completely abandoned, wanton and rude, hiding nothing, hers completely because she had been the one to take me in hand and spank my bottom when I needed it.

Even when I had come down and she had taken her hand off my pussy she still cradled me, allowing me to suckle on the big nipple in my mouth for just as long as I wanted. For a long moment of perfect submissive bliss I held on, finally pulling away when a touch of embarrassment penetrated my dazed wits. She chuckled and gave my red bottom a gentle pat as I stood up.

'That was wonderful, thank you,' I managed. 'Just what I needed.'

'Shock treatment, like I said. It works wonders.'

'It does, and being comforted. That was special, thank you.'

'A pleasure. Nothing like a good old-fashioned spanking and a cuddle afterwards.'

I bent to kiss her, a very genuine thanks for what she had done. It was what I had wanted Emmeline Young to do to me, or more exactly what Emmeline Young should have done to me if she'd had any sense. She hadn't. Possibly it was something that had never crossed her mind. Laura had done it, and in the

154

space of a few painful but exquisite minutes had earned my gratitude, my friendship and a fair bit of loyalty.

Despite my utter submission her attitude to me didn't change at all. As we washed together we discussed punishment technique, equal and dominant once more. We considered the rival virtues of the tawse and the cane, of making a girl bend over or rolling her up on her back, and even whether objects should be inserted in the victim's vagina and anus during beating. By the time we were decent again and had fresh mugs of coffee in our hands we were giggling together as we swapped stories of our slave girls' amusing or ridiculous reactions to their pain.

We talked for hours, on dozens of topics, most but not all related to our shared sexuality. Despite very different backgrounds and ages, we were similar in many ways, the only real exception being in our attitude to men. She was happy to have men as friends, but hadn't had conventional sex since the 70s. Her sadomasochistic experiences were strictly with women. Yet she could see the pleasure I took in having Jasmine and Caroline perform for me, arguing only that if I was to do it I should be prepared to take it myself. I had to agree, which in turn helped me come closer to terms with what I had done at the Red Ox.

I was allowed to try her uniforms on too, and we spent a happy hour dressing up, until I was having to make a serious effort not to offer myself for a caning. Not wanting to attempt the A40 on my bicycle in the dark, I declined her offer of dinner and started back for Oxford while there was still plenty of light. It had been a wonderful day, and I was feeling extremely happy, running over what had happened in my mind again and again. Finally I was forced to turn off the main road and into the lanes, find myself a secluded copse and bring myself to a hasty climax with my hand stuck down the front of my panties.

All in all it had been ideal, the precise opposite of my last attempt at meeting women with similar tastes to my own.

Nine

As with Emmeline Young, I had a bit of a schoolgirl crush on Laura, and I knew it. This time it was good, because she understood, and would spank me when I needed it. There was to be more too, because we had agreed to swap and share our slave girls, which I was looking forward to immensely.

Then there were the uniforms, which I was to be allowed to try whenever I pleased. They were genuine, most of them, and all, save for one of the really smart ones, were designed for men. On Laura these were more than a little baggy, and really only for show, but on me all it was going to need was a little padding at the shoulders, a slight adjustment of the waist and hips and they would be the next thing to perfect. I could picture myself very easily and, while I had felt it would be unfair to ask to borrow one when it was only the first time I'd met her, I knew I would be back.

She had also helped me to a greater understanding of my sexuality, if not quite in the way I'd expected. As she was so forthright, I had assumed she'd always been that way, but it was not the case. In fact it had taken her a long time to achieve the confidence I so admired. Jasmine and Caroline both had far more for their age. I did too. While there was an element of disappointment, it did make her more approachable, as a friend rather than simply as a mentor, which was how I had first imagined her. She would be able to attend to my occasional need for submission, while also being a perfectly equal playmate when we worked together in dominant roles.

I wanted to see her again, but I was also a little cautious of being over-eager and spoiling what promised to be a good relationship. There was plenty to do at college anyway, with our mods exams coming up at the end of term and the possibility of being thrown out if we failed. Everybody was in a state over it, but on Thursday Duncan assured me I would be fine just so long as I kept the standard of my essays up, then spanked me pink just to make sure he'd got the point across. I sucked his cock afterwards, another first since the Fieldfare Hall disaster.

Tierney had been a nuisance, constantly trying to be familiar and seemingly always where I was. The temptation to complain to Duncan was high and growing higher, but the prospect of having my behaviour at the Red Ox given an open airing did not appeal. So I did my best to ignore him and by and large succeeded, until the Saturday of the first week.

It was hot, and I was by my window, sipping iced tea and watching the comings and goings in the quad. I caught a familiar laugh, then the sight of Jasmine's pale blonde hair, and was about to wave when I realised she wasn't alone. Caroline had appeared, and Tierney, the two walking a little behind Jasmine. I felt my lips purse in annoyance, which grew as I realised my instinctive response, to pull Jasmine and Caroline's panties down and wallop them until they howled, was not practical, at least not with Tierney around. It would be exactly what he wanted me to do. So I made sure my door was unlocked and went to sit down, making sure they found me holding a deliberately icy pose.

Half a minute later there was a knock on my door. I responded with a deliberately sharp command to come in and the door swung wide, to reveal Jasmine, who looked worried, Caroline, who bounced cheerfully onto my bed, and Tierney, who gave me an oily grin and sidled over to the fireplace.

'Well?' I demanded, letting my reaction to their treachery show in my voice.

'We want you to come up to the Ox this evening,' Caroline responded enthusiastically. 'We're stripping, and –'

'Caroline,' I interrupted, 'you know I cannot possibly come up to the Ox. I –'

'Oh, come on, Isabelle, please! Never mind what happened with the poker game. You shouldn't be upset about that, it was the place in Thame it went wrong.'

'Yeah, right,' Tierney put in.

'Please, Isabelle?' Jasmine added.

'It ... it's not what happened,' I answered in exasperation. 'It's ... it's you, Tierney. How do you think I could go up there with you around after the way you tricked me?'

'I didn't do nothing! Come on, Isabelle love, come up the Ox, have a laugh.'

'You didn't do nothing? I sometimes wonder if you employ those double negatives deliberately, Tierney, I really do.'

'You what?'

'Never mind.'

'Please!' Caroline repeated, bouncing off the bed again and onto her knees in front of me.

She put her hands up to her chin and looked up at me with her huge eyes, an imitation of a puppy begging that normally melted me in an instant. Even then it was hard to resist, but I shook my head.

'No, not possibly. Anyway, you know what it's like when I go there. All I get is nasty remarks about students and –'

'Not when you stripped you didn't,' Tierney chortled.

'I am not stripping, and that is final!' I snapped back, absolutely outraged that he even dare suggest it.

'You'll come, then?'

'No!'

'Please? Pretty please?' Caroline pleaded as Jasmine got down beside her on the floor.

'Stop it, you two,' I snapped, 'or you'll be going on stage with bruised bottoms, and no, I do not mean in front of you, Tierney. Anyway, what's so special about tonight?'

'Mike's set up a competition,' Jasmine explained. 'There are girls coming from all over, not just around Oxford, but London, Birmingham, even Leeds! The first prize is a grand!'

'Great, but what's that got to do with me? You're in with a chance, you have to be, especially if you do a double act.'

'No way,' Jasmine answered me, 'not the two of us. We're local, and the judges won't want people to think it was fixed, but if you're there, a student, then we're in with a chance!'

'I am not stripping at the Red Ox,' I answered firmly.

'You don't have to!' Caroline insisted. 'Just top us on stage, something really stylish, in full Victorian gear. You won't have to show so much as an ankle! Please, Isabelle, for us?'

'Well . . . well maybe,' I answered her, cross with myself but just not able to crush her enthusiasm.

She immediately hugged herself to me, smiling happily as she pressed her head to my chest, Jasmine also squeezing in. I put my arms around both of them, wishing I could find it in myself to be just a little tougher.

'I haven't said yes,' I insisted, 'and anyway, if you want me to dominate you for this competition, what have you brought this lecherous old goat for?' I asked, nodding towards Tierney.

'To apologise to you,' Jasmine answered me.

'I ain't done nothing, like I said,' Tierney answered, 'but all right, if it makes you happy and you come. I'm sorry, Isa.'

'Thank you,' I answered, really unable to stop myself despite a feeling that an apology was insultingly trivial after what had happened. 'I will at least think about it.'

'Pretty, pretty please?' Caroline asked, and nuzzled her face into my crotch.

'Stop it! Bad girl!' I answered, but it was impossible to keep the laughter out of my voice, and while she did stop, Tierney was leering.

They left half an hour later, Jasmine and Caroline to make adjustments to dresses, Tierney probably to go and pull on his dirty old cock somewhere private. Jasmine and Caroline had wanted me to come with them, but I had refused, needing to think on my own before making a decision. The last thing I wanted to do was hurt their feelings, or do anything that might risk alienating them. Yet they had really put me on the spot, and it was impossible not to feel angry. Some of it was at myself too, but they obviously thought I was just being sulky, and there was a nagging suspicion in the back of my mind that they were right. After all, I had been willing on the night of the poker game, eventually. If to an extent I had been tricked into what I'd done, then it had been a wonderfully strong submissive experience, for all the men might think of it as just a bit of fun with a dirty college girl. I wasn't even absolutely certain that I had a right to be angry with Tierney. Then there were the Line Ladies, who were either genuine and had made an honest mistake, or were the Rattaners and had simply reacted to me trying to push in as I might have reacted in the same situation. In fact, when it came down to it there was only one person to blame for the entire fiasco – myself.

It was not a pleasant realisation, but to swallow my pride and go to the Red Ox that evening was a big step. I didn't want to do it. In fact I wanted Tierney to have tricked me and to have the right to wallow in my misery, but the more I thought about it the more unlikely it seemed. He just didn't have the intelligence or the organisational ability to set up such an elaborate scheme, while he did seem genuinely hurt at being accused. At worst all he'd been doing was protecting his own interests.

I needed to clear my head, and went for a walk, aiming vaguely towards the meadows along the Cherwell, where I could be alone. After meeting Laura I'd thought I'd managed to sort myself out, but clearly I'd been wrong. Now it seemed that I not only had to come to terms with myself but also admit it had been my fault in the first place. If I accepted it, I could just see that before long I'd end up back on Stan Tierney's cock, and it stung.

Yet there was no suggestion of anything of the sort at the striptease show. The Red Ox would be packed, and not only with the regulars. I'd be on stage, well away from the men, and we could leave before any of them started to have any ideas. Meanwhile I could see that not going risked a rift between Jasmine, Caroline and I. I was their Mistress, yes, but ultimately our relationship worked by mutual consent, and I had to provide for them just as they provided for me.

I'd reached Rainbow Bridge by the time I'd decided I had to go, and was looking over the rail at the Cherwell. It was more crowded than I'd imagined, with plenty of people soaking up the warm spring sunshine in the meadows and both students and tourists out punting. I crossed the river, thinking to walk down the opposite bank as far as Magdalen then cut across to the Cowley Road and Jasmine's.

It was lonelier, but far from empty, with couples enjoying themselves in the tall grass and a few people with picnics. Still keen on solitude, I turned my path away from the river, only to almost tread on a couple with a rug spread out in the shelter of a hedge of scrubby hawthorn and willow. Both were women, one face down and wearing a bikini, and at the same instant I spotted the warm red of recent spanking I realised that her companion was Sarah Finch. I apologised hastily and moved on, the whole thing simply too sudden to allow me to introduce myself.

So Walter had been right. Sarah's girlfriend did get spanked, and to judge by the colour of her bottom she had been attended to that afternoon, presumably with her bikini pants pulled down among the bushes. She'd been really quite red, and a good deal of her deliciously cheeky bottom had been spilling out around the frankly inadequate pants. Whether they were Rattaners or not, I simply had to introduce myself. Not to do so was foolish, and cowardly. The girl had been spanked, no question, so, embarrassing though it was, it could not be anything like as bad as with the Line Ladies, even if they told me to mind my own business. Yet it was not easy. Laura would have done it, I was sure, and Jasmine, and Caroline. All it took was a little courage, a little determination . . .

I turned about, my heart absolutely hammering in my chest. They were still there, Sarah's bright yellow frock easily visible across the meadow, the hedge now acting as a backdrop and not a screen. I had to speak, to find my words in maybe a hundred yards of walking ... fifty yards ... ten, and I was standing next to them feeling very sheepish indeed as Sarah looked up and the girl rolled over.

'Hi,' I managed after a moment, realising that I could hardly admit to spying on them, or claim that Walter Jessop had mentioned them. They wouldn't even know who he was.

'Yes?' Sarah answered me as my face went slowly crimson.

'I ... I'm Isabelle Colraine,' I said. 'I ... er ... a student ... at St George's. I er ... I think we have something in common.'

It was what I'd said to Emmeline Young, and seemed really stupid in the circumstances. Both of them were looking at me as if I were mad, Sarah puzzled, the girl giggly. I forced myself to go on, talking to the girl and pushing out every word.

'I ... I just couldn't help noticing that ... that ... that ... your bottom is rather pink. You've been spanked, haven't you?'

The last bit came out in a great rush, and it was all I had in me. My cheeks were burning, my lungs felt as if they were going to burst and I was sure I was going to pee in my panties at any second. Both were staring, as speechless as I, amazed, maybe shocked, and then the girl burst into giggles, her face flushed with embarrassment, but it was Sarah who answered, her voice cool and measured.

'So you'd like a bit of the same, would you? Portia?'

'Ooh, yes, you can spank her,' the girl answered

immediately. 'She's cute, and so cheeky! Just so long as I get to watch.'

I made to speak, but changed my mind. This was not the time to press the issue of who was spanking who. Sarah was still looking at me, and for one moment I thought she was waiting for me to get over her knee, then and there in the meadow with the absolute certainty that somebody would come past while my bare bottom was being reddened. In fact I could already see a man coming towards us. Then she spoke again.

'The Eagle and Lamb, one o'clock tomorrow, prompt.'

After two failed attempts to make some sound come out of my mouth I nodded, and left. I'd done it, yet the urge to run away was so strong, and it was really hard to keep walking at an even pace as I crossed the meadow. She had understood, or else wanted time herself, so that either of us could back out if we felt the need. It was the sensible decision, yet as I glanced back to find them now standing, Portia pulling on her jeans and the man I'd seen some halfway between us, I was wishing she'd been anything but sensible.

I was wishing she'd done me then and there, in front of the man and anyone else who came by, panties down across her knees, my pussy and bottom hole flaunted as I was spanked hard, punished for my insolence. It was a very strong image, and there was no question in my mind that I would be getting that spanking, albeit not in quite such an exposed position. Yet it looked as if she'd taken Portia into the bushes, and possibly the display of reddened bottom cheeks had been an addition to the punishment, deliberate, to humiliate by showing off what had been done, a wonderful way to handle a spanked girl.

Being me, it was impossible not to imagine myself getting the same treatment. I just work that way. Put a fantasy in my head and it runs and runs. Making contact with Sarah and Portia had me elated, which didn't help either, and the thought of taking a public spanking from her had me trembling. I wanted to masturbate then and there, thinking of my agonising humiliation as my panties were taken down in a public meadow, of the man who'd passed seeing, of he and Portia watching, watching my shameful bare bottom punishment . . .

I couldn't, not beside the Marston Road, any more than she would really have spanked me, and maybe less. Yet it was ten minutes' brisk walk to Jasmine's, and I was determined to try out Duncan Appledore's theory. A true dominant does exactly as she pleases sexually, including having her bottom smacked.

It took me eight minutes to get to Jasmine's, where she and Caroline were busy adjusting two of their Victorian dresses to make them practical striptease garments. The workroom was strewn with dresses, corsets, underwear, bits of cloth, scissors, thread and more. I'd let myself in and both turned as I pushed the door wide, smiling as the clatter of their sewing machines died.

'I'm coming tonight,' I announced, 'but first, you should both know that I have just propositioned Sarah Finch, as well as her girlfriend, who is called Portia.'

'Excellent!' Caroline answered me. 'Are they going to play?'

'I'm meeting them tomorrow,' I explained, and decided to embroider a little, 'although she did threaten to spank me in the Meadows.'

'She didn't!?' Caroline squealed in delight.

'Cheeky bitch!' Jasmine put in.

'She did,' I responded, 'and in consequence you two are now going to do exactly what I say.'

'We're a little busy . . .' Caroline began.

'Caroline! At my feet, now!'

She came, hurrying over to kneel at my feet and shower kisses on the toes of my shoes. Jasmine also rose, standing with her head bowed.

'Good girls,' I told them, seating myself on Caroline's work stool. 'Jasmine, lick.'

She came immediately, down on her knees to bury her face between my thighs as I lifted my skirt. Caroline looked a little hurt, but I reached out to ruffle her hair as Jasmine began to nuzzle my pussy through my panties.

'You can play too,' I promised Caroline. 'First, remember, I am your Mistress, I do as I please. Now tell me what Sarah should have done to me in the Meadows.'

'But, Mistress . . .' Jasmine began, lifting her head.

'Shut up and lick!' I ordered her, pulling my panty crotch aside and pushing her head firmly back into place. 'Yes, like that . . . yes, of course you can lick my bottom too. Come on, Caroline . . .'

I leaned back against Caroline's sewing machine, allowing Jasmine to get at me properly. She kissed my anus, very tenderly, then began to lick, teasing my bottom and pussy with her tongue. I kept my hold in her hair and cupped one of my breasts, closing my eyes as Caroline began to speak.

'I think you'd have put up a fight, Mistress . . . but . . . but there were two of them, and, well . . . you'd have lost. Sarah would've been angry by then. Maybe you'd have ripped her blouse open . . . and her bra, so her boobs were hanging out. People would see, and she would be furious, scratching and pulling your hair . . . and before you really knew it they'd be

167

sitting on you, Sarah on your back, Portia on your legs. You'd still be struggling, but Sarah would take what was left of her bra and use it to tie your hands behind your back, really tight ... so it hurt. Then they'd strip you, real slow ... Sarah would have nail scissors in her bag, and she'd slit your dress, and ... and rip it open up the back, all the way, opening it up so you'd be in just your bra and panties, still struggling, but helpless as your bra strap was cut ... and your knickers were slit and ripped open, showing off your bum, your bare bum, Isabelle, showing in the Meadows, with about fifty dirty old men leering over you, some of them wanking their cocks ... over you, Isabelle ... over your bare bottom, as ... as Sarah began to spank you, really hard, until you lost it, and starting kicking, showing your pussy off ... showing your bottom hole off as you were spanked and spanked and spanked and spanked ...'

I just came, full in Jasmine's face, the single word 'spanked' going through my head again and again as Caroline repeated it, driving me up to an exquisite peak just as Jasmine eased two fingers up my pussy and a third into the mouth of my bottom hole.

The Red Ox was even more packed than I had imagined it would be. We had to park in a nearby street and walk, in full Victorian dress, which drew laughter and catcalls from the groups of men moving towards the venue. It was ironic when we were showing far less than any of the women there, in our full skirts, gloves and bonnets, but they knew what was going to happen, and seemed to like the idea.

Caroline and Jasmine had really gone to town. Caroline was in red, a gorgeous silk gown that made the best of her opulent chest and hips, while the elegant S-curve corset she wore beneath had pulled her waist in to a tiny 21 inches. The corset was also red, and everything else white: chemise, split-seam drawers and all three layers of her petticoats. Jasmine's clothes matched exactly save for her panel-back drawers, but were in a rich blue that set off her hair and made a perfect contrast to Caroline. I was in pure black, a Governess outfit, my hair up, my block heels lifting me to six foot two, which was enough to leave me looking down on the heads of most of the men. I also had my cane, which drew plenty of ribaldry and one or two looks of genuine alarm.

The car park was solid, and the inside of the club a heaving mass of men, who had already begun to spill out through the big double doors. We went to the back, to be greeted by a flustered Mike, who showed us to the tent he'd erected to serve as the girls' changing rooms. It was not good, with a hastily arranged stand pipe producing cold water, two ancient dressing-tables, one of which had no mirror, and a single glaring spotlight that threw everything into a confusing pattern of shadows.

I wasn't taking any of the money if we did win, on principle, but that didn't stop me assessing our competition. There were a lot of girls, but a good half conformed to what I suppose must be regarded as the working man's concept of female beauty – slim, dyed-blonde hair, enlarged breasts. A few stood out, a beautiful black girl in nothing but a lime-green bikini and heels, a tiny girl with blonde curls and an impish face, and a pair so alike they seemed to be twins, both tall, dark and elegant, maybe Spanish or Portuguese.

Mike had set up a running order, which was causing some problems, none of the girls wanting to be first on, or last. I let them get on with it and helped myself to beer, which was not only warm but had to be drunk from the bottle. It was too hot in the tent anyway, so I went outside, where it was nearly dark, the spring day already cooling and oddly still beside the raucous music and buzz of coarse voices coming from the club.

Eventually I went back to the tent, where things had been worked out. The opening act had just gone on, one of the cloned blondes, and with our own piece worked out in detail there was nothing to do. We were on late, and I did want to watch, but not if it meant standing among the crowd of men with their cigarettes and beer and sweat. There wasn't much space left over, but I managed to slip in behind a drape, from where I could watch both the crowd and the girls without being seen.

By no means all of it was erotic, for me anyway, but it was fascinating. The girls' routines varied, some sensuous, some athletic, some blatant, some pretending to be coy. All but two went nude, and those down to the most minute of thongs, and they suffered, with the crowd demanding they strip bare and booing them for being prissy. The black girl I'd so admired was very conventional, really just dancing as she had so few clothes to tease with, but she did have the most glorious bottom. She was also very rude, flaunting herself to make sure the men got a good look at every detail of her sex and even pulling her cheeks apart to show off her bottom hole. Her act was the first to leave me feeling aroused, and I was hoping she would earn a place.

Another blonde followed, then a very sensuous girl with multicoloured hair, tattoos, pierced nipples and labia, then the little curly-haired girl. She was the rudest yet, stripping nude in seconds, pouring water over herself as she danced and as a climax filling her pussy with water and squirting it over the audience. I

170

was impressed by her sheer cheek, and also by the open delight she took in showing off her naked body, while many of the girls projected a sense of reluctance, however openly they put themselves on display. I knew I would have been the same.

Next came the twins, who were spectacularly good, first announcing themselves as sisters, which drew a shocked and excited buzz from the men, then going through a slow, elegant routine, undressing each other article by article, turning and turning about until both were nude. By then a hush had fallen over the audience, not absolute, but it became so when they began to kiss, stroking each other's bodies, mouths open together, apparently with real passion. I was beginning to feel wet by the time they finished, with a reverse bow to show their bottoms, and then they strutted off, arms around one another's waists.

The crowd were thoroughly enjoying themselves, cheering and clapping, as vulgar as ever, and giving out as much crude insult and praise. I could see Big Dave, his head looming up above others near the back, and Jack, right at the front, amusing his cronies by finding fault with the appearance or style of every single girl. Tierney I couldn't see, nor the other poker players, but I was sure they would be there and looking forward to going on stage.

We were on in two acts, and I moved away to join Jasmine and Caroline. Both were a little nervous, but no more, and so was I, despite my teasing and dominant role. By the time the girl before us came off my stomach was fluttering, but as Jasmine and Caroline came on and curtsied prettily to the audience I was enjoying the thought of the men's consternation when I came out but revealed nothing.

I could see through the curtain as the girls began to undress each other, their movements as much pose as dance, yet precise and elaborate, also sexual, including kisses and caresses as arms, shoulders, and finally chests came bare, each undoing the other's chemise. With their breasts in each other's hands I stepped boldly forwards onto the stage, my chin held up, my face a mask of cold formality.

Both immediately went into a little shocked dance of fluttering lace and silk, their hands to mouths open in Os of surprise and then fear as I rapped the cane on the boards. They froze, stood still, bent their heads in meek resignation, turned their bottoms to the audience and touched their toes. As I stepped forwards with the cane Jack called out from the audience, calling me a kinky bitch and demanding I strip. I ignored him, hiding my smile by turning my back as I began to strip Jasmine for her caning.

I did it slowly, standing well to the side of her. First I took her petticoats up, one by one, hoisted onto her back to expose the taut seat of her drawers, her slim cheeks tight against the cotton, the panel buttons straining just a little. I began to open them, popping each button with my face set in haughty disdain. It was easy to imagine her feelings as her panel came slowly loose, each button revealing a little more creamy flesh, then everything as the last dropped away and her little pink bottom hole and pouting pussy lips were put on show to the entire room. She was shaking, her cheeks quivering in her emotion, something I was sure would make all the difference to the display – and if feelings intensified the display, so would her pain when I caned her.

Caroline got the same treatment, petticoats hauled high to show off the bulging seat of her splitters, which I tugged wide with a single angry gesture, exposing the full, cheeky globe of her bottom. Like Jasmine, she was trembling a little, and I made a point of walking slowly around them to make sure the crowd got a good look at every detail of their bodies, all the time aware of the progress of our music. It was an Edwardian music hall piece, very different from the other choices, but right.

I got to my place at exactly the right moment, lifted my cane and gave Jasmine six hard cuts, fast, in exact time to the rhythm. A step forwards and I was beside Caroline, waiting for my moment, then again applying six quick, precise cuts, to leave both bottoms decorated with half a dozen neatly planted welts and the girls shivering in their sudden pain. The crowd, most of whom I was sure would never have seen a girl beaten before, had gone absolutely quiet, only for the silence to be broken by Jack's rasping drawl.

'Now you strip, you la-di-dah bitch, and I'll give you a real whacking!'

One or two others echoed the sentiment, but I simply smiled and turned away. They didn't understand, but that was not my business, while it was very satisfying to sense Jack's frustration as I walked coolly off stage and the girls began to retrieve their discarded clothing. There were two acts to go, and while both the twins and the curly blonde had matched us for sheer shock value, I had no idea what the audience would have thought. I had no idea how the competition was being judged, either, save that it was by a panel of 'striptease experts', which presumably meant dirty old men.

Back in the tent Jasmine and Caroline were excited, sure that the twins were the only real competition. I wasn't so sure, but kept my opinions to myself, until Mike came in to announce the result. Third place had gone to one of the blondes, a girl whose act had been completely ordinary as far as I was concerned, and my heart sank.

'I thought so,' I sighed in Caroline's ear. 'What else can you expect from that lot?'

' . . . and we have a tie for first place,' Mike went on, 'between . . . Diamonds and Gold of Manchester, and our very own Jasmine and Caroline, not forgetting Mistress Isabelle, of course.'

For some reason I immediately found myself thinking of how it had felt to be face down in a lavatory while Stan Tierney sodomised me, but the girls were jumping up and down in glee, with others either congratulating us or throwing jealous looks over. Mike raised his hand for silence, of which nobody took the slightest notice, then went on anyway.

'For the grand prize, by popular demand, there will be a tie-break. Get your best routines ready, girls, 'cause this is a lot of cash!'

He held up a bundle of twenty-pound notes, took a deep sniff of it and made for the entrance with a parting shot. 'Five minutes. You're on first, Jas.'

'What are we going to do?' Caroline demanded. 'We're going to have to make it different.'

'I agree, but what?' Jasmine answered.

'I don't know. I don't even have any other outfits!?

'How about a doggie training session?' I suggested. 'It's not really striptease, but . . .'

'They won't go for it, not that lot,' Caroline objected. 'We can do something like that, though, only get Mike to make the tie-breaker a dirty show instead of a striptease. The lads will love it, and those two wouldn't dare get as mucky as we can.'

'You've got it,' Jasmine agreed and began to strip, pulling what remained of her clothes off with a complete indifference to her exposure unlike anything shown on stage.

I ran inside, not really sure what we were doing but hoping for some props. The storeroom was a great deal less full than it had been, with the great towers of beer now reduced to stumps, and behind was something that immediately gave me an idea – catering tins. I could hear Mike announcing the coming strip, and grabbed the nearest two, stacked them in the corridor and joined him. As I'd left the tent the twins had been going through a selection of costumes and talking in a worryingly professional way, so rather than argue I simply took the microphone out of his hand. The crowd burst out laughing, then went silent.

'A slight change in program, gentlemen – as our tie-breaker we won't be doing striptease, but a full sex show!'

They went wild and I ducked quickly out under the drapes, leaving Mike to calm them down. Jasmine and Caroline were ready at the back, nude but for panties which they'd obviously borrowed.

'Just do as I say,' I instructed, picking up my tins.

Caroline nodded. Jasmine stuck her head out through the drapes and signalled to Mike. Music started, some pop song or other, and we stepped out. The crowd were clapping, those we could see behind the lights red faced and expectant, projecting a drunken lust that took me aback. I had to force myself to stay calm as I once more took the microphone.

'Good evening, gentlemen – do you like my slave girls?'

There was an immediate chorus of agreement, with a few voices demanding that I strip, or worse. I ignored them and continued.

'And they are my slave girls, gentlemen, and they will do exactly as I say. Perhaps I might have some suggestions?'

Again came the answering roar, worse this time, many suggesting throwing the girls to the crowd to be fucked, others having them perform together, with me, and Jack demanding I be beaten myself. I wagged my finger at him, secure in my position on the stage and the presence of Mike's bouncers, then held up my hand for silence.

I didn't get much, but it didn't matter. They couldn't make out everything that had been suggested any more than I could. Pointing over the heads of the audience, I yelled into the microphone, causing an ear-splitting screech of feedback. It wasn't what I had intended, but it worked. I pointed over the heads of the crowd, at random, and spoke.

'What was that, sir? A little slapstick to start with? What an excellent suggestion, sir, and also wonderfully British. Jasmine, Caroline, hold out your panties.'

Both obeyed, looking a little worried and a little puzzled as they stuck their bottoms out and eased their waistbands open, providing me with a fine view of creases and welted cheeks down the rear of each panty pouch. The men were laughing, making rude remarks and sniggering together, and a murmur of amusement and not a little disgust ran through them as I lifted the first of my tins, five kilos of baked beans.

I peeled the lid off, making very sure they could all see, including Caroline and Jasmine, who were looking back at me with horrified expressions, to the delight of the crowd. The lumpy, orange surface of the beans was revealed and I lifted the can, looking first to Jasmine, who hung her head in mute submission, then to Caroline, who made a disgusted face. It was a mistake, which she found out as I emptied the contents of the can down the back of her panties.

There was too much, far too much. Her panty pouch was full before half the can was down it, and then the beans were spilling over her waistband to fall squashily to the floor. Her panties were already bulging badly, and a big orange stain was spreading up the seat. I took her hand away, letting her waistband snap back against her flesh, then pointed to her pussy. Her face was already set in utter disgust, and it grew worse, but she did it, straightening up, sticking her little tummy out and opening her pussy pouch to show me the plump, shaved mound of her sex.

I tipped the rest of the baked beans down the front of her panties, again filling them in an instant so that most of them went on the floor. There was a good half-can down her panties, though, which were stuffed full back and front, heavy with beans, some of which had begun to ooze out around the leg holes. It was a truly disgusting sight, and the crowd were in fits, laughing, yelling for more and commenting on the way Caroline's panties bulged and sagged.

'And now for Jasmine,' I said sweetly, and took the second can.

I had no idea what it was, having simply grabbed the nearest two. She had, though, and was really struggling to hold her meek expression as she stared at the garish picture on the tin and the legend – 'Faggots in Gravy'. I just laughed, completely carried away, and leaned out, to make a show of peering down the back of her panties, at the little pink bottom cheeks within, neat and feminine, well caned and, above all, clean. Slowly, now smiling because I was simply enjoying myself too much to pretend to be cool, I began to tip the can of faggots, bringing the thick, grey-brown gravy to the lip, and over.

Down it went, filling her panty pouch and immediately soaking into the cotton, then the faggots, fatty-looking lumps of glistening brown I would not have put in my mouth for the world, plopping down her panties one by one, to pile up inside, until her entire pouch was full. Grinning sadistically, I pinched her hand, making her let go of her waistband. It snapped back, leaving her panty pouch a lumpy bulge, sodden through with gravy, more of which had begun to run down her legs. I snapped my fingers.

'Pussy now. Stick it out.'

She stood up, the load of faggots in her panties shifting disgustingly as she moved, to hang heavy under her bottom as she took hold of the front of her panties and opened them up. Once again I tipped the big can, and once again saw the gravy run down her panties, only now coating her pussy and making a pool, which overflowed as the first of faggots went in. There were plenty left, a good half, and it seemed a shame to waste them. Taking the can, I tipped some over her breasts, leaving both brown and mucky, then up-ended the can on her head, so that she was wearing it like a ridiculous crown, with gravy running down her beautiful blonde hair and over her face. I was grinning like a maniac as I stepped back to admire my results, and I couldn't stop myself, nor could I resist up-ending the bean can onto Caroline's head to leave her in the same sorry condition.

They looked absolutely comic, and I was laughing as I stood away, as were my audience. I bowed, and as I took the microphone once more the weight in Jasmine's panties finally proved too much. They fell down, hitting the floor with a squashy plop and spilling meatballs out over the stage. Again I spoke to the audience.

'A fine sight, gentlemen, I'm sure you'll agree. And now, what do you think they deserve? What was that, sir? Make them eat it? Really, sir, is that fair?'

There was a concerted yell of 'Yes'. I shrugged and turned to Jasmine and Caroline.

'Sorry, girls, don't blame me. Head to toe you go, then, and bon appetit.'

Caroline gave me the most wonderful look, at once sulky and worshipful. Jasmine's was simply dazed as she stepped out of her filthy panties and got down onto her back, her ridiculous crown falling off to roll into the crowd. Her legs came open and the brown mess smeared over her pussy parted to show the pink interior for at least a second, before a trickle of gravy ran down into her open hole. Caroline climbed on, her bulging panty seat over Jasmine's face, then in it as she deliberately sat down. The crowd went into wild clapping as the huge soggy bulge settled over Jasmine's features. Caroline laughed as she looked round at them, gave a cheeky wiggle, reached back and pulled her panty pouch open, to deposit a good kilo of beans over Jasmine's head.

It did look good, a classic queening, crown and all, but she was being a sight too impudent for my liking. I picked up Jasmine's discarded panties, took the tin off Caroline's head and put the panties in its place, pulling them well down to squash bits of faggot out into her hair and face and leave her looking more ridiculous than ever. Putting my fingers onto one of the few clean bits of her back, I pushed her down between Jasmine's open thighs.

'It's over when you've both come,' I announced.

They didn't need to be told. Jasmine already had Caroline by the thighs and was licking her juice smeared pussy, apparently oblivious to everything else. Caroline returned the favour, sucking pulped faggot from the groove of Jasmine's sex and swallowing it down, then starting to lick. Both were urgent, rubbing their filthy faces in each other's crotches, groping and spanking at filthy bottom cheeks and thighs, licking and probing, bottom holes as well as

179

pussies, completely wrapped in each other, the crowd staring in silence.

I felt completely triumphant. It was my doing, and I was fresh and clean and not even undressed, while they were squirming in mess, so far gone they didn't care about having a huge crowd of men watch them lick each other's bottoms. They were going to have to see to me, just as soon as we were in private, but for the time being I was content to watch and enjoy what I'd done.

Jasmine came first, with her face completely smothered in Caroline's ample bottom, tongue in the hole, blind with gravy and baked-bean sauce, her thighs wrapped hard around Caroline's head. Caroline followed, moments after Jasmine had come down, squirming her filthy bottom about as she was licked, and still with her head trapped firmly in place. As her orgasm died I turned to the audience and curtsied.

They were pretty excited, pressing forward to the stage, and the smell of sweat and arousal was like a wall, of which I'd been completely unaware just moments before. I gave them what I hoped was a disarming smile and beat a retreat, once more thinking of my bog-washing and buggery at the hands of these same people I had now driven into a frenzy.

Jasmine and Caroline followed, both giggling and cuddled up to each other, out of the club and into the tent. Most of the girls were gone, just three still packing their things away. None had watched us, except maybe the twins, who were not there, and the state of my two was greeted with amazement. They washed together at the stand pipe, drinking beers at the same time. I took one too, downing most of it at a gulp. Before it had been pretty foul, but now it was immensely refreshing, and I took a second and a third in quick succession as I wondered what I should do with the girls for the climax of my own evening.

They put their drawers and chemises on, nothing more, and we trooped back inside, just in time to see Diamonds, or possibly Gold, deliver the full contents of her bladder in her sister's face. The crowd were screaming in delight and disgust, and I realised that we did after all have some serious competition. It was good to watch anyway, with her mouth wide open to catch the full force of the stream, yet plenty still escaping from the sides to run down over her breasts and belly to her sex. She was already masturbating, and came with the piddle still bubbling out of her mouth, then finished by putting her mouth to her sister's pussy and returning the favour, to wild applause.

It was so good, and I had to come, and soon, preferably with both of them to work on me as well as Jasmine and Caroline. They were dirty, as bad as us, and there would be no difficulty this time. It just needed a word, I was sure.

Mike had seen us peeking, and beckoned us out to join them. The roar of the crowd grew louder still as we appeared, and I was sure they would rush the stage at any second and simply have us, whether we liked it or not. I could just imagine it, all five of us stripped nude, fucked, made to suck cock, greased up with the faggot gravy and sodomised . . .

There were hundreds of them, on the edge of losing control, and I was shaking as I stepped up beside Mike. He seemed oblivious, and simply raised his arms until he was able to shout loud enough to be heard, the speakers whining and bumping as his voice boomed out, telling the crowd that the judges had reached a decision, and that the winners were Diamonds and Gold.

I felt a sharp hit of disappointment, far stronger than I had expected, but then one of the sisters was kissing me and the other was hugging Jasmine and Caroline, her hair and chest still wet with pee. It was my moment, and I took it, giving Mike just long enough to present the prize money before taking my new friend by the hand and leading her quickly out to the back.

We all knew what was going to happen if we stuck around, and we all knew what was going to happen if we didn't. I could already hear the swirl of water around my head and imagine the taste of faggot juice and worse on a cock recently pulled from my anus as I was made to suck on it. Deep down I wanted it, but common sense told me otherwise and I was the most urgent of all, stuffing our things into a bag and running for the car with the others laughing as they came behind.

There was no question of where we were going. We piled into Jasmine's car, all together, laughing and kissing and touching each other, high on sex and our power over all the men we'd left high and dry. At Jasmine's we tumbled out again, into the house and straight up the stairs, the five of us piling onto the bed in a tangle of limbs and hair and breasts and bottoms, stroking and licking and kissing. I was naked almost before I knew what was happening, and I'd come soon after, with Gold's face pressed to my bottom from behind as she licked me and I in turn licked her sister. From then on it was a blur, my one clear memory a bare, sticky bottom lifting from my face and revealing the window with dawn lightening the curtains.

Ten

Morning was not a pleasant experience. I hadn't drunk that much at all, unlike the others, who had put back a bottle of vodka between the four of them. They were out cold, and I would have loved to join them again but had to be in The Eagle and Lamb by noon. My head hurt and I felt weak, presumably from the smoke in the club, general lack of air, dehydration and the exertions of having dirty lesbian sex for several hours non-stop.

I didn't even know Diamonds' and Gold's real names, or if they were actually sisters, making it my first anonymous sexual experience, in a sense. Had we not got out so quickly, it would have been my first anonymous sexual experience with a vengeance. It had been a great night, and I wanted to be pleased with our escape from the clutches of the Red Ox men. Logically, I knew that the situation had been genuinely threatening. Many of the regulars knew about the poker night and would have expected much the same as I had given then. They had been drunk and aroused, and while we might have coped with a few, there had simply been too many to handle. We would have been put in the storeroom or the loos, and fucked and fucked and fucked. Knowing them they'd have sodomised us too, and come in our faces, between our breasts and a dozen other dirty acts. Doubtless they'd have had fun with the revolting mixture of beans and faggots in gravy Mike had scraped off the stage as well. It was an idea that terrified me, yet left my pussy warm and tingly as I cycled down the High towards Carfax, and it was impossible not to feel that I had missed out.

It was five to twelve when I chained my bicycle up outside The Eagle and Lamb. I'd made an effort to look right, dressing in the same casual but refined manner I had seen Portia in the first time, with my most expensive pair of trousers and a light blouse tucked into it. It was also a style I felt made the best of my figure, especially the way the trouser seat hugged my bottom, allowing the shape of my cheeks to show without squashing me. I had also determined not to put my foot in it, but to let Sarah lead. If she was a Rattaner, then it seemed reasonable to assume she would know I had been rejected. That meant she was either interested in me personally, or I was being given a second consideration. If she was not a Rattaner, it could not hurt to let her make the decisions, and dominate. Certainly I had no intention of pressing the issue of switching roles.

Both Sarah and Portia were already there, seated in an alcove in the back bar but keeping a lookout. Portia came out to me and bought a round of drinks, tomato juice laced with Worcestershire sauce and Tabasco in my case. She was grinning cheekily as we walked back to where Sarah was, and even patted my bottom. Sarah gave me a cool little smile as I sat down, then took a slow sip from her glass of white wine and spoke.

'So, you're the young lady who wants her bottom spanked.'

'Yes,' I managed, looking round quickly at the

students, tourists and shoppers packing the pub as Portia dissolved into giggles.

'I think we might be able to do something about that,' Sarah went on, 'but I would like to know a little about you first.'

'Of course, and likewise.'

'You should answer my questions first, I think.'

'As you please.'

'Good. Why do you like to be spanked?'

I hesitated only briefly, then spoke, sure that she was grilling me for more than just the pleasure of humiliating me.

'It . . . it just seems right, instinctively right, but I do know where it comes from. I was brought up to see sex as wrong . . . well, not wrong, but something to be ashamed of, definitely a sin, and corporal punishment to be the best way to deal with sin. So spanking and sex go together. There's something about the shape of a woman's bottom too, that just makes me want to spank it . . . including my own when I look in the mirror.'

I'd added the last bit quickly, keen to establish my credentials as submissive yet aware that if she was a Rattaner she would already know I switched roles. Unsurprisingly, she latched on to the point, but not in the way I would have expected.

'Aren't you a little young to want to be doing the spanking?'

'Young?'

'Yes. How old are you?'

'I'll be twenty in three weeks, more or less.'

'Oh we must give her a birthday party,' Portia squeaked, 'and twenty of the cane with one for luck!'

'Be quiet, Portia,' Sarah answered. 'Isabelle, do you not think yourself a little young?'

Again I hesitated, wondering what she knew. I had to assume it was everything, and answered carefully.

'I . . . I do feel I should be spanked, but . . . but that's part of me, of who I am. So is the desire to spank, but I am happy to be flexible, to suit my behaviour to a partner's needs.'

'It is a matter of age, Isabelle, not personality at all. Young girls like Portia and yourself should be spanked, and regularly. It is what you need. Who better to do it than a mature woman like myself, with experience and the same needs?'

'You were spanked yourself, then, when you were younger?'

'Yes, naturally, but that is not the issue. If you do genuinely want to come under my discipline, you must accept how we stand. I really ought to spank you right now, for impertinence. If it wasn't for social convention, I would.'

She was testing me, she had to be, being deliberately provocative. Two could play at that game.

'I wish you would, right now, and on the bare of course.'

Portia burst into giggles, Sarah gave a quiet smile and I knew it had been the right thing to say. I was going to get spanked by her, in front of Portia, and the thrill of it was rising inside me.

'How shall we go about it then?' Sarah said evenly.

'Outdoors, perhaps?' I suggested. 'That was what I was thinking about after I met you.'

'Riding,' Portia cut in. 'Take her riding, up to Wytham – it would be perfect!'

'It would, wouldn't it?' Sarah agreed. 'Riding it is then, Isabelle. Meet us here, next Saturday, eleven o'clock. We'll arrange everything, and we may even have a little surprise for you.'

I answered with a nod, a thousand questions on the tip of my tongue, not the least of them why she didn't simply take me home and put me straight across her knee. They remained unsaid, any one likely to spoil the situation she had put me in, because the surprise simply had to be that they were Rattaners.

'Thank you, Sarah,' I said eventually, 'and you, Portia. I'm sure you'll find you've made the right choice.'

'Oh, I think we have,' Sarah answered. 'Another drink?'

'Please, yes,' I answered, 'the same again; last night was a bit heavy.'

She stood up, and I was left with Portia, her face lit up by a smile that was pure mischief.

'You will love it,' she assured me, 'but one rule – Sarah is my girlfriend, and has been for two years. No going behind my back.'

'I understand,' I assured her. 'You're in your third year, then?'

'I'm a post-grad,' she answered, 'doing my Master's at Bede's. I was at Erasmus first, reading chemistry.'

'St George's, history, and still in my first year, with mods coming up.'

'Don't worry. Only idiots get thrown out at mods.'

'Let's hope I'm not an idiot then!'

She laughed, not the girlish giggle that the slightest mention of spanking seemed to provoke, but a richer, more womanly sound. That, with her manner and accent, suggested upper-middle class, even genuine upper class, while there was an innocence to her that went with her obvious intelligence to suggest she had never really had to struggle in her life. It was hard to see her being tough about anything, including keeping secrets.

'How did you meet Sarah?' I asked, probing, but gently.

'Because she smacked my bum with a spoon for being late in the cafeteria,' she laughed. 'She had guessed what I was like, just from the way I am!'

187

'I can imagine. So what's her background? She said she used to get spanked?'

'And how! When old Lizzie used to spank her she would give her an enema with soapy water first. Can you imagine!?'

'Lizzie? Not Elizabeth Hastings?'

She was going to answer, but Sarah was coming towards us, the drinks in her hands. Portia gave her spanking giggle, making me absolutely certain that not only had she said something she should not have done, but that Elizabeth Hastings had been Sarah's mentor.

I was absolutely flying as I cycled back to college. With a little effort and a little luck I had found myself Laura Soames, Sarah and Portia, as well as the twins. Even if the Rattaners did prove to exist only in Stan Tierney's twisted little mind, I had found myself a fine set of playmates. True, I didn't have full control of my own fate, but that would come with time. I was also 95 per cent sure that the Rattaners did exist, and that Sarah wanted me as a member. The question then became simply whether she had the influence within the club to swing my membership against Emmeline Young and Hope Ashdene, at worst.

On a different level, if I had felt it was wrong to punish Laura Soames, the opposite was true for Sarah Finch. She too was older than me, but whatever I had said I did not agree with her attitude. Turning her across my knee and proving to her that a young woman could dish out a spanking as well as any other appealed to me, while I was sure it would delight Portia. Physically, there was a womanliness to her that made the idea of taking her panties down for a rousing spanking not only appropriate but immensely satisfying.

Her attitude also revealed the secret of the Rattaners' philosophy. Young women had their bottoms spanked, older women did the spanking. It was not a concept I'd encountered much during my internet researches, except as an accepted truth for stories and particularly picture stories, yet for all that I disagreed with it I could understand the reasoning behind it. It would also be very convenient for a woman like Margaret Coln when seducing young college girls into accepting punishment.

The riding idea appealed too, and I was hoping that the secret would prove to be the presence of a few more members of the Rattaners for my punishment. They'd take turns with me, and it was sure to hurt, providing me with that glorious mixture of anticipation and fear all the way back to St George's. I had to come, and despite being sore from the previous night's excesses I stripped off and lay down on my bed the moment I'd reached the haven of my room.

It was hard to decide what to come over: what was going to happen to me for real, or my fantasy of turning the tables on Sarah. After a moment of idly stroking my breasts and tummy I chose. To come over anything to do with the Rattaners was tempting fate after what had happened the time before. It had to be Sarah. I could imagine how, too – when we went riding, when she expected to spank me. Her indignation when it was her who got it instead would be simply wonderful, and all the more so for it being in front of her girlfriend.

I could do it too, because for all Sarah's confidence she could never dominate me physically. She might think she could, and try, attempting to force me down across her legs, perhaps sat on a tree stump somewhere deep in the woods. I'd fight back, to her immense surprise, then horror as I picked her up bodily, put her down across my lap and gave her the spanking of a lifetime. I would do it bare, of course, stripping her slowly to really let the consternation build up in her head. Portia would be giggling crazily as her Mistress's jodhpurs and panties were hauled down, one layer after the other, revealing Sarah's full, womanly bottom. I would expose her breasts too, just to add an extra element of humiliation, and leave them dangling nude under her chest as her bottom was smacked . . .

My legs were wide open, my fingers busy with my pussy, my eyes closed, everything focused on the image of Sarah held over my lap, struggling, cursing, begging Portia to help her. None of it would be to any avail as I stripped her body, laying her bare from chest to knees, or completely, to make her go nude in the woods, bare and wriggling over my lap as the spanking began.

I'd do it hard from the first, a real punishment spanking . . . no, I'd do it slowly, playfully, to bring home the utter helplessness of her position as she was gradually warmed, brought on heat, her arousal rising despite herself. Maybe she'd cry, maybe she'd disgrace herself, but I wouldn't stop, spanking and spanking until her whole bottom was a warm, rosy ball of flesh, her cheeks well parted, her pussy on show. She'd be wet, soaking, and after a while I would start to masturbate her, rubbing her pussy between every set of fifty spanks or so.

When she realised she was going to be made to come she would go berserk, really thrashing, scream-ing and begging for it not to be done. Portia would be silent by then, wide-eyed with excitement, rubbing her own pussy through her jeans as she watched her helpless Mistress being punished. I'd hold on, tight, alternately spanking and rubbing, until at last she gave in and came, in ecstasy yet also misery as I took her to orgasm.

It would break her will to dominate me, and she would go down to order, kneeling nude between my thighs with her hot bottom stuck out behind. First she would kiss my anus, in willing submission, then set to work to make me come. Portia would get down too, her pretty impish face beside Sarah's, both naked, both licking me, attending to my aching pussy and my bottom, vying for the privilege of making me come . . .

Which was exactly what I was doing, my mind set on the image of Sarah fighting as her panties were hauled down and my body jerking and shuddering in climax. I could almost hear her outraged squeals as it all came on show, which faded to the noise of some students in the quad below my window as I came slowly down.

I fell asleep after my orgasm, with my hand still pressed between my thighs, and I didn't wake up until the light had begun to fade from the sky. For a moment I was completely disorientated, not sure if it was dawn or dusk, or what I was doing stark naked on my bed. Memory returned fast enough, though, first of the meeting with Sarah and Portia, then the night before. I had meant to go back to Jasmine's in the afternoon to find out what was going on with Diamonds and Gold, and who they were as people rather than purely sex partners as well.

They would certainly have gone, but I wanted to talk to the girls anyway. I also wanted to eat, and it was too late for hall. So I splashed water in my face to wake myself up properly and cycled over, finding them padding around the house in bras and panties, just starting to think about getting dressed properly so that they could go and get some food. I told them about Sarah and Portia, and that we would be meeting next week, but not about my coming spanking. They in turn explained that the twins had rushed off shortly after midday, needing to get back for an evening booking in Bolton, and that they had not given their true names, nor revealed if they were really sisters.

We ordered a Chinese, far more than we were ever going to eat, but with their four hundred pounds for second place in the striptease competition the girls were feeling flush. I accepted some money to buy a couple of bottles of Champagne as well, which I felt I could live with as I wasn't being paid directly, but I had to walk all the way down to St Clement's to get them.

By the time I got back I was ravenous, and sure the food would not only have arrived but be cold. Fortunately the delivery man was just drawing up outside Jasmine's as I turned the corner of the street, but unfortunately he wasn't alone. A group of three men were at the door with him, one unmistakably huge even in the twilight: Big Dave. The others were Jack and Stan Tierney, who for some reason had his overcoat on only one arm with the other sleeve pinned up at the front as if he thought he was Napoleon Bonaparte.

I smiled bravely as I approached. They leered back, Stan and Big Dave just plain dirty, Jack with a touch of aggression. I opened the door for them and paid the delivery man with what I had left from Jasmine and Caroline's money, then followed them in. By the time I'd put the Champagne in the fridge, as I was not opening it with them around, and helped Caroline with cutlery and crockery, they had spread themselves out in the living room, beers in their hands. I hadn't seen Tierney at all the night before, and I immediately discovered why.

'. . . came from fucking nowhere, he did,' he was explaining to Jasmine as he displayed the plaster cast enclosing his right arm. 'I never even fucking saw him!'

'Stan was involved in a hit and run last night,' Jasmine explained, 'just a couple of streets from the Red Ox.'

'Oh, I am sorry,' I responded.

'So am I, believe it!' he answered. 'And I'm a sight fucking sorrier now Dave and Jack told me about the competition. All that and I'm up the fucking Radcliffe having gravel scraped out of my arse!'

'Ouch!' I answered, wincing at his description. 'It was a good show, though, sorry you missed it.'

'Yeah, well, that's what we come about,' he answered.

'Yeah,' Jack put in. 'See, we reckoned the three of you might give Stan a bit of a private show, you know, to make up for it.'

'What, now?' Caroline demanded. 'Give me a break, Jack, we were up all night, and we haven't eaten since yesterday.'

'Yeah, yeah, have your tea first,' Stan answered her, 'no rush or nothing.'

'Up all night, what, with those two Scouse tarts?' Jack demanded.

'They're from Manchester.'

'Fuck me, five in a bed! What, they'd do that pissing stuff with you?'

'Not in my bed,' Jasmine answered him, 'but yes, they stayed over. It was good.'

'Good! I bet it was fucking good.' Stan sighed.

'Nah, you need a man, five maybe . . . well, fifty maybe, for you dirty bitches!' Jack said. 'So what, did you use dildoes and stuff?'

'Mind your own business,' Caroline answered.

'You might've invited a few of us,' Big Dave complained.

Caroline just stuck her tongue out and began to spoon sweet and sour pork balls onto the bed of lemon rice and mushroom chow mein she'd been making on her plate. Jack was chewing his lower lip thoughtfully, Stan drinking beer. Big Dave adjusted his cock in his trousers. I began to make pancakes with shredded duck and hoi sin sauce, too hungry to really care about anything but the food.

'So what?' Jack demanded after a while. 'Does Stan get his private show?'

'Maybe,' Jasmine answered tartly and I glanced at her, wondering where she got the energy and the sheer dirty-mindedness. 'It's up to Isabelle.'

I hid a sigh. It was the answer she should have given, deferring to me, but I was really not in the mood to take charge. I also felt genuine sympathy for Stan Tierney. Not only did it look like he had been telling the truth, in which case I'd wronged him, but the thought of being hit by a car horrified me, as it must every cyclist. It wasn't as if we hadn't done things for him before, either.

'Definitely not until we've eaten,' I told them. 'What did you have in mind, anyway?'

'Some stuff like what you did with the food,' Big Dave answered. 'Stan'd love to see that, wouldn't you, Stan?'

'Too right, I would,' Stan answered. 'Baked beans and some brown shit, wasn't it?'

'Faggots in gravy,' I responded. 'That was OK on stage, but we can't do it here, can we? Think of the mess! Anyway, we don't have any faggots in gravy.'

'There are baked beans,' Caroline stated casually before feeding a forkful of Chinese food into her mouth.

'Mess is about right,' Big Dave laughed. 'Mike's cleaners are going to be well pissed!'

'You could roll the carpet back,' Stan suggested.

'Yeah,' Jack agreed, 'only we want all three of you. That was good, what you did, real dirty-bitch stuff, and you should've won, but we reckon you ought to take your share, Isa.'

'I do,' I reminded him. 'How about what you did to me after your little poker evening? You're the ones who don't take your share, not me.'

'Yeah, but we're blokes, ain't we?' Big Dave put in.

'I don't know, you tell me,' Caroline asked. 'Leave Isabelle alone, you lot. She did what we asked her to. I was the one who worked out our routine, you know.'

'Don't you want us to give her a good arse whacking?' Big Dave queried.

Caroline giggled, nearly losing her mouthful, but Jasmine responded before I'd decided what to say.

'Isabelle does as she likes, exactly as she likes. I do as she tells me, and so does Carrie.'

'Thank you, Jasmine,' I responded. 'That is how it works, gentlemen, which you never seem to understand. Domination within the context of a bisexual relationship is not something which –'

'Do we get our show or what?' Jack interrupted. 'Come on, Isabelle, don't be so stuck-up. Poor old Stan's had his arm busted, and –'

'Yes, I suppose so.' I sighed. 'When I say, and what I say.'

Big Dave immediately gave a double thumbs up, which Jack answered, and Stan with his good arm. All three were grinning as I went back to my food, and I was wondering what would be fair. Jasmine seemed game, Caroline too, and all I really had to do was lie back and issue instructions, perhaps while I sipped on a glass of chilled Champagne. A strip, a mutual spanking, and they could take Stan in their hands, and the other two if they wanted. As Jasmine said, it was up to me.

Having talked us into doing it, they didn't seem in any great hurry. They'd bought a six-pack of beers each, strong lager, and were content to drink it and chat, mainly about the show the night before and the approaching climax to the Association Football season. I opened one of the Champagnes, a couple of glasses of which made me feel a great deal better, even restoring some of the old sense of mischief-making with which the girls performing with Tierney had once provided me.

By the time we'd finished our food and taken a leisurely time to digest I was beginning to feel very much in control. The men were getting excited, and Caroline had begun to tease, deliberately bending as she cleared the plates so that the tiny skirt she'd put on rose to show off her panties. I decided to have her spanked, and to let one of the men do it. Big Dave's eyes were bulging out of his head as she bent again to pick up the half-finished takeaway cartons, which was not surprising with the fullness of her bottom more or less in his face. Tierney could hardly do it, and Jack had to learn to be at least a little more respectful, so he was the choice.

'Caroline,' I said, casually, 'get over David's knee, now.'

She gave me a look of surprise, then cast an uneasy glance at him, or more exactly at his hands. They were huge, and rough, the hands of a man who has spent his work life on a car-production line, and each big enough to just about cup one of her by no means little cheeks.

'Now,' I repeated, 'spank her hard, David, she has plenty of padding.'

'Hey, that's not padding, that's me!' Caroline complained, but she had put the cartons down and come to his side.

'I don't know about this spanking stuff, but I'd love a feel of your arse, Carrie,' he said, reaching out to slide one massive paw up her thigh to the seat of her panties.

'Feel all you like,' I offered generously, 'but spank her too, it's what she likes best, and don't worry if she makes a fuss.'

He nodded, his eyes on Caroline's bottom as she laid herself down over his knees, her skirt riding up with his groping hand. Her panties were wholly inadequate, little more than a thong, with big slices of bottom cheek spilling out to either side, plump and creamy. He tucked the skirt up to get a proper view, then began to stroke her bottom.

'Do take down her panties,' I instructed. 'She likes to show.'

'Yeah,' he grunted, then grabbed her waistband and jerked her panties smartly down, and off, leaving her naked from the waist down.

She gasped as she was stripped and I felt a familiar flush of pleasure in reaction to her emotions. Her glorious bottom was quivering a little, with the chubby lips of her shaved pussy just showing between her thighs – a beautiful sight, which all three men were drinking in, Stan with his hand on his crotch, nursing a very obvious erection through his trousers.

'Jasmine, go and help Stan with that,' I instructed.

'Yes, Mistress,' she answered immediately.

Tierney's face broke into the dirtiest of leers as she crossed to him and sat herself neatly down on his lap. She had simply thrown a long T-shirt over her underwear when they came in, and it rode up at the back, showing her panties. Tierney took hold of her bottom as she pulled his fly down and, very clinically, extracted his cock, which she began to masturbate.

'Wade in, David,' I instructed, nodding to Big Dave, who was idly fondling Caroline's bottom. 'Make sure Stan has plenty to watch.'

'Yeah, right,' he answered, and began to spank her, really quite gently, but hard enough to set her wriggling and gasping for his sheer power. He stopped.

'That was fine,' I told him, 'harder, even. Ask her if you're not sure.'

'You all right, love?' he queried.

'Shut up and spank me,' Caroline breathed.

'Pull her breasts out too,' I ordered.

Big Dave shrugged, stuck his hand under Caroline's chest to haul her top and bra up and flopped her breasts out, leaving them squashed to his massive leg as he set to work on her bottom, properly now. I was laughing immediately, as he laid in with a series of pile-driver slaps and she went completely crazy, thrashing in desperate pain, her limbs and hair everywhere, her bottom squashing out like so much dough, her pussy flaunted as she lost control of her thighs. He stopped again, looking puzzled, and this time all her cheek had gone. She lay limp across his lap, gasping for air, one hand back to stroke the red skin of her slapped bottom cheeks.

'Oh, that was hard!' she complained. 'More, Dave, please, but not so hard, not at first.'

'Warm her up,' I explained, 'with middleweight smacks; you can do it really hard when she starts getting excited. That's the thing with spanking, there's a pain barrier to get over.'

'Come over here and I'll put you through your pain barrier!' Jack answered. 'You're the one who needs it, Isabelle.'

I ignored his outburst as Big Dave went back to spanking Caroline, better now, hard enough to make her jerk and wriggle but not to really hurt her. He might not have really been into it, but Tierney certainly was, groping and patting Jasmine's bottom as she masturbated him. She had stuck it out obligingly and had also pulled out his balls, which she was tickling with her long nails as she tugged on him. He looked ready to come, while the mixture of lust and envy on Jack's face was a picture.

The spanking was getting to Caroline too, her legs now cocked wide to make her pussy available and her fingers clutching at Big Dave's leg and the arm of the chair, still in pain, but coming towards that crucial point. I was little different, my pussy warm and needful and my nipples hard, but I held my poise, controlling the scene to order as the girls expected.

'Harder now, David,' I instructed. 'Jasmine, I think you'd better take that in your mouth – we don't want any unnecessary mess, do we?'

'No, Mistress,' she answered promptly, and with no more than a trace of disgust on her face went down on Stan Tierney's cock.

Almost immediately her cheeks bulged out and the disgust was replaced by surprise as he came in her mouth. She couldn't hold it either, sperm and spittle erupting from around her lips as her mouth filled, then from her nose as she began to choke. He paid no attention, his eyes closed in bliss, pumping his hips out to fuck her mouth, still groping her bottom, only with his hand in her panties, toying with her anus as he came. When at last she got up there was a froth of sperm bubbles on her chin and upper lip. She was gasping for breath, and showing off the white mess in her mouth, but she made no effort to get his hand out of her panties, merely turning to me with a dazed look.

'Good girl,' I thanked her. 'You can stop now, David.'

Big Dave responded, grudgingly, finishing Caroline off with a last salvo of really hard spanks before letting her go. She leaped up, to snatch at her reddened cheeks, rubbing and clutching at her flesh as she jumped up and down on her toes, speaking only when she finally managed to get control of herself.

'Ow, my poor bottom! That was some spanking! Thank you, Dave.'

He looked a little surprised as she bent forwards to kiss him, not bothering to put her panties back on, and more surprised still as she got down on her knees between his legs. She turned to me.

'May I say thank you properly, Mistress, pretty please?'

'Of course,' I answered. 'You are a very lucky man, David.'

He didn't answer, but helped her with the fly of his jeans, to pull out his cock. It went straight into her mouth, her face setting in dirty ecstasy as she began to suck. Her bottom was stuck well out, the hem of her little skirt half covering the big red cheeks, her pussy and bottom hole showing between, moist and glistening with sweat and her juice. I poured myself another glass of Champagne and sat back to admire the view, wondering if I dared have the girls lick me in front of the men.

'What about us, then?' Jack asked suddenly. 'You need your share.'

'I need my share, yes,' I admitted, 'but not from you.'

'Bollocks! Suck on this, you stuck-up bitch!'

'You really know how to charm a lady,' I answered him as he pulled his cock out.

'Shut up, Jack,' Big Dave groaned. 'I'm getting my knob polished here.'

'Yeah, and I want mine,' Jack insisted, 'from Lady Muck here.'

'I'll do it if I must,' Jasmine said, finally rising from Tierney's lap.

She looked enchanting, having wiped her mouth, with her T-shirt barely covering her pussy, her nipples erect beneath the thin cotton and her panties halfway down at the back. Jack was not impressed.

'No thanks, Jas. I want Isabelle to learn how it feels to get a dose of her own medicine.'

'I already do, Jack, as you very well know.'

'Yeah, only because we fucking made you.'

'No. It was what I wanted, at the time.'

'Bollocks! You're just a stuck-up bitch, that's all. We had you 'cause you were too fucking scared to try and stop us. If you want to prove you ain't, suck my cock!'

'Fucking shut up, Jack!' Big Dave grated, making me immediately grateful, even if it was only because Caroline was sucking his cock.

'I shall prove it,' I stated, thinking just how easily Big Dave would be able to handle Jack if it came down to it. 'Excuse me, Caroline.'

Caroline came off Big Dave's cock, a bit reluctantly, because she had started to stroke her pussy and clearly wanted to come over what I'd made her do. I put my Champagne glass down, stood up and walked over to Big Dave, cool and calm. He looked up, grinning and holding his wet cock up, for my mouth. I got down, drew in the thick cock scent and took him in, making a deliberate show of working on him for his pleasure.

'Fuck, she's good,' he groaned, and took me firmly by the hair.

Jack's response was a envious grunt, which was immensely satisfying. I pulled up for just a moment.

'Touch me, Caroline, you too, Jasmine – make me come as I suck on David's lovely big cock.'

Caroline already had his balls out, and I began to lick them, showing off as the girls got down beside me. Jasmine's hands came around my waist, to pop the button of my jeans and ease my fly open, allowing her to pull them down, panties and all as Caroline lifted my top to take my breasts in hand.

'Make it dirty,' I told them, and gaped wide, to take the full bulk of Big Dave's scrotum into my mouth.

I took his cock, tugging gently as I sucked on his balls, rolling them over my tongue and mouthing on them, as rude as could be, all the while very aware of Jack's stare. I was showing behind, my bottom hole as well as my pussy, and as Jasmine's thumb slid up my hole I gave him a little wiggle, speaking as I pulled up from Big Dave's balls.

'You can masturbate if you like, Jack.'

Tierney gave a chuckle and I threw him a mischievous grin before taking Big Dave's cock back in my mouth, to suck more firmly, in the hope of getting a mouthful just as I came myself. I was going to as well, before too long, with Caroline holding me and stroking my breasts, which she'd laid bare, and Jasmine with her thumb in me as she teased my pussy and stroked my bottom.

'Stick some Chinese on it, Dave,' Tierney joked.

'Sure,' I answered. 'Caroline, a little sauce for Dave's cock, please.'

She giggled and one of the little polystyrene sauce cups was placed on Big Dave's spreading gut. It was the one for lemon chicken, bright yellow and so thick it didn't so much pour as ooze when I turned it up over Big Dave's erection. He let me get on with it, grinning down at me as the sauce spread slowly over his cock head and began to run down the shaft. I took him back in, sucking greedily as I gave my bottom a wiggle to return Jasmine's attention to bringing me off.

Her response was to slip the top of one finger up my bottom hole. I stuck it out, no longer posing at all as I was penetrated, but wanting to come and not really caring how. Big Dave was close too, his grip in my hair now tight, forcing me to keep my head down and jamming his erection deep into my throat. Jasmine's hand left my pussy and I gave another wiggle, more urgent, only to feel something round and squashy pushed to my hole as she began to feed the remains of the pork balls up my vagina.

It was hardly slavish behaviour, but I didn't care, sticking my bottom out for more. I got it, my pussy crammed full, ball after ball stuck well up with her fingers until I felt bloated, while the juice was stinging my flesh as it ran down between my lips. Her hand came around, under my belly, and she was masturbating me once more, now with my bottom on full show to the room, my stuffed hole plainly visible as I lifted a little to flaunt myself, thinking of Jack's anger and jealousy at how dirty we were being.

Caroline came down beside me, another tub in her hand, easing my head from Big Dave's erection to pour the glutinous brown hoi sin sauce over the cock head, even as I caught Jasmine's squeak of protest and her finger pulled from my bottom hole.

'Let a man do a man's job,' Jack grated, and even as Big Dave stuffed his sauce-laden cock back into my mouth, my hips were taken, hard.

I tried to struggle, wanting fucking but not by him, but they had me tight, ignoring the girls' protests. Then it was too late, and Jack's cock was in my hole. I was being fucked, at both ends, and there was nothing I could do about it, and I didn't really want to. The girls sensed my willingness, shutting up as their hands went back to my breasts and pussy, helping me towards orgasm even as I realised that Jack couldn't actually get his cock up me for the pork balls. His finger went up instead, scooping most of them out, then once more I'd been taken firmly by the hips and penetrated.

'You know the best thing about women?' he asked as he eased himself deep into me.

'What's that, Jack?' Big Dave responded, his voice thick as he pushed his cock head deep into my windpipe, the hoi sin sauce burning my throat.

'They're full of holes!' Jack laughed and began to fuck me.

I felt a pork ball burst in my pussy as he jammed himself deep, and a second, squashing out of my hole and into Jasmine's hand. He got faster, fucking in a tube of meat and soggy batter and sweet and sour sauce, making me feel impossibly bloated, bits of it squeezing out around his cock with each pump, but the feeling that I was about to burst only growing worse.

Jasmine was rubbing hard, and whispering to me, soothing me even as I was used, and Caroline too, kissing my shoulder and back as she pulled at my nipples. My body began to go tight, my pussy and bottom hole pulsing, even as Big Dave forced his cock deeper still into my windpipe, and as I began to choke I began to come.

'Like a pig on a fucking spit!' Tierney called from behind me, and Big Dave had come down my throat, his sperm pumping into me, milked out by my agonising retching, more and more, even as my body locked in orgasm.

A filthy mixture of sperm and mucus and yellow-brown sauce exploded from my nose and suddenly I could breathe again, snorting mess all over Big Dave's front as my whole body went into violent, involuntary contractions. Dimly I heard Jack grunt in ecstasy and knew that my pussy was now full of sperm as well as meat paste and batter, which brought me to my true peak, writhing, mindless orgasm, squirming on their cocks as they pumped me full of sperm, Jasmine's fingers still working on my clitoris, mess plopping into my dropped panties, every muscle in my body locked tight in the perfect, most glorious blend of agony and ecstasy.

Eleven

My fucking had really hurt, and left me bruised and sore. They had thoroughly abused me, or at least Jack had, yet I could hardly deny I'd enjoyed it. My climax had been so good, and for all I pretended to be angry once I'd finally finished coughing up sperm and Chinese sauce, I hadn't mean it, and it had showed.

Jack's argument was that with my rear view so rudely flaunted I was giving him an open invitation. I hadn't been, but I had been deliberately taunting him, and had wanted to be fucked, and he was the only man in the room who'd been in a position to do it. He also quite clearly enjoyed the idea of it having been against my will, so in the end I shyly admitted that it was what I had wanted all the time and left it at that.

I had to face facts. However much pleasure could be had with the crowd from the Red Ox, they simply didn't understand how sadomasochism works, at all. As Jasmine and Caroline explained to me as we sat drinking Champagne after the men had left, they divided women into two groups, wives and sluts. Subtleties such as sexual orientation and personal choice for who and how and when and where simply did not come into it. Jasmine and Caroline stripped and were therefore sluts. I was their friend and therefore also a slut. They didn't mind, regarding male behaviour with the same sort of resigned good humour they might have applied to a flood or some other natural disaster.

It was a little different for me because, while the men's basic need from Jasmine and Caroline was to get their cocks attended to, with me there was an element of spite, at least from some of them. Dave, Mo and many others but above all Stan Tierney took that attitude, deriving extra enjoyment from my pain and humiliation simply because I was a student and from a landed family. Big Dave was simply an oaf, and pretty rough, but with no real malice to him. Mike could be tough when it came to things like ensuring that strippers went all the way, but was kind enough underneath, as well as generous. Jack alone was a genuine misogynist.

Nasty or nice, I could have done without the lot of them had it not been for one thing – the sheer intensity of what they did to me. It was submissive heaven, and not something I wanted to lose, but they had to be controlled, at least at first. Once I was high they could do as they pleased, but it had to be on my terms. Jasmine and Caroline felt the same, more or less. They could handle it far better than I, and would not want to give it up. For them the occasional session at the Red Ox was about right, but for me it was simply not a safe place to be. There was too much spite mixed in with the lust.

Nor was the Rattaners going to be enough for me, not any more. As I'd abandoned my commitment to dominance in the pure form, so had I abandoned my commitment to lesbianism. I needed cock, if only in the context of my submissive desires, and I felt better for admitting to it for all the resulting aches and pains. There was considerable irony in that I now seemed to have a realistic chance of being accepted by the Rattaners, but I was more than happy to shelve my principles, at least for the time being.

That meant keeping Tierney sweet, and so on the Monday evening I took him a big box of chocolates and some flowers, then smeared a rose cream all over his cock and gave him a leisurely suck. He was suitably appreciative, and even apologised for not warning me when Jack was about to fuck me the night before. I accepted it, and even kissed him on the cheek before I left, having extracted his solemn promise that he would say nothing about my behaviour to Emmeline Young.

I took the rest of the week easy. Thursday was spanking day and I let Duncan do it, first over his lap and then touching my toes for a half-dozen of the belt with my panties in my mouth to keep me quiet. He then fucked me, doggy-style, before taking me to dinner at Gray's. The evening left me with a general feeling of well-being and a smarting bottom, which helped me to a pleasant but gentle orgasm before sleep.

Saturday was very much on my mind all day Friday. I was determined to behave, and not actually wrestle Sarah over my knee and spank her pink, despite the temptation. As well as behaviour, dress was obviously important. To judge by Portia, and Katie, and the whole Line Ladies thing, they liked their girls a little soppy and a little sassy. A Little Bo Peep costume would have been overdoing it, but not by much. It would also have been very difficult to ride in. Side-saddle was impractical, as was going stark naked but for a hard hat and boots, despite the temptation. In jodhpurs and pinks I was going to look a good deal more dominant than Sarah, but it was really my only choice. In the end I decided to soften it by going for a bottle-green jacket I managed to pick up for five pounds, a loose blouse with a slight frill, no bra and my hair in bunches tied with dark green ribbons. Inspecting myself in the mirror on the Friday evening it was hard to decide if I looked cute, like something out of a Thelwell cartoon, or both.

It was going to have to do, and at least I felt a great deal less silly than I had dressed up as a cowgirl. I set off, on foot, down to Carfax and the Eagle and Lamb, arriving early but with Sarah and Portia already there, and like me in full dress. We took a brief stirrup cup, our conversation strictly neutral, and left. Both of them looked wonderful, Sarah in pinks with her full bottom filling out her jodhpurs beneath the hem so nicely I didn't know if I wanted to smack it or kiss it. Portia was much like me, only in a black jacket and expensive corduroy jodhpurs, again making a glorious display of her bottom. She also had long black leather gloves, which gave her a dominant touch, and I wondered if Sarah had decided that she was senior enough to spank me.

There had to be a moment when the younger girls were initiated into dishing it out rather than taking it, and maybe Portia's was now. Maybe the younger girls even continued to take it until a replacement could be found, in which case that replacement looked like being me. The idea left me feeling excited and rebellious all at once, and as we drove out through West Oxford I was on edge, talking stupidly about the most trivial things while Sarah held her cool and Portia giggled between sidelong glances at me.

We stopped at a riding stable a good three or four miles beyond the Ring Road, in pretty wooded countryside with the villages nestling among little hills. The owner, a buxom blonde woman with a voice like a foghorn, seemed to know Sarah and Portia well, promising them their usual mounts and eyeing me with a gaze that I was not sure was entirely professional before selecting a fine bay hunter called Lady Louise. As we saddled up and mounted I was wondering if the stable owner was a Rattaner, but she gave no hint, and nor did we meet any others. If my surprise was to be introduced to the rest of them it was coming later, and we simply rode up into the woods as if nothing were out of the ordinary. I couldn't stop trembling, though, just from knowing that once we were deep enough in my panties were coming down.

Sarah really knew how to build up my tension, several times stopping and openly considering one site or another, most embarrassingly public, only to dismiss each in turn. We had ridden maybe four miles and I was lost beyond a vague idea of the points of the compass when she turned down a firebreak among a stand of mature pine, somewhere she seemed to know well. Sure enough, after a quarter of a mile it ended in a clearing, just over the brow of the hill we were on, with thick scrub and a pretty well impenetrable undergrowth of bramble, bracken and nettles in front of us. We were hidden, completely, and certainly a good distance from the nearest house.

'Here will do nicely,' Sarah stated, reining her horse in. 'Come up beside me, Isabelle, and I think for the time being I should be Miss Finch to you.'

'Yes, Miss Finch,' I answered, again feeling both rebellion and submission as I steered Lady Louise up beside her.

Portia had also come to a halt, almost directly beside me, her eyes bright with mischief.

'Bend forwards, Isabelle,' Sarah ordered. 'Take hold of her neck. I'm going to spank you.'

'Like this, on horseback?' I queried, but going down.

'It's not the first time Lady Louise has had a brat spanked on her back,' Sarah answered, 'and I did not hear you call me Miss Finch.'

'Sorry, Miss Finch.'

'You will be. Portia, find me a flower, something pretty.'

Portia dismounted, moving to the big pines behind us, beneath which were grasses and ferns and flowers. Sarah leaned out, her hand finding my bottom, to stroke the taut seat of my jodhpurs, gently, caressing me, then giving a little pat to each cheek.

'Very firm,' she remarked as she pushed her thumb down the waistband of my jodhpurs. 'Firm, but full. I shall enjoy this.'

Then my jodhpurs were coming down, slowly, peeled off my bottom as I lifted it to make it easier for her. My panties came on show, the tuck of my cheeks, the cup of my pussy mound, all thrust out above the saddle in a thoroughly rude pose that was about to get a great deal ruder.

'Nice and slow, let her feel it,' Portia remarked from behind me as Sarah took a firm grip of my panties.

I looked back. She had picked a little bunch of buttercups and was watching me with an impish smile as my panties began to come down, ever so slowly, my bottom laid bare inch by inch, the air cool on my skin, on my cheeks, between them, on my anus . . .

'Oh, what a rude bottom hole!' Portia laughed suddenly. 'All brown!'

'It's . . . it's just the way I am!' I sobbed, my rising humiliation hitting a sharp peak at her words.

She just giggled as Sarah took my panties down another few inches, and it was all showing, my bottom spread across the saddle, on blatant display, big and white and ready for punishment, a punishment anybody who came by was going to see, in detail. My legs were well splayed, my jodhpurs and panties taut between them, well down, hiding nothing but framing my bottom between them and my coat tails to make my exposure yet more extreme, more shocking for a viewer and more humiliating for me.

'Hand me your whip,' she instructed, 'and stick your bottom right up.'

I passed it across to her, then lifted my bottom. She turned the whip in her hand, the rounded base towards me, and I realised it was to be put up me a moment before it touched the mouth of my vagina and was pushed inside. I moaned as I was filled, thinking how absurd I'd look with a riding whip sticking out of my pussy hole. It was right, where my whip should go, to make me look foolish and show I had no right to use it, that or up my bottom. I was fairly sure that was where the flowers were going.

'Portia, the vase,' Sarah ordered.

Portia giggled as she peeled one glove off, then stuck her finger in her mouth. I felt my bottom hole twitch in expectation as she reached up, then open, along with my mouth as her spit-wet finger was pushed in, and not just a little way, but deep, right into my rectum.

'Portia, behave,' Sarah stated patiently.

All she got out of Portia was a giggle, but after a little more rummaging her finger was pulled out of my bottom.

'Can I make her suck it please, Sarah?' Portia asked.

'I suppose so,' Sarah sighed, and Portia's finger was presented to my mouth, wet and sticky.

I did hesitate, but the wicked, joyful gleam in her eyes was too much for me. My mouth came open, her finger went in and I was sucking on it as she went into a fresh fit of delighted giggles. I was shaking when she finally pulled her finger out, from the sensation of being open behind, of being used. She'd made me take the taste of my own bottom in my mouth, and now she was going to use my anus as a vase.

The flower stems touched my hole, all at once, then I felt them slip up, and it had been done, a pretty yellow posy now sprouting from my bottom hole to go with the whip up my pussy. I could picture myself, my bottom spread naked on Lady Louise's back, framed in dropped panties and coat tails, the whip sticking out, and a puff of yellow concealing my bottom hole and pussy lips.

Sarah edged her horse a little closer, took my bottom in hand, stroking me, then started to spank, little stinging slaps delivered with her fingertips, making my cheeks quiver and setting the flowers and whip trembling. I'd closed my eyes, concentrating on my humiliation and the slow warming of my bottom as my sense of submission rose, and my arousal. She kept spanking, gradually firmer, bringing me ever so slowly on heat, until I had let go and began to wriggle my bottom on the saddle, and to whimper.

'Forwards a little,' Sarah instructed. 'Put your sex on the pommel. You may masturbate as I whip you.'

I obeyed, rising to press my pussy to the smooth wooden saddle pommel. It was the perfect thing to rub on, round and hard, like an impossibly large cock head. I started, firmly, so that I could feel the whip wiggling in my pussy. The flowers were tickling my bottom, keeping in my mind how rude and silly I looked from the rear as my pleasure rose. Sarah was going to whip me, but it was not the moment to complain about marks. I wanted them, to show what I'd taken, and if Jasmine complained I'd give her the same treatment, only twice as much . . .

Sarah's riding whip cracked down on my bottom and I screamed in pain, a line of raw fire springing up across the flesh of my bottom as yellow petals showered down around my bottom and legs. For a moment I was off the pommel, then back, rubbing harder still. I screamed again as the second stroke caught me, harder and lower, really slamming into my bottom, but my pussy stayed on.

I was close, and getting closer as she laid in, whipping me mercilessly, perfectly, hard and fast, turning my bottom to a ball of pain as I screamed and gasped and writhed on the pommel. Then I was there, in a beautiful blend of pain and pleasure, rubbing myself as I was beaten. Portia was giggling madly, the little yellow posy sticking out of my bottom hole, the whip from my pussy, my flared cheeks hot and welted, in agony, and in ecstasy as it all came together in one long, glorious orgasm. Sarah was beating harder and harder as my holes went into contraction on their loads, and I was yelling, begging for more, and to be done harder, squirming my naked pussy on the pommel, my bottom wobbling crazily behind me, and still jumping to the cuts . . .

Which finished the instant my climax broke, Sarah timing it perfectly. I sank down, hugging Lady Louise's neck and whispering a thank you for her patience into her long, horsey ear. She gave a snicker in response, and mouthed up the sugar lump Portia was holding for her.

'She knows she gets one when she stays still,' Portia explained, and I managed a weak smile before finding my voice.

'Thank you, Sarah, that was glorious, so naughty . . .'

'That's Miss Finch to you, young lady,' she answered. 'We're not finished yet.'

I nodded, determined to take it, and give her pleasure in turn, however she wanted me. Not that I could move very easily, with the whip still in me, while my bottom crease was beginning to itch. Portia dealt with me, coming behind to ease the posy from my anus then extract the riding whip, which she stuck in my mouth. I sucked obediently, swallowing down my own cream, then dismounted at Sarah's command.

My legs felt a little weak, but I stood, knowing better than to try and sit down or to pull up my panties and jodhpurs. Sarah flicked my bottom with her whip, sending me stumbling to the centre of the little glade.

'Stand still, hands on your head,' she instructed. 'We're going to play a little game. Portia, her blouse.'

I'd put my hands on my head, and I kept them there as Portia came to me, smiling as she took my pussy in her hand, slipping her fingers between the lips to feel my wetness, then up, into my vagina.

'Portia!' Sarah snapped.

'Sorry, Miss Finch,' Portia answered, all insolence, but moving quickly enough.

She began to undo my blouse, popping the buttons open one by one until the last was done, then taking the sides and holding them apart to display my breasts. I closed my eyes as she took them in hand and stroked my nipples, scratching gently at the skin until I had once more begun to tremble.

'Enough,' Sarah instructed, just as I was beginning to wonder if Portia would bring me off again. 'Now, Isabelle, you will do exactly as I say.'

'Yes, Miss Finch.'

'Pull up your knickers.'

I obeyed, slightly puzzled, but bending to tug them up over my bottom as she came close, the riding whip in one hand. Standing beside me, she tapped it on my bottom, sending a little shiver of apprehension through me. I'd just come, and my cheeks were already smarting from the dozen or more hard cuts she'd laid in as I masturbated on the saddle. Yet if she wanted to whip me cold . . .

'Keep your hands in your waistband . . . a little forwards. Yes. Now, knickers down!'

It took me an instant to register and then I had pushed them down again. Immediately the whip cracked down on my bottom, wrenching a gasp from my mouth and leaving me shaking my head in reaction.

'Slow,' she stated, 'very slow. You will have to do better than that. Obey immediately and you will avoid the whip.'

'Yes, Miss Finch.'

'Knickers up!'

I jerked my panties up as fast as I could, but still shut my eyes in expectation of pain. It never came, Sarah speaking softly instead.

'Good girl, much better. Now . . . Knickers down!'

My panties were back down in an instant. I'd been expecting it, and it was impossible not to feel a little smug.

'Good girl,' she repeated, and her hand found my bottom, stroking her fingernails along the fresh welts she herself had inflicted.

I stayed still, letting her bring me slowly back on heat, then reacting the instant she gave the command, my panties once more pulled up and held in place, my thumbs in the waistband, ready to take them down again to order. She chuckled, then gave the order again, casually.

'Knickers down.'

They came down, smartly. Had they not done so I knew full well I'd have earned a whip stroke. Still the act of exposing myself had provoked a touch of humiliation, and I stayed apprehensive of her whip. Again she chuckled, and again she spoke.

'Knickers up. Good. Stick your bottom out a little. Yes, like that, nice and rude. Knickers down! Very good ... Portia is right, you do have a very rude bottom hole. Maybe you should put on weight so it doesn't show quite so blatantly when you're stripped, or maybe not ... Knickers up! Good girl, very fast, very obedient. Knickers down! Excellent. Knickers up! Knickers down! Knickers up! Knickers down! Knickers up! Knickers down! Knickers up! Knickers down! Knickers ...'

I reacted, jerking them frantically up and down, covering and exposing myself, in greater confusion and feeling a little jolt of shame every single time my pussy and bottom came on show. At last she stopped and I was left, my panties at half mast, the waistband gripped firmly in my hands, panting a little and feeling utterly humiliated, and ready to serve her, and Portia too. She came in front of me and tilted my chin up with her finger.

'Do you know what a conditioned reflex is, Isabelle?'

'Yes, Miss Finch, I think so. It's when an animal is taught to react instinctively to a signal. Someone did it with dogs, didn't they?'

'Yes, Pavlov,' she answered, 'and it is a technique I have borrowed in order to deal with brats like Portia and yourself. You see, Isabelle, a girl can be given a conditioned reflex, just like a dog. Even if I were to whisper my command to Portia, in the High perhaps, she would react. Obviously she would catch herself before she actually pulled her knickers down in public, but the urge would be there. I intend to do the same to you.'

'Yes, Miss Finch,' I answered, horrified at the idea of having it done to me yet extremely aroused by it.

'By the end of term we might already have you trained, with luck,' she went on. 'Knickers down!'

I whipped them quickly down and she laughed. Portia was behind her, still smiling, but a little nervous now. I could imagine why, if she'd been conditioned to pull her panties down to Sarah's order and had just heard the command so many times in succession. I smiled back, thinking it was about time she was punished herself, even if it was side by side with me. It was Sarah's choice, though.

'Would you like to come again, Isabelle?'

'Please, Miss Finch, yes,' I answered quickly, 'unless you would prefer me to serve you, or Portia, of course.'

'Perhaps,' she said, 'although I am not certain that is a privilege you have yet earned. What do you think, Portia? She wants to lick me?'

'I think you should tie her to a tree with her panties stuffed and make her watch me do it,' Portia answered, in good humour, but with a touch of jealousy nonetheless.

'Sorry, Miss Finch, sorry, Portia,' I said quickly. 'I didn't mean to intrude.'

'I'm sure you didn't, my dear,' Sarah answered, 'but it is rather a nice suggestion anyway. Come then, Portia, run along.'

Portia ran giggling into the trees, and to my horror began to pick stinging nettles. There were plenty about, lush green ones that looked as if they would sting dreadfully, and my trembling grew abruptly worse. I could imagine the pain, although I'd never been nettled whipped, because I'd been stung often enough, and this would be on my bottom, my bare, welted bottom . . .

She didn't take long, emerging from the woods in about a minute, with both hands full of bushy, bright green nettles. With her gloves and jacket sleeves she was fine, but I wasn't, still holding my panties down and completely vulnerable, front and back. My hands would be worse, I knew, so I quickly put them on my head, a gesture they took as surrender.

Portia came behind and my stomach went tight. Sarah took my panties down a little further. One bunch of nettles was pushed rudely down them, prickling my thighs with stings which grew to hot pain in an instant. My panties and jodhpurs were held out, the second bunch stuffed down and the whole lot hauled up around my bottom. Immediately my skin was suffused with an agonising tingling, which grew quickly worse, until I was gasping for breath in my pain yet with my thighs clamped tight together to spare my pussy and the sensitive skin around my anus.

I craned back over my shoulder, carefully, to find the whole rear of my jodhpurs bulging out, fat and lumpy with the packed nettles. Portia stepped forward again, beckoning me as she started towards the stand of pines where she had picked the posy for my bottom hole. I followed, with awkward little steps, yet every one was still hot agony, and worse for my whipping, the stings turning my welts to lines of liquid fire. They were both in among the pines long before I got there, and by the time I did I was gritting my teeth against the pain, and the sheer frustration of it too. The first of my tears broke free as I reached the little patch of grass where they were standing, and as Portia saw her sadistic grin turned to sympathy.

'Are you OK?'

'Yes. Just let me cry.'

She gave an understanding nod and reached into her pocket, to pull out a length of brown gardening twine. Sarah just watched as I was pulled gently backwards and my hands taken behind the tree, squashing the packed nettles yet tighter against my skin and adding fresh stings to my misery. My hands were tied, lashed together around the trunk to leave me completely helpless, my bottom and thighs on fire, struggling not to wriggle because I knew it would only make it worse. It had made my bladder feel weak too, and I was shaking my head against the reactions of my body as Portia went to Sarah and knelt down.

Sarah looked cool, wonderfully poised, even as she pushed down her jodhpurs and the silky black panties beneath. Bare, she crossed her hands against the trunk of a big pine directly opposite me and stuck her bottom out, full and feminine, her cheeks parted to show the swelling lips of her sex and the pink dimple of her anus. Portia shuffled close, put her face between her Mistress's bottom cheeks and began to lick.

I was wishing it was me, and imagining the taste and feel of Sarah's pussy, her bottom too, because Portia had started by inserting her tongue in her Mistress's anus. She was going to do herself too, I realised as she quickly raised her hips to push down her own clothes, exposing her beautiful meaty bottom to me. Her cheeks were full and round, every bit as spankable as I had imagined, and lickable. Between them her anus was a glistening pink hole, and her pussy plump and pink and wet, the mound shaved like Caroline's.

She was licking Sarah firmly, and I wanted to do the same to her, to be the slave's slave, my tongue in her bottom hole and on her clitoris even as she gave her Mistress the same service. Had I been free I'd have done it, grovelling behind her, or laid flat to let her sit on my face. I couldn't, capable only of watching them take their pleasure as I squirmed in my pain.

My reserve broke as Sarah began to sigh in ecstasy, and I was wriggling my bottom in the nettles, in serious pain, near blind with tears, yet rubbing myself in wanton submission. Suddenly my legs were wide, allowing the nettles to my precious pussy lips and between my cheeks, even as Sarah cried out in ecstasy, a sound echoed by Portia moments later as they came together. Still I writhed, now desperate to come myself, my vision a blur as I squirmed my open bottom against the tree, rubbing the nettles on my anus and on my pussy, then stopping as I heard Sarah's voice.

'Pull down her knickers, Portia, then untie her and let the poor thing put herself out of her misery.'

'Please, yes . . . ,' I gasped. 'Please, Miss Finch.'

Portia came to me, quickly tugging the knot at my wrists loose. I stepped forwards, to push down my jodhpurs and panties, desperate to touch myself. My whole bottom was a great burning ball of tortured flesh, throbbing with pain, agonisingly sensitive, too tender to touch by far, yet it was exactly what I wanted to do, what I needed to do. My hands went back, to caress the swollen hemispheres of my cheeks, stroking the punished flesh. My skin felt oddly thick, and hard, and hot to the touch. Portia's gloved fingers found the groove of my pussy and she was rubbing me, my pleasure rising to the point of orgasm immediately.

I pulled my cheeks open, finding my crease full of nettle leaves which stung my hands, and my anus too as I penetrated myself, deep in, to probe my slippery little hole as I was masturbated. She put one finger up my vagina, pushing more nettle pulp in, and I was screaming as I started to come, squirming myself about in blinding ecstasy, my whole existence centred on the pain of my bottom and between my legs.

She took me off, very casually, all the way, still rubbing until I slumped down in total exhaustion, dizzy and weak, but so, so thankful, both to Portia and to Sarah.

Twelve

Rattaners or not, Sarah and Portia certainly knew how to handle me. The idea of being trained to make submissive responses by instinct was truly sinister, and appealed immensely. They had taken me far beyond where I had expected to go as well, and not because I'd felt I had to, but because I'd wanted to. It had hurt like anything after my second orgasm, and riding back with my bottom covered in nettle rash was agony, so bad I had to stand in the stirrups most of the way, which Portia inevitably found hilarious.

They had said nothing about the Rattaners, and I hadn't asked, sure that if they wanted to tell me they would do so. Even when we parted, after a friendly cuddle with Portia and a more reserved kiss from Sarah, I was still unsure if they intended to introduce me or wanted me to themselves. It did occur to me that it might be done gradually, one new person at a time, either so as to break me in gently, or because of internal club politics.

What I was sure of was that the Rattaners existed. Portia had mentioned 'Lizzie', obviously Elizabeth Hastings, again, and drawn a sharp look from Sarah. Also, the day had been planned from the first, every detail worked out in advance. Why else would Portia have been wearing leather gloves if not to protect her hands from the nettles? She had had twine in her pocket too, and they'd known about the glade we'd used. That suggested experience and a body of knowledge more typical of a club than individuals. They'd spanked me in the saddle too, as I'd asked to be spanked at Fieldfare Hall, although this time on a real horse, a horse who was used to having girls beaten while riding her. Lastly, they had told me my conditioning would begin in a few days, and that someone would come and collect me. If somebody other than the two of them turned up, it would be the final proof.

I was on tenterhooks from then on, starting at every knock on my door, and leaving little apologetic notes even when I went to hall or to visit people. Tierney wasn't going to be back at work for a while, so I couldn't ask him questions, but I did want to talk. I told Jasmine and Caroline almost the entire story, and even showed Caroline the mess of welts and nettle rash on my bottom, which she thought so funny I had to put her over my knee then and there.

There was also my birthday to think about, and I was determined to make the best of it. If I'd been accepted by then, Portia's idea of giving me a birthday caning might be made real, while I also wanted to celebrate in style with Jasmine and Caroline, and maybe Laura Soames too. It might mean two parties, but I could live with that.

The knock came on Wednesday. I was in my room, polishing up my essay with a few annotations, which Duncan always liked to see. I heard a footstep on the landing and my heart gave the now familiar jump. For a moment nothing happened and I thought the visitor might be for my neighbour, then came a tap, barely audible.

'Come in!' I called, turning in my seat to see a head poke cautiously around the door, a blonde head, with a bob haircut, a snub nose and freckles – Katie.

'Hello!' I greeted her, not even attempting to keep the sheer delight out of my voice. 'I didn't expect you, I must say! Sit down.'

'Thanks,' she answered. 'I'm not bothering you, am I? Because if this isn't a good time ...'

'No, no, I've nearly finished.'

She sat down and folded her hands in her lap, looking desperately embarrassed, with her cheeks and neck flushed pink, so that I wondered if she had been told to do something rude, or even to accept some humiliation from me.

'I ... I've been thinking,' she began, obviously struggling to get the words out, 'about ... about what you said at Line Ladies that evening.'

'Yes?'

'Well ... well ... would you? I mean ... do you? No, this is really stupid of me, I ...'

'No, not at all,' I said quickly as she made to get up, her face now flaming scarlet. 'Whatever it is, Katie, just say! I understand.'

She stopped, and sat down again. I realised she was actually crying, and went over to her, taking her hand in mine. They had obviously made some really severe demand of her, perhaps more than she could cope with. I wanted to make it all right, and to find out what it was.

'Don't worry, Katie,' I told her, 'you can tell me, whatever it is. After all, look at me at Fieldfare Hall, it can't be worse than that!'

She managed a tear-stained smile, wiped her hand across her face, then spoke.

'It ... it is that. That's what I want to talk about. I ... I ... I want to be spanked.'

She had closed her eyes, her face screwed up, a picture of misery and shame. I took her in my arms, kissed her, and very gently pulled her to her feet. She came, looking uncertain, her body shaking hard as I sat back down on my hard chair, taking her with me, across my lap.

'It's all right,' I soothed as she gave a little whimper. 'Just let me take over.'

Her response was a single, miserable nod. She was still crying, but she made no effort to get up. Her bottom was a dream, a perfect ball of cheeky girl flesh in her low cut white jeans, and she was pushing herself up on her toes, which could only mean one thing. She wanted to go bare, or at the least down to her panties. It seemed odd that she was so shy, but with her across my lap it was not the time to argue about it.

I slid a hand under her tummy, to find the button of her jeans and pop it open. She gave another little whimper as I eased her zip down, and again as I began to push her jeans off her hips. They were tight, and I had to use both hands, squeezing her soft, pale flesh to expose the top of her bottom crease and a pair of little pink panties, taut over her cheeks. She held still, letting me take her jeans right down to her ankles, then laid herself down on my lap, bottom high and quivering slightly. There was a faint scent of perfume, something vaguely citrus I didn't recognise.

She clearly needed to be soothed, and I spent a moment stroking her hair and the nape of her neck, then her bottom, smoothing the pink cotton out over the roundness of her cheeks. The urge to just twist her arm into the small of her back and give her a thorough spanking was strong, but I held back, uncertain of her mood. She gave no response to my touches, completely given over to me, but still sobbing gently, and I decided to take it as easily as possible.

'May I pull your panties down, Katie?' I asked as I took hold of them.

She nodded, a single urgent motion, and I did it, easing them down over the smooth creamy skin of her cheeks, exposing her fully, her crease a dark valley with the little lines of her anal star just visible. I wanted to push a finger up, and make her suck it the way Portia had done to me, but again I was sure it would be too harsh. Instead I adjusted her panties around her thighs, well enough down to make sure she knew her pussy was showing at the back, tucked my arm around the slimness of her waist and gently, methodically, began to spank her.

At the very first pat she let out a long, heartfelt sigh, as if I had tapped some great well of emotion. Why it should be so strong I had no idea, but I was determined to make a thorough job of her and continued to spank, making my slaps gradually harder, with my own passion rising too. Soon she'd begun to pink up, her pale skin taking on colour very easily, and her cheeks to bounce and part, showing off the tight pink bud of her bottom hole. She had stopped crying, but was giving little gasps with each slap.

'There, is that better, Katie?' I asked. 'Is that what you wanted?'

'Yes,' she sighed, 'that is lovely . . . so lovely . . . thank you, Isabelle, thank you . . . and you can be a little harder if you like.'

'I do,' I answered, and gave her a full-bodied swat across her cheeks to make her squeal and buck.

She didn't complain, and I kept at it, her squeals rising in pitch and volume as her pain grew, and the slaps of my hand on her bottom flesh began to echo around the room. I stopped, her bottom now a glowing ball of pink.

'You . . . you don't have to stop,' she gasped. 'I can take more . . . I think.'

'I'm sure you can,' I answered, 'and I'm not stopping. It's just getting a little noisy, that's all. You wouldn't want all the people walking through quad to know you have to have your bottom smacked, would you?'

She gave an embarrassed giggle as I leaned out to pull the window catch to. I was aroused, but no more than she was, her perfume now lost beneath the aroma of excited pussy. Still I thought it best to ask, but I was already pushing the first of her trainers off as I did so.

'I'm going to strip you,' I told her, 'and put your panties in your mouth so you don't squeal too much. Then I'm going to give you a proper spanking.'

'Yes, Isabelle,' she answered meekly and I felt the familiar thrill of sadism and control.

Her shoes off, her socks followed, then her jeans, and the little pink panties. She needed her breasts out too, or rather I did, and I quickly tugged her top up and spilled them out of her bra, taking a moment to feel the twin handfuls of heavy, soft flesh and the hard nipples on top of each. She was bigger than me, for all her small size, if not so generous as Caroline, and it felt wonderful to have her in my hands, bare and yielding. It was hard to let go.

'Do . . . do you normally feel a girl's boobs when you spank her?' she asked after a while.

'If it pleases me,' I answered. 'Now open wide.'

I picked up her panties and presented them to her mouth, pushing them in between her lips, all the way, until only a tiny puff of pink cotton showed between her teeth. Taking hold of her waist once more, I went back to her spanking, now hard. She was rosy, her bottom really glowing, with the goose-pimples coming up and a sheen of sweat beginning to rise. Her pussy was juicing too, the scent thick in the air, and her open bottom hole twitching to the slaps, as if she were winking at me. I got harder still, thinking of how I would make her lick me when I'd finished with her, have her kiss my anus, sit on her face maybe . . .

She stuck it up, suddenly, right up, her cheeks spreading to show off her bottom hole and pussy lips in detail. I slapped my hand in, right over her pussy, where the fat of her cheeks met her thighs, and again, and again, as hard as I could as I realised she was coming, spanked to orgasm by the sheer effect of my slaps on her clitoris. Her anus was pulsing, her pussy hole too, squashing out white juice then opening, ready to be filled as she came in a shuddering, heaving climax, her bottom cheeks still bouncing under the slaps, her legs holding her bottom rigid in the air.

I stopped the moment her muscles went slack, panting, my hand stinging crazily and much the same colour as her bottom. She'd spat her panties out and was gasping for breath, still limp across my lap, then she was on the floor, her face crimson with embarrassment. I took her into my arms, quickly, cuddling her to my chest before she could speak and holding her there, her body shaking hard. She made to speak, but I had to come, and with her, which was only fair.

'Sh!' I told her. 'My turn. Come on.'

'Wh – what?'

'You're going to lick my pussy. Don't you want to?'

She nodded, looking up at me wide-eyed as I released her. Her expression was full of uncertainty, but I was having no nonsense, and quickly pulled up my dress and eased my panties to the floor. Spreading my thighs, I took a gentle hold of the back of her head and pulled her in, not hard, but just firmly enough to let her know I was determined. There was no resistance. Her mouth met my flesh, her tongue came out, and she was licking, clumsily but eagerly enough, big, wet laps running from my pussy hole right up to my clitoris.

I looked down, watching her, her pretty, freckled face framed in bedraggled blonde hair, her boobs swinging free, her red bottom stuck out behind, her tongue busy with my sex. She looked absolutely enchanting, so beautiful and so naïve, so innocent yet so wanton. I was going to come, and tightened my grip in her hair, pulling her in, and down, her little snub nose on my clitoris, her mouth over my bottom hole.

'Lick,' I gasped as my climax hit me, 'lick my bottom . . . show me you're really grateful.'

There was a moment of resistance, and then she was doing it, her tongue tip licking up and down in my crease, deep between my cheeks, on my anus and in my vagina as I rubbed myself off in her face, using her nose to frig on. I screamed out as I came, far too high to care who heard, completely focusing on my own body and on Katie's and what I had done to her, what I was doing with her face.

I let go the moment I had started to come down, almost slipping from the chair. She sat back, her pretty face smeared with my cream, wide-eyed and blushing, her little plump breasts heaving with her gasps. I smiled and leaned forwards to kiss her, tasting myself on her lips, and in her mouth as it came open under mine, our tongues meeting in a long, sticky snog.

'Thank you, Katie,' I sighed when we finally broke apart. 'That was lovely, and not at all what I expected.'

'What did you expect?' she asked shyly as I passed her a tissue.

'Some ferocious old domina, I suppose,' I answered. 'I certainly didn't expect to be doing the spanking, but I'm glad I did.'

'So am I,' she answered with a giggle. 'That was sweet, and ever so rude! You are terrible, what you made me do. But how do you mean you were expecting a domina?'

'From the way Sarah goes on I didn't think I was going to be allowed to give spankings, not for ages!'

'Sarah?'

'Sarah Finch.'

'I don't know her. Is she into spanking too? Does she spank you?'

'Yes . . . of course. You must know who I mean. She's the catering manager at Erasmus Darwin. Dark-haired, medium build. She sent you, surely?'

'No, really. I came because . . . because I wanted to come. I've wanted to come since the night I met you and you said . . . what you said to Emmy Young.'

'Emmeline Young told you to come, then? Maybe Sarah spoke to her.'

'No, nothing like that. I . . . I've just always had this thing about being spanked, but . . . but I thought it was weird, that I was the only one . . . and . . . and then there was you.'

She shrugged. I gave her another kiss, just for reassurance, then stood up, adjusting my dress and kicking my somewhat soiled panties off. I took a new pair, wondering why the Rattaners would simply not admit their existence to me. Surely, after Sarah, and now Katie, I could be trusted? Maybe Katie had been sent as a test, to see if I would spank her?

I'd had enough.

'Tidy up and get dressed,' I told her. 'We're going to Bede College, to see a girl called Portia.'

'Why?'

'I suspect you know very well why.'

'Is she into spanking?'

'Is she into spanking!' I snorted.

She did as she was told, ever so meek as we walked the short distance from St George's to Bede's. I found out where Portia's room was from a surly and ancient porter, took Katie firmly by the hand and led her after me, across a tiny quad and up a flight of stairs, to a first-floor room with a neat hand-written label beside the door – Portia Anson-Jones. I knocked, and Portia herself opened the door, her face wreathed in wicked smiles the moment she saw me, then she looked puzzled but no less wicked as she realised Katie was with me. Wicked, yes, but there was not the slightest glimmer of recognition.

'Sit down,' I ordered, pointing to Portia's bed, the surface of which was almost entirely hidden beneath cuddly toys.

Katie went quickly. Portia made to speak but obeyed, looking a little sulky as she moved an enormous green and yellow dragon to make space for herself.

'Do you two know each other?' I demanded.

'No,' they chorused, and shared a look.

Portia tapped her finger meaningfully against her temple. Katie just looked worried. I sighed.

'Portia,' I went on, 'tell me the truth, or I am going to take your panties down and spank you until your bottom is the colour of a Victoria plum . . .'

'Yes, please!'

'Shut up, I'm being serious. Katie here is a member of the so-called Line Ladies, as I am convinced you know. So is Lady Emmeline Young, the wife of your Master here at Bede's. She was a close friend of Elizabeth Hastings, who also introduced Sarah Finch to spanking, and to the Rattaners' Club. Yes?'

'Elizabeth who?'

'Portia, do not play games. That is a very fine long-handled hairbrush on your dresser, and I am in the mood to use it on your bottom.'

'Any time, but I don't know what you're talking about.'

'Elizabeth Hastings, Portia,' I said patiently. 'Lizzie, who used to give Sarah enemas before she spanked her, as you told me.'

'No.'

'Yes you did.'

'No, I didn't. That's what Lizzie used to do to Sarah, sure, only I wasn't supposed to tell you, and if you tell her she'll –'

'Shut up, Portia, you're wittering. Did Elizabeth Hastings . . . Lizzie Hastings if you prefer, introduce Sarah to spanking? Elizabeth Hastings, pupil to Dr Margaret Coln, lately Reader in English Literature at Lady Maud College? I know all about it, you see.'

'No, not Lizzie Hastings, whoever she is – Lizzie Abbott, Dr Eliza Abbott. She was a biologist, an ethologist to be exact, hence the conditioned reflex.'

'Dr Eliza Abbot? But . . .'

'Yeah, she was really into it. Sarah was working in the kitchen at Erasmus . . .'

'Never mind that. So you don't know about Elizabeth Hastings? You must do! How did Sarah . . .'

A dreadful truth was dawning on me as she went on, her voice even, playful, completely honest.

'I was telling you. It was fifteen years ago, when it was just about getting OK to admit you were lesbian. Lizzie was in the original university lesbian society,

233

which is why Sarah went to her, but she found she'd bitten off a bit more than she could chew, at first anyway. She may seem confident now, but not then. I'll tell you what Lizzie did – she conditioned Sarah so that at the command "wet!" she'd pee herself. How cruel can ... actually, I shouldn't really have said that.'

'Never mind,' I answered her. 'Seriously, don't you know anyone else who's into spanking, or anything else kinky?'

'No. Only you, and we have a few contacts on the net, but not in Oxford, and ... maybe you?'

She had turned to Katie, the wicked look back on her face. Katie blushed.

'Never mind Katie, just answer my question,' I insisted, although I was now sure she was telling the truth. 'You promise? Not Lady Emmeline Young?'

'Lady Young! You have to be joking!'

'No, I'm not,' I managed, almost begging. 'Haven't you heard of Margaret Coln? Hope Ashdene? You two really don't even know each other, do you? Katie? Please tell me ...'

I was close to tears, and both of them looked genuinely concerned.

'I ... I thought there was a club,' I went on, 'for people like us, I really did. Tell me, please? You know you can trust me ... you certainly do, Portia!'

'It's a wonderful idea,' Portia admitted, 'but I've never heard of it.'

'Nor have I,' Katie added.

'But that's just not possible!' I insisted. 'Everything made sense, everything Tierney told me ...'

'Tierney? Stan Tierney?' Katie queried.

'Yes. You know him, then?'

'Sure, he sweeps up after Line Ladies' evenings. He's been doing it for donkey's years, so Emmy says.'

Stan Tierney had made a complete fool of me. He had worked the whole thing out, based on his knowledge of the Line Ladies, and of me, from first to last. It was immensely galling, not only because of the way I had been used, but because I had been so easily duped. I was supposed to be the intelligent one, and even if Tierney did have something like forty years of experience on me, there was really no excuse for my naïvety. He might be a college servant, vulgar, coarse and ill-educated, but he was no fool. On the way back from Bede's I swore to myself that I would never again make the mistake of assuming somebody was stupid simply because their place in life suggested it.

I sulked until the Thursday, and that afternoon allowed myself to be put across Duncan Appledore's knee for a long, hard spanking. I didn't tell him, but in my head it was a punishment for being so stupid, and it certainly made me feel better. Afterwards I gave him a long, loving suck, licking his balls and anus too, which delighted him, then going back across his knee to be masturbated to orgasm. The experience left me feeling castigated if not fully resolved, and I decided that, Rattaners or no Rattaners, I was having my birthday party.

Duncan was an obvious choice for a guest, although I wasn't sure he would risk coming, given that he was a don. To my delight he accepted, stipulating only that the party be well outside Oxford. I had to agree. The city was out of the question for a venue, college premises for obvious reasons, Jasmine's house in case we got gatecrashed by the entire regular mob from the Red Ox. Hiring Fieldfare Hall struck me as an amusing possibility, but there was a much better first choice, which was Laura's.

She agreed with enthusiasm, asking only that I keep the number of men to a reasonable minimum and make sensible choices in general. I gave her my promise and set to work selecting a suitable group. None of my fellow undergraduates were even worth a thought, except Rory, and it was hardly fair on Samantha to invite her boyfriend to a sex party.

Portia was good, so wholesome, so proper, yet so dirty. She was spoilt, no question, but the delightful thing about her was that she knew it, and what should be done about it. Obviously I would have to invite Sarah as well, and I did want to. The thought of getting Portia alone for a little spanking play and sex then taking the consequences from Sarah was intriguing in the extreme.

With Jasmine and Caroline, Portia made three submissive girls, Katie four if she could get over her shyness and insecurity. Laura had said she would attempt to get Pippa to come, which then made five, which was surely enough to keep me busy. What Sarah would make of it I wasn't sure, but the non-existence of the Rattaners had somewhat changed our relationship, at least from my perspective.

I wanted more men, but the right men. There was really only the crowd from the Red Ox, and then only the ones who could be counted on to behave. Mike was at least responsible, and if I wasn't entirely trustful of Big Dave, his presence would at least ensure that any local gatecrashers could be dealt with. That made three, which was quite enough.

Another good reason for inviting some men from the Red Ox was that I could do so in front of Tierney, and pointedly not include him. It was a pretty pathetic revenge, but I was going to do it anyway. Jasmine and Caroline were stripping at the Red Ox on the Friday, which made it ideal to issue my invitations in front of him, but obviously not giving away the venue.

I drove up with them and came in by the back, early, when only a few people were about. Mike was there, and Big Dave, as well as Jack, Mo and the other Dave, playing cards around a table with two men I didn't know. Stan Tierney was also with them, laughing at some joke as he lifted his pint of Guinness to his mouth, with the arm that was supposed to be broken.

He never even saw me coming. Five swift paces took me across the room, and his pint was in my hand even as he lowered it to the table, then over his head as I poured it out. He was spluttering and swearing on the instant, then cursing me and calling me a mad bitch as he realised who it was. It didn't stop me, and his cursing grew rapidly worse as I grabbed him by the collar, hauled him to his feet and threw him down across my knee as I dropped into a chair.

The instant he realised he was to be spanked he went absolutely berserk, trying to hit me, trying to kick me, swearing and cursing, calling for his friends to help. They just stared, amazed, as I laid in, holding on like grim death to his thrashing body and be-labouring his scrawny little buttocks with every ounce of strength in my body.

I heard Caroline's laughter behind me, then Big Dave's, and suddenly they were all laughing, except Tierney. He kept cursing and swearing and threatening, but I kept spanking, indifferent to his fighting, to the stinging of my hand, to the flash of Mike's camera, and to the exclamations of shock as half a dozen other regulars came in the door.

Only when he had finally managed to writhe himself off my lap did I stop. He fell on the floor and I stood up, breathing hard, to look on him as he crawled quickly away, scrambled to his feet and ran.

For a moment there was silence, then Caroline began to clap, and Jasmine, and Mike, laughing too as I walked back the way I had come. In the end it was Jasmine who issued the invitations.

My actual birthday was on the Thursday, for which Duncan spanked me, presented me with a pearl necklace, took me to dinner and presented me with a real pearl necklace. It was a wonderful evening, and the night as good, spent in bed with Jasmine and Caroline, who provided immaculate service.

The session with Duncan meant I'd had my birthday spanking, and I was having no nonsense about my role at Laura's. Jasmine, Caroline and I drove up early, to adjust one of the uniforms. Laura had selected it, cavalry dress with captains' insignia. There was a superbly cut scarlet jacket, black trousers with a red stripe down the leg, as well as a peaked cap, which was not strictly correct but added another couple of inches to the six foot two I made in my heels. With my hair up and the barest trace of make-up, I might have been mistaken for a young male officer, slightly effete perhaps, and it wouldn't work close-up, but I was immensely pleased with the image.

Laura dressed to match, a rank senior, and with a certain mature authority I had to envy, but not really carrying it off the way I did. We put Caroline and Jasmine in work detail fatigues, baggy green outfits that made them look a fine pair of little scruffs. Yet it was still cute, with the material stretched taut over their bottoms and in Caroline's case her breasts, with the buttons absolutely straining, to show off a good slice of soft pink cleavage.

Pippa arrived while we were still finishing. She was a pretty, brown-haired woman of about thirty, with a natural shyness that appealed immediately to me as submissive, despite her being so much older than me. Laura ordered her to get a private's uniform, straightforward battledress, then opened a bottle of wine. In no time the five of us were chatting as if we'd known each other intimately for years.

The next person to arrive was Duncan Appledore, bringing a magnum of Champagne. He was delighted by our look and, in full black tie himself, fitted in well enough. As we started on our second bottle I was already considering the possibilities for play, and when Mike phoned from the town to be given his final directions I decided that with the men there we would need a little show to break the ice. After that I had one or two little debts to settle, but not until my victims were drunk, aroused and had been lulled into a false sense of security.

Mike and Big Dave arrived with Katie, who they'd found looking lost in the lane and had tried to chat up on principle. Big Dave was actually in black tie, and looked every inch a bouncer, while Mike had put on a shiny blue suit straight out of the 80s. Katie was simply in jeans and a roll-necked top, but still looked very sweet, especially as she was fidgeting and pink-faced with embarrassment. She accepted a glass of Champagne and quickly allowed herself to be taken under Laura's wing as Jasmine, Caroline and I looked after the men and Pippa prepared food.

I had almost decided to start anyway when Sarah and Portia finally arrived, both in their riding gear. By then I was already feeling a little drunk, and ready to play, but with so few of them knowing one another and so many of the women lesbian it was clear to me we would need Laura and Pippa's performance. Pippa, fortunately, had no qualms whatever, and as she was the one who was going to be exposed, that was what mattered.

With everybody seated, drinks in hand, I told Laura she could start at her leisure and brought Katie over to sit on the sofa with Jasmine and Caroline. I caught a lust filled glance from Big Dave as I gave her bottom a pat to send her in the right direction, and wagged a finger at him. If Jasmine had done her work then he knew what he was and was not allowed to do: basically what I and the other dominant women permitted.

I settled back to watch, with my arms around Jasmine, and Katie and Caroline curled up at my feet. It felt particularly good, being entirely in control, with three pretty submissive girls as mine and a show about to be performed to my order. Not only that, but it was all the result of my hard work, risk-taking, and not a few upsets, never mind the assorted spankings and humiliations.

Pippa came out from the carriage, marching smartly to a spot at the centre of the room, where she came to attention. Laura followed at an easy walk, a swagger-stick in one hand, which she tapped menacingly against her palm as she made a slow circle around Pippa. Coming to the front again, she spent a moment looking at the bulging chest of Pippa's uniform with every evidence of distaste, tucked the swagger-stick under one arm, put her hands into the front, and ripped it wide.

We'd fixed the buttons, but it still looked great as they popped off, the blouse beneath ripping, and the bra too, leaving Pippa with two plump little breasts sticking out at the room, bare and round. Her nipples were big, puffy, and distended, so that they looked like teats. I could just imagine her embarrassment, and she was shaking hard as her tunic was jerked down from her shoulders to trap her arms at her sides.

Again Laura made a slow circuit. Pippa stood still, but with her naked breasts quivering in her emotion and a muscle in one leg twitching slightly. Laura reached the front, used the swagger-stick to tilt Pippa's chin back up, and continued. Behind, she paused once more, then took hold of the hem of Pippa's skirt and tugged it smartly up, exposing frilly blue panties over a full bottom, round, soft and very spankable.

Pippa's trembling was growing harder as her skirt and the tails of her tunic were tucked up, leaving her big panties on full show. Again Laura made a circuit, letting Pippa's humiliation sink in with her breasts bare and her panties exposed, then whipped them smartly down, one smooth motion and it was all bare. I heard Pippa sob as she was stripped, but she stayed put, with now her back and front, breasts, pussy and bottom all nude among the tangled mess of her uniform.

I thought she'd get it standing, which would have been a treat, but Laura was not finished. She clicked her fingers, pointing at Pippa's boots with an order to touch the gleaming toecaps. Pippa went down, her full bottom spreading as she reached for her toes, to show off the thick fur of her pussy mound, chubby pink lips and a soft, well-puckered anus. Her cap fell off, rolling to near my feet, so I quickly picked it up and balanced it on Pippa's back, as if her bottom were her face. Big Dave laughed, but the others stayed silent, watching as Laura stood back and tapped the long swagger-stick carefully across the meatiest part of Pippa's bottom.

It was given hard, twelve firm cuts, every one of which Pippa was made to count, with her trembling and the richness of emotion in her voice rising each time. She was a brave girl, though, braver than I'd have been, and never broke her pose, or cried, merely snivelling slightly with the final three. With it done, her beautiful bottom was left decorated with a dozen parallel lines and her pussy was more than a little juicy. As she was married I wondered if Laura would allow her to be fucked, and what her husband made of her bruises.

Beaten and humiliated, she was sent into one corner to stand with her hands on her head, breasts and reddened bottom still on show, supposedly in rueful contemplation of her sins, but undoubtedly wishing she could sneak away and bring herself to orgasm. No such privacy was to be allowed. Thinking the show was over, Duncan began to clap, as did Big Dave and Portia, only to go quiet as Laura acknowledged them with a slight bow and moved behind Pippa.

There was a curt command, Pippa stuck her bottom out, and once more the full rude details of her pussy and anus were on show. Laura moved a little to one side, making sure we all had a good view, turned the swagger-stick in her hand and quite casually slid the rounded base well up into her girlfriend's pussy. Pippa moaned as she was penetrated, earning a slap across her welts. The stick was pulled out, put in the groove of her pussy instead of the hole, and rubbed.

It took about a minute for Pippa to come, and as she did so she was squirming as much in embarrassment as in ecstasy. I would have been the same, with an audience admiring the way my pussy and bottom hole clenched on air and my cheeks and legs shook in involuntary ecstasy. It left her gasping and knock-kneed, still showing everything as the end of the swagger-stick was eased in up her bottom and left there.

Laura took another bow, and this time everybody clapped, except of course poor Pippa, who knew better than to come out of the corner. She was not interfered with further, but left standing, the swagger-stick protruding from between her bottom cheeks, to make an ornament as the rest of us got on with the party. Personally, I'd seen enough to want to play myself, and a glance around the room showed I wasn't alone.

Portia was snuggled up close to Sarah, who in turn looked bright-eyed and eager. Caroline and Jasmine were much the same. Duncan was distinctly red in the face, and both Mike and Big Dave looked fit to burst, their cocks making long bulges in their trousers. Katie alone betrayed little arousal, and had been watching quietly. Had I not known she was genuine I would have worried, but this was the girl who had come to me to ask for spanking. She just needed a little help in order to express herself.

I did it very casually, changing my grip just a little and hauling her down across my knee so that her face went into Jasmine's lap. She squeaked, and for a moment was resisting, but I took a firm hold around her waist and gave her a pat on the bottom. She went limp, but began to sob, and shake too, knowing it was her turn, and compliant, but not having an easy time of it. I was going to do it, though, and bare, my hand slipping under her tummy as Jasmine began to stroke her head.

Caroline moved around to help Jasmine soothe Katie, whose sobbing became abruptly more intense as she felt my fingers on the button of her jeans, and stronger still as it popped open. I drew down her fly, took hold of her waistband and began to push. She wasn't helping, her body limp and trembling, her fingers clutching at the material of the sofa as she was exposed. I'd already decided her panties were coming down, and took them with her jeans to avoid any fuss, and at least spare her the specific humiliation of being shown off in her underwear before she was stripped naked.

She had to be bare, though, for her own sake, and I took the jeans and panties far enough down to make sure it all showed, if only to Laura. What mattered was that she knew, and as I lifted my knee to make her show off the rear of her pussy she burst into tears, really blubbering. I gave her a moment, to let her rise if she wanted to, but she stayed down and so I began to spank, as I had dealt with her before, gentle pats rising slowly in force.

Nobody spoke, the sheer intensity of her emotion enough to silence even Big Dave as she bawled out her feelings across my knee. I held tight, spanking gradually harder and trying to hold back from my desire to really lay in. Only when she finally began to push her bottom up did I use any real force, to set her lovely cheeks bouncing and parting too, revealing her anus and the wet mouth of her pussy.

She was ready, but I was not having her fucked, not by anybody, not my Katie. That was a far more appropriate fate for Jasmine and Caroline, who would appreciate it. Katie had to come, though, it was part of her lesson. She was eager, her bottom lifted, still crying but deeply aroused. Again there was a moment of resistance as I slid a hand under her pussy, but it stopped the instant I touched her clitoris. I began to rub and the next instant she was squirming herself against my hand, fully on heat, as wanton as any slut with a hot bottom could ever be.

Still I spanked, firm and even, right under her cheeks, to make them bounce and wobble. Each slap closed her cheeks, which then came wide to show her off, and as her pussy and bottom hole began to go into contractions I knew she was coming. She gave the sweetest little whimper as it hit her, and then she was writhing in wild, abandoned ecstasy, all her shyness gone as she revelled in being masturbated and spanked.

Her shyness came back, quickly, blushes suffusing her face the moment her orgasm was over and she had turned to me. She thanked me, though, and the girls, kissing each of us in turn before giving a brief flash of her pink bottom to the room as she started to pull up her panties. I wagged my finger.

'Best not. Into the corner with you, beside Pippa, keep your clothes down and put your hands on your head.'

'But, Isabelle . . .'

'It's for the best, Katie, go on.'

She bit her lip, but nodded, and with a quick glance to the watching men she shuffled over to stand beside Pippa. They made a fine pair, with their clothes disarranged and their red bottoms showing to the room, and I was wondering how it would look to have a line of five spanked girls when Jasmine leaned close to whisper in my ear.

'Best to get Mike and Dave despunked, don't you think?'

I nodded. She was right. They were behaving, so far, but there had to come a point when they would no longer be content merely to watch. Once they'd come, both would be grateful, and more easy-going. I could also tell that Jasmine was keen to be under orders, with a cock in her mouth and another in Caroline's.

'Let's have you bare first,' I stated. 'Those fatigues aren't made to leave a spanked girl any modesty.'

Her fatigues closed at the front, and she was bare chested underneath. I pulled the zip down and hauled them off her shoulders and arms, leaving her topless with the dull green material bunched around the slimness of her waist. Her nipples were hard, and I spent a moment playing with them, until she had begun to sigh gently, then took her by the scruff of her neck.

'Over you go, then,' I instructed, and took her down across my knee.

She went easily, her bottom lifted obligingly to let me get at her fatigues and push them right down, exposing the little pink peach of her bottom with her cheeks well apart and the tiny thong not even covering the lines around her anus. I pulled it down anyway, just to make sure she had nothing hidden whatsoever, and set to work, spanking her hard to set her bottom shaking and her tiny breasts quivering beneath her.

It didn't take long to push her over the edge – maybe fifty spanks and her little cries had stopped and her kicking subsided. Her bottom came up, offered to my punishment, and to the same treatment I had given Katie. I obliged, curling my hand under her tummy to find her sex and masturbating her. Immediately she was wriggling and panting, her bottom cheeks squeezing even as they were slapped.

I stopped, and lifted her off my lap. She stood up, a little unsteady, looking at me in surprise and clutching at her lowered panties. I snapped my fingers, pointing at the two spanked girls in the corner. She went, making three in a line, which was shortly going to be four, as Sarah had taken Portia down over her knee and was in the act of stripping her. That I wanted to watch.

There was considerable consternation on Portia's face, and she kept glancing at the men. It made no difference whatsoever, Sarah simply hauling down her jodhpurs and panties as one and setting to work. I'd seen Portia bare, but I hadn't seen her spanked, and it was every bit as arousing and every bit as funny as I had imagined. For all that she needed it, she gave every impression of hating it, especially with the men watching. The expression on her face when her panties came down was a treat, and it grew better as the spanking started, with pain added to her self-pity.

Sarah spanked hard, and with no thought for Portia's modesty. When Portia began to kick Sarah dealt with it immediately. One leg was hooked into place, trapping Portia's thighs and spreading her bottom to show the fleshy pink knot of her anus and her shaved pussy lips. As the spanking began once more I beckoned to Caroline. It was all the instruction she needed. Kneeling up, she peeled down the zip of her fatigues and bared her chest. Her fatigues were pushed down to her knees, and she turned quickly to stick her tongue out at the men as she bounced her meaty breasts in her hands.

I patted my lap. She came across my knee, her big white panties came down and two well-fleshed bottoms were being spanked in unison. Sarah got harder, bringing Portia up into a real frenzy, and I followed suit, determined to get a bigger reaction out of mine. I knew Caroline would make a big fuss – she always did. Portia was wriggling her bottom about and swearing in a most unladylike manner, but I'd barely got Caroline's bottom pink when she burst into tears. For a moment it almost drowned out Portia's protests, only for Sarah to pause, reach into her bag and extract a big, silver-backed hairbrush.

Portia was immediately begging not to have it used, only for her protests to break to squeals as it slapped down on her bottom. I spanked harder in turn, indifferent to my stinging hand as I brought Caroline up to a howling, struggling crescendo, and stopped. Caroline got up, taking her bottom in hand. Her big cheeks were a rich red, her face streaked with tears. I gave another snap of my fingers and she waddled over to join the punishment line. Sarah also stopped, gave Portia a curt order, and she too went into the corner.

Five pink bottoms showed to the room. I took a sip of my Champagne and sat back on the sofa, glancing sidelong at the men as I did so. Mike caught my eye and blew his breath out. Big Dave was squeezing a very obvious erection in his trousers. Both knew I made Jasmine and Caroline service Stan Tierney, and more, yet both looked uncertain.

'You seem a trifle flustered, gentlemen?' I addressed them.

'Not at all,' Duncan replied, quite coolly. 'I am merely enjoying the show.'

'Well, I'm fucking flustered,' Mike said. 'I've never seen a row of bums like that, not even on competition nights.'

'Competition nights?' Laura queried. 'Do you run spanking competitions?'

'Only stripteases,' I answered for her. 'Spanking competition might be a little exotic at the Red Ox. For some reason the audience always wants the girl doing the spanking to get it herself.'

'Dead right,' Big Dave said.

'Well, this is how it should be,' I told him, 'with those who wish to dominate in dominant roles, and those who wish to submit in submissive roles. Don't you agree?'

He merely made a face, no doubt wanting to tell me that women ought to be spanked on general principle but not wanting to ruin his chances. I

248

laughed, enjoying my complete control, then gave my fingers another snap.

'Jasmine, Caroline, I think the boys need to be relieved. See to it.'

They went, both of them, without argument, and even Jasmine with no more than a trace of reluctance as she got down on her knees in front of Mike. Caroline went to Big Dave, both girls quickly unzipping their men to pull out fully erect cocks. The cocks went in their mouths and I settled down to enjoy my Champagne and watch, wondering how I should take my own pleasure when the time came.

The thought of having all five submissive girls at my feet was good, and if Sarah was the only person likely to want to deny me, that made the thought of having Portia in the line up all the more appealing. I would sit on her face, pussy to mouth, while Jasmine attended to my bottom hole from the rear. Because Katie was so shy it would be good to make her pose, in some thoroughly rude and undignified position, touching her toes or perhaps with her legs rolled up, both of which would leave every detail of her pussy and anus on blatant display. Pippa could also pose, to provide me with the satisfaction of having a mature woman under my orders, and in a position no less dirty than Katie's. Caroline could then attend to my breasts and neck while I enjoyed feeling her body.

All that would come, with time and a little skill. For now it was important to get the two men 'despunked', as Jasmine put it. It was going to happen soon too, the girls with their heads bobbing up and down in time, each with her mouth wide around a thick cock shaft and her hands busy with a sac full of balls. The sight and smell were making me want to suck cock myself, and I decided I might take Duncan aside later and do it privately.

Jasmine's eyes popped, her cheeks bulged, Mike grunted and I knew that he had come in her mouth. He was jammed well in, but she struggled to swallow, coming up with just a trace of sperm on her lower lip. She hadn't come, and as she turned to me with an imploring look I knew she wanted permission to masturbate, but that was not part of my plan.

Caroline was less lucky, Big Dave locking his hand in her hair just as he started to come, and forcing his cock head into her windpipe at what for her was exactly the wrong moment. Like Jasmine, her eyes popped as her mouth was spunked in, but instead of taking it in her cheeks it came out of her nose, mixed with mucus and spittle in a great dirty gush. Big Dave didn't even notice, but just milked what was left down her throat and lay back with a low moan of satisfaction.

'Nice,' Mike sighed as Jasmine wiped her mouth with a tissue. 'Thanks, Jas.'

'Thank my Mistress,' Jasmine said meekly as she stood up.

'Thanks, Isa.' Mike laughed and turned to Laura. 'Got another beer, love?'

Caroline had run into the bathroom, either to clean her face or be sick, but came back a moment later and snuggled up by my side. For a while we drank and talked, everyone now getting on easily as the girls had shown their bottoms and the men had had their cocks sucked. We let the other three leave the corner, Katie coming straight to me. She pulled her trousers and panties up, though, while both Jasmine and Caroline were topless with their fatigues bunched around their waists. Pippa's front was still open but her trousers were up. Portia had also dressed, and she was first on my debt list.

'Time to play, I think,' I announced, standing.

'Sarah, would you like to swap brats? Caroline for Portia.'

She gave me a wonderfully forceful look, clearly wanting to tell me that I was the brat and ought to get straight over her knee. I could tell Caroline appealed to her, but it was clearly a close thing, so I played my trump card.

'Two for one?' I offered. 'Jasmine and Caroline for Portia.'

She nodded, a touch frostily, and I gestured to the girls. Both crawled over to Sarah's feet and I gave Portia a smile which was answered by a wonderfully uncertain look.

'May I take these two into your dungeon, Laura?' Sarah asked. 'I think they need to be taught a little proper discipline, from a mature woman.'

'You're right,' Laura answered her. 'I'll join you. Pippa, look smart, at the double.'

Pippa responded instantly, marching smartly from the room, with Caroline scampering after her, and Jasmine squealing as Sarah led her away by the ear. I'd been going to suggest to the men that they watch, but they didn't need to be asked. Both Mike and Big Dave followed the little troop of women. Duncan remained, casually sipping Champagne.

'Would you look after Katie?' I asked him. 'Katie, may Duncan punish you?'

She went bright pink, hesitated, then gave the tiniest of nods. There was a dog lead nearby, one Laura had been showing Sarah, and I quickly fastened it around Katie's neck to mark her firmly as mine, then gave the end to Duncan.

'Be careful with her,' I told him. 'Right, Portia, you're mine.'

Her expression was pretty sulky, so I reached down and took her by the ear, just as Sarah had with

Caroline. She squeaked, but came, protesting faintly as I dragged her up into the carriage, choosing the unaltered compartment for my operations. There was no real fight in her, and I didn't know if her resentment was genuine or put on to play the brat. I didn't care, either. Placing her with her back to the window I barked a command.

'Knickers down!'

A nervous spasm shot through her body, both her hands going to the waistband of her jodhpurs before she caught herself.

'Don't do that, Isabelle!' she gasped. 'It sends a shock right through me!'

'That's the idea, and why are your knickers still up?'

'Well . . . I'm older than you are, Isabelle. I should be doing this to you, shouldn't I?'

'Not in my books. Now come on, let's have those panties down. I want a better look at that adorable bottom. Oh, and let's have your blouse open too.'

'What are you going to do to me? I've been spanked . . .'

'Yes, and a fine sight you looked too. Now come on, knickers down!'

This time they came down, her jodhpurs too, with her face set in a little moue of resentment as she exposed herself. Her pussy looked sweet from the front, a little plump mound of baby pink flesh with no more than a trace of her inner lips showing in the crease.

'Now your breasts,' I instructed. 'Come on.'

She was still looking sulky as she unbuttoned her blouse, but there was more than a touch of pride as she pulled up her bra to reveal twin breasts the size of large oranges and about as round, and very firm. Her nipples were not too big, pale and very hard. I took one between finger and thumb, tweaking it gently. She gave a tiny squeak and made to cover herself, so I took her wrists and placed her hands on her head.

'Whatever is to be done with you, Portia?' I questioned, stepping back to admire her dishevelled nakedness. 'The cane perhaps? A riding whip? After all, you enjoyed watching me being whipped, didn't you? Yes, you did, Portia, but that wasn't all you did, was it?'

She shook her head, looking genuinely scared.

'Stay,' I ordered her, and walked coolly from the compartment.

I could already hear Caroline's squeals of pain and the slap of leather on girl flesh from next door, but wasted no time. There were leather gloves in the uniform compartment, and I quickly pulled them on, then jumped down from the door at the end of the carriage and snatched up a good handful of the long nettles growing between the sleepers. There were also lilies, heavy orange blooms of some fancy hybrid, and I treated myself to two before running back inside. Portia was where I had left her, hands on head, breasts, pussy and bottom all bare and awaiting my attentions.

'Two things, Portia darling,' I told her as I put the nettles down. 'The vase and the nettling. For the vase, at least I am giving you the chance to wear these beautiful lilies rather than a simple posy of buttercups. Kneel on the seat.'

She went, keeping her hands on her head and looking back anxiously as she climbed on. Her bottom was half covered by the tails of her coat and blouse, which I lifted, exposing the full, cheeky globe.

'Stick it out,' I ordered, and her cheeks spread to reveal my targets, the tight pink knot of her anus and the moist crevice of her pussy.

Her eyes were fixed on mine and she was trembling hard, making her cheeks quiver. I lifted a finger and stuck it purposefully in my mouth, letting her watch me suck before it went between her cheeks. She gave a little moan as I touched her bottom hole, her muscle squirming against my finger, then around it as her ring popped. I pushed deep, immersing my finger in the hot mush of her rectum and slipping two more into her pussy.

'Do you remember how you made me suck your finger?' I asked.

She gave a sob in response.

'Good,' I answered. 'Open wide.'

Her eyes had shut as I began to masturbate her, and they stayed that way, but her mouth came open, slowly, but wide, her lower lip trembling as she waited to be made to suck on the finger I was working deep up her bottom. I really wanted to make her feel it, and took my time, opening her until she had become slimy, and pushing so deep I could feel a little something inside. Only when she began to whimper did I pull my fingers out and stick all three in her mouth.

'Suck,' I ordered. 'Taste your own bottom, Portia, just like you made me taste mine.'

To my delight she began to suck immediately, her face working with emotion as she mouthed on my fingers, her breasts quivering, but her hands staying firmly on her head. When I was quite sure I'd been sucked clean and that the full effect of what she'd done would have sunk in, I pulled them out.

Her bottom hole was slack and mushy with spit and her pussy agape, with white juice running from the open hole, both making fine targets. I took the lilies, quickly crushed each end and stuck them in. The first slid easily up her pussy, the second met a little resistance before her anus gave, and like me, her rear end had been made a flower vase.

'Very pretty,' I told her. 'Look back, and you can see yourself in the mirror above the seat opposite.'

She did, looking more chagrined than ever as she inspected her penetrated bottom. I gave her a little slap to make the flowers wobble, wishing I'd had the sense to bring a camera to record her humiliation. Laura had one, I was sure, but by the sound of it she was busy next door, with the noises of Pippa's pain now added to those of Caroline and Jasmine. There would be other times, though, I was sure.

'Good girl,' I instructed Portia. 'You're being very obedient. Now twist around. Show me your breasts.'

'Not my breasts, Isabelle, please,' she begged even as she stuck them up for me. 'I didn't do your breasts!'

'Shut up,' I answered as I opened her jacket and blouse to make sure I had access to the full area of both fat little globes.

She kept her eyes shut, tight, shaking harder than ever and biting her lip. I made her wait. I picked up the nettles and gave them a couple of experimental swishes, then thrust the entire bunch full against her chest. All she did was giggle, as if being tickled, but as I began to twist them around on her naked breasts the giggles turned to gasps, then screams as the pain bit.

For one moment she had pulled back, then she was deliberately jiggling her breasts in the nettles, even as she called me a bitch and more. I just kept on, grinning as I tortured her, thoroughly enjoying both her reaction and my revenge. She was aroused too, with a vengeance. Her nipples had come right out, and her breasts were swelling to two angry red globes of hurt flesh, each topped by its fiery bud. Her neck and belly were spotty with nettle rash too, and I could just imagine the pain.

'Now your bottom and pussy,' I told her as I at last pulled the nettles back, 'and you can come while I do you.'

'You wicked bitch!'

'I think that's Wicked Witch, darling. Now stick it out.'

She moved, pushing her bottom up and out, to leave both lilies thrust high over her spanked cheeks. Sarah had done her hard, and she was starting to bruise, while her pussy was swollen and ready. Her hand went back, straight to her clitoris, and she was masturbating, rude and wanton in front of me, utterly abandoned to my torture. I pushed the nettles in, tickling the swell of her bottom to leave a trace of white prick marks that quickly changed to a red deeper even than that of her punished skin. A second, slower stroke and the full width of her bottom was left prickly with rash, a third and the tiny bumps had begun to blend to an even swelling of tender skin.

'Ow!' she sobbed as I began to rub the entire bunch over her buttocks. 'That hurts ... oh, my poor bottom ... oh, Isabelle, you vicious bitch ... you vicious, vicious bitch ... you ... you ... angel ... my angel ... hurt me ... really hurt me!'

As her voice broke to a scream she was coming, her lilies quivering madly in her holes as her body shook, her fingers working frantically in her pussy. She was in the same agonised state she had put me in, and the blend of arousal and revenge singing in my head had risen to become one of the finest feelings of my entire life.

I took the nettles away the instant she had finished, and she collapsed sobbing onto the seat, her blazing, swollen bottom stuck high in the air, her skin wet with sweat. She was crying, and I kissed her tears away and gave her a hug, then stood again, feeling immensely strong and completely in control. I wanted to come, and to have every one of them watching me as I did it, queened on my beaten victim, and I knew whose face I wanted under my bottom – Sarah's.

A quick visit to Laura's implement room provided me with a tawse, as well as a collar and lead, which I clipped to Portia's neck. She let me, and followed, meek as a puppy, as I led her to the playroom. Sarah was still there, and all the others bar Duncan, Katie and Laura. Jasmine and Pippa had been stripped and put in the cage together. Caroline was in the pillory, her uniform trousers and panties well down, her big bottom wobbling to hard whip cuts as she was thrashed. Sarah had her back to me, her jacket off, and the taut seat of her jodhpurs pushed out, and she hadn't seen me come in. I had to do it.

'Wet!' I snapped, and smacked the tawse down across her cheeks.

I'd expected her to jump, the way Portia had, no more. Making her submit was to come later. What she did was pee her panties, then and there, the urine simply squirting out into her gusset and emerging from where her jodhpurs were pulled taut over her pussy in a little fountain before she even realised what had happened. Then she had jumped up, clutching at herself in dismay, but it was too late, piddle squirting from between her fingers even as she tried to stem the flow, and already soaking into her seat. She rounded on me, her face red with anger and embarrassment, still clutching herself.

'Just do it,' I ordered.

Her face set, stern, determined, then something inside her had snapped, her eyes were closed and she was sobbing her heart out as the pee bubbled from the front of her jodhpurs and down her legs, to patter onto the floor in a rapidly spreading puddle. She was crying hard, genuinely upset, and in an instant all my sadistic glee had dissolved.

'Sorry,' I managed, limply.

She stood straight. There was real anger on her face, and I really thought I had spoiled everything. Then she had it under control.

'You are in real trouble, Isabelle, but no more so than my brat ... Portia, you ... What the hell have you done to Portia!'

'I nettle-whipped her,' I admitted.

'No more than she deserves,' Sarah answered, and was going to continue, but stopped as Laura came in, bearing a huge chocolate gateau heavily decorated with whipped cream.

'What's happening?' she asked, glancing at Sarah's sodden jodhpurs.

'I am about to punish Isabelle,' Sarah answered.

'Well, it is her birthday,' Laura answered casually as she put the cake down on top of the cage. 'May I help?'

All I could do was shrug, feeling a touch of the same consternation that Portia had suffered. I was trying to be fair, taking my punishment, and they were now making a joke of it. With the memory of Sarah's face as she wet herself I was quite unable to refuse.

'Yes, of course,' Sarah answered, 'if you could tie them while I change. Might I borrow a uniform?'

'Anything you like,' Laura offered. 'Right, you two, strip to your knickers and get on the floor. Now!'

She really shouted it, and Portia's finger went straight to the flower in her bottom hole. I had already begun to strip, peeling off my beautiful uniform with my sense of consternation growing ever worse as I came bare, right down to my panties, as ordered. The men were watching, and the girls too, from their cage. Only Caroline was unable to see.

'Head to tail,' Laura ordered the moment we were both in panties. 'Portia on top, as it's really Isabelle who needs to be punished.'

As Portia climbed on top of me Laura left the room. My head was a whirl of emotions, dominated by the now burning consternation, yet my guilt was too strong to let me rebel, and as Portia's bottom swung over my face the focus of my arousal began to waver. Laura quickly came back, with an armful of rope. I was telling myself it was right to give in, that I could always retrieve my dominant role later, and then I was helpless as our waists were lashed together and it didn't matter what I thought. Our wrists followed, mine and hers tied together in the small of her back. Then it was our legs, her ankles tied behind my head to leave my face pressed into the seat of her panties, mine hauled high and tied off to our wrist knot, trapping her head.

No sooner had she finished than Sarah came back, now in one of the majors' uniforms, and holding a swagger-stick. She gave a puzzled frown as she saw the position we were in, then got down and pulled Portia's head back by the hair. The next instant my panties had been wrenched up and the swagger-stick was being applied to my bottom.

It was hard, furiously hard, setting me writhing in my bonds and screaming into Portia's panties in an instant, but there was no let-up, and all the while Laura was casually cutting my birthday cake into pieces above me. I almost fainted with pain, and was left gasping and babbling apologies and begging Sarah's forgiveness. Her response was to slide the full mass of her fist into my vagina.

'Sopping,' she remarked as I began to squirm on her hand like some sort of demented glove puppet. 'What a slut.'

'There's only really one punishment for bad little dykes,' Laura answered her. 'Give them to the men.'

I felt Portia stiffen. Sarah's hand was eased out of my vagina, leaving me gaping to the room as Big Dave spoke.

'Nice idea, love. We'll punish 'em for you.'

He laughed.

'Thank you, Dave,' Sarah answered sweetly. 'Yes, I think it would be just what they need.'

'Isabelle should have some of her cake first, though,' Laura said, then bent down, opened the rear of Portia's panties, dropped in a slice that must have been a good quarter of the cake, and let go.

Portia's waistband snapped shut, trapping the slice as a huge bulge in her panty seat, right in my face, with chocolate icing and cream already squeezing out at one side. Big Dave and Mike were already advancing on us as Laura took my hair and pulled my head up, the mess in Portia's panties squashing against my face. Sarah laughed. My face came away sticky, and as I looked up I saw Big Dave looming over me, just stepping out of his trousers and pants.

'Feed it to her on your penis,' Sarah suggested as Big Dave sank down.

His cock was flopped in my face, thick and musky, even as Mike took hold of my thighs. Something squashed onto my pussy, more cake, then Portia's face as her head was pushed down.

'Suck them,' Sarah ordered and I felt the roundness of Mike's balls on my pussy as his cock was fed into Portia's mouth.

Big Dave put his in mine and I was doing it, sucking cock with Portia's panty bulge right in my face, already sticky with cake. As his cock began to grow he took hold of her bottom, pulling her panties aside to bare her, revealing the revolting mess of cake and chocolate and cream smeared over her pussy and between her bum cheeks.

'Now fuck them,' Sarah demanded, 'and don't think twice if you want to use their bottoms.'

Mike's hard cock was slid up my pussy, taking a great wad of cake with it.

Dave was fucking my mouth even as Mike did my pussy, and in a moment he had pulled out, hard and long. It went up Portia, and I heard her moan, chocolate and cream squashing out of her hole and into my mouth as she was filled, then his balls were there as well as he squatted down on my face. I could barely breathe, smothered in hot, sweaty flesh, his anus right on my nose, but only for an instant, and then his cock had been pulled out and stuck back in my mouth, now laden with cake and Portia's juices.

I struggled to swallow, gagging on cock and cake, with Mike still fucking me. Big Dave's cock came out again, into Portia's filthy bottom crease and back into my mouth. I was being fed, fucked, and Sarah had said I could be buggered. I was sure to be, and my hole was slimy with cream, an easy target for cock. Again Dave's cake-laden penis was plunged into my mouth, and again, forcing me to swallow the cake so fast I was starting to feel sick – only when he did stop, it was to put his cock head to Portia's bottom hole.

She gasped in horror as she realised she was to be sodomised, then moaned as he began to rub his cock in the cream, to make her ring soften and spread, opening immediately as he pushed. His balls were dangling in my face, then slapping in it as he began to force himself up her in a series of little jerks, her anus pulling in and out, brown cream squashing from her empty pussy hole. She took it badly, whimpering and grunting as her rectum filled with cock, right to the hilt.

I felt Mike leave my own hole, followed by relief at the wet sound of Portia's mouth being filled, then despair as the rounded cock head pressed to my slimy anus. Up it went, jammed in with me no more ladylike in buggery than Portia, my rectum stuffed. As Portia's head pressed to my pussy they began to rock us, back and forth, cocks up bottom holes, laughing and grunting in glee as we were used.

Portia was licking me, I had a cock up my bottom, and I was going to come, like it or not. For just a second I tried to resist, holding off from committing what seemed like the final indignity in front of Sarah, Laura, and my own girlfriends too. Big Dave did it, jamming himself hard up Portia's rectum as he filled it with spunk, then pulled out, to offer his filthy, steaming cock to my mouth, the tip still dribbling sperm . . .

I took it, right in, my orgasm bursting in my head as the taste of chocolate and sperm and Portia's bottom filled my mouth, then pee, as she took her revenge and let go, full in my face. Her urine was splashing everywhere as I came, over and over, sucking on Big Dave's filthy cock with wanton relish, my bottom hole pulling in and out as Mike buggered me and at the very peak of my ecstasy came in my rectum.

It took ages to untie us, the knots pulled tight by our thrashing about as we were used, and most of them slippery with cream. When I was free I could barely stand, and simply squatted down on the floor, my eyes closed in exhaustion, mess dribbling slowly down my body. Laura took me to wash, and I was still in the bathroom when Duncan came in, smiling, a glass of wine in one hand and Katie's lead in the other. There was come in her hair.

'Your girlfriend, I believe, Isabelle?'

'Thank you, yes.'

He handed me the lead and Katie nuzzled up to my thighs. As I began to stroke her hair he went on.

'This is . . . wonderful . . . exquisite . . . but we must be discreet.'

'Naturally.'

'I was thinking – perhaps a club of some sort, to make it formal and thus ensure our members' loyalties.'

'I agree. I even have a name.'

The Rattaners might never have existed, but they did now.

NEXUS NEW BOOKS

To be published in May 2004

CRUEL SHADOW
Aishling Morgan

Peter Williams is a sales supremo who lives for the road. Infatuated by the inviting bottom on the cover of an erotic novel, Peter is determined to enjoy a spell with its owner, the lustrous Linnet, and her friends. Peter prides himself on driving a hard bargain, but with Linnet in his car, things get harder than he bargained for. Fry-ups, flagellation, hot tarmac and hotter sex follow as Linnet and her friends take Peter along a series of sexual byways that weren't even on his roadmap before.

£6.99   ISBN 0 352 33886 5

COMPANY OF SLAVES
Christina Shelley

Michael is a twenty-one-year-old high-flying graduate beginning a career at Lovelace Fashion and Design under the tutelage of the haughty Chief Executive, Emily Lovelace. His prospects are good. What Michael really wants, however, is to spend his life as Michele, his masochistic she-male alter-ego. To his surprise, fear and excitement, LFD have the perfect opening for a man of his predilections. Sheathed in silks and satins, subservient and suitably restrained, Michael might just fit the brief . . .

£6.99   ISBN 0 352 33887 3

EMMA'S SECRET DIARIES
Hilary James

Emma has decided to keep a diary of her masochistic adventures. Having left her cruel mistress, Ursula, but still craving the sensation of lesbian domination, she swiftly becomes infatuated with the icy Isabella and then a Romanian countess whose keenness for administering bizarre punishment would not have embarrassed Sade. A holiday retreat becomes a dungeon of depravity – how will poor Emma return to civilisation? A Nexus Classic.

£6.99   ISBN 0 352 33888 1

To be published in June 2004

PRIZE OF PAIN
Wendy Swanscombe

Britain is to host the most bizarre TV game show ever, as hopeful submissive males enter a lottery to appear on 'Prize of Pain'. One day soon discreetly perfumed black envelopes will slip through the letterboxes of five lucky men and they will receive their instructions from the Domina de Fouette. Public humiliation awaits, and attempts to cheat will be detected and cruelly punished. Four men are unworthy and will fail the ordeals She sets them: one only will win through to the ultimate prize. The prize of pleasure . . . and of pain. Who wants to enter Mistress's Lair? And no coughing!

£6.99   ISBN 0 352 33890 3

DOMINATION DOLLS
Lindsay Gordon

Is it a beauty treatment? A fashion statement? Or the costume of a sinister cult? How do these masks of transparent latex transform ordinary women into beautiful vamps, dominant mistresses, and ruthless femme fatales? A timid socialite and her shy maid suddenly become merciless exploiters of male weakness; a suburban mother changes into a cruel mistress who takes an assertive interest in a prospective son in law; a mysterious female traveller leaves a trail of bound, disciplined and thoroughly used men behind. These are some of the stories of the Domination Dolls and the men they walk upon. Confessions collected by the librarian chosen to work in London's secret fetish archive, a woman who turns detective but soon succumbs to the temptations of female domination.

£6.99   ISBN 0 352 33891 1

LESSONS IN OBEDIENCE
Lucy Golden

What would you do if a young woman arrived unannounced on your doorstep one day to make amends for someone else's sins? And what if you detected, beneath her innocent exterior, a talent and a willingness to submit you'd be a fool not to nurture? Faced with that challenge, Alex Mortensen starts carefully to introduce his pupil to the increasingly perverse pleasures that have always featured in his own life. But what should he do when she learns so fast, catches up with him and threatens to overtake? A Nexus Classic.

£6.99   ISBN 0 352 33892 X

If you would like more information about Nexus titles, please visit our website at www.nexus-books.co.uk, or send a stamped addressed envelope to:

Nexus, Thames Wharf Studios,
Rainville Road, London W6 9HA

✂ -

Please send me the books I have ticked above.

Name   ....

Address   ....

             ....

             ....

             .... Post code...................

Send to: **Virgin Books Cash Sales, Thames Wharf Studios, Rainville Road, London W6 9HA**

US customers: for prices and details of how to order books for delivery by mail, call 1-800-343-4499.

Please enclose a cheque or postal order, made payable to **Nexus Books Ltd**, to the value of the books you have ordered plus postage and packing costs as follows:

UK and BFPO – £1.00 for the first book, 50p for each subsequent book.

Overseas (including Republic of Ireland) – £2.00 for the first book, £1.00 for each subsequent book.

If you would prefer to pay by VISA, ACCESS/MASTERCARD, AMEX, DINERS CLUB or SWITCH, please write your card number and expiry date here:

....

Please allow up to 28 days for delivery.

Signature ....

Our privacy policy

We will not disclose information you supply us to any other parties. We will not disclose any information which identifies you personally to any person without your express consent.

From time to time we may send out information about Nexus books and special offers. Please tick here if you do *not* wish to receive Nexus information.   ☐

- - - - - - ✂ -